About the Author

Tue Elkjær lives in Copenhagen, where he works with content production and digital marketing. In his late teens and early twenties, Tue was a fixture in Copenhagen's gay party scene, while he studied textile design. He started his career in the Danish fashion industry before he started working in fashion journalism and digital media. In his spare time, he enjoys haunting upscale hotel bars, watching classic movies and reading Russian realism.

A Queer Object

Tue Elkjær

A Queer Object

Olympia Publishers
London

www.olympiapublishers.com
OLYMPIA PAPERBACK EDITION

Copyright © Tue Elkjær 2023

The right of Tue Elkjær to be identified as author of
this work has been asserted in accordance with sections 77 and 78
of the Copyright, Designs and Patents Act 1988.

All Rights Reserved

No reproduction, copy or transmission of this publication
may be made without written permission.
No paragraph of this publication may be reproduced,
copied or transmitted save with the written permission of the
publisher, or in accordance with the provisions
of the Copyright Act 1956 (as amended).

Any person who commits any unauthorized act in relation to
this publication may be liable to criminal
prosecution and civil claims for damage.

A CIP catalogue record for this title is
available from the British Library.

ISBN: 978-1-80074-409-7

This is a work of fiction.
Names, characters, places and incidents originate from the writer's
imagination. Any resemblance to actual persons, living or dead, is
purely coincidental.

First Published in 2023

Olympia Publishers
Tallis House
2 Tallis Street
London
EC4Y 0AB

Printed in Great Britain

Dedication

"To Jan, the love of my life and to my dear parents. Thank you for your unrelenting love and support."

Acknowledgements

I'd like to acknowledge all my ex-boyfriends, my affairs, all the sexists and homophobes I've had the misfortune to meet, as well as everyone who has upheld destructive and objectifying beauty ideals. Thank you for the trauma, I wouldn't have had anything to write about, if it wasn't for you and your bullshit.

Chapter 1

He was sitting and staring daringly into the pale face of his reflection, looking for faults, that might be mended, trying to get ahead of any disapproving eyes.

Pinching his cheeks, he desperately wished he had marked, chiseled features, with high cheekbones and a definite jawline. Stretching out his long neck, he tried to will it to be even longer, to prevent his chin from drooping. Even though he was a little underweight and had a long, thin and bony body, his face was round and apple-cheeked, like a child and he hated it. His round cheeks and childlike chin made him feel so fat, that he wanted to vomit from self-repulsion.

Men didn't like him fat, he thought, but they did like his likeness to a young child.

Shifting his attention, he stretched out the skin under his eyes with his fingers. At an age of twenty-one, he was terrified of growing older and each day he imagined time taxing him for his good times and taking a bit of his youth. From an outside perspective, he was a young, very thin and very tall young man, with a charming babyface and notably pale complexion. Most people would probably compare him to a porcelain doll, but he couldn't see it himself. He was terrified of not being attractive enough or good enough. Being the proactive and defensive type, he only saw his faults and the possible ways he could correct them.

In exhaustion of his own critical thinking, he dropped his

face in his hands and growled out loud, in desperate dissatisfaction: "ugh" His outburst quickly evaporated and was replaced by his characteristic desire to get on with things and so, he got up from his makeup table and started his day. As he stood up, his body felt sore and heavy and his head ached from last night's liquor. Despite only having slept for three hours, he felt a need to get out of bed and start his day.

As he walked groggily across his bedroom floor, he felt something icky under his left foot. It was a condom from last night. He scanned the room, with sleepy, droopy eyes and picked up one, two, three, four condoms and put them in the trash.

Now he remembered, Jason had come over last night. Had they really gone through four condoms? He checked his bed stand, Jason had left a wad of cash. He took the wad and habitually put it away in the bed stand drawer, to accompany all of the other wads of cash, from other night time visitors.

This was all standard procedure. Every day started with the same routine.

He would stop on the way to bathroom for a second inspection of himself in the full length mirror and grunt again.

Despite the classic pajamas, stylish robe and lavish velvet loafers, he never saw a beautiful man looking back at him in the mirror, not really. There was nothing he wanted so much as to be beautiful and desirable. He was always disappointing in his own gaze, he didn't desire himself as he wanted to.

Desirability meant power and beauty, to be of a higher social order, to be beyond it all, in a metaphysical state of higher being. Beauty was not so much about looks, but about ability, skill and talent – it was about factual aesthetic genius, like Wallis Simpson. He had indulged in such lofty and pretentious ideas since age seven, when he'd started school. It was the same time, he'd begun fretting about his looks and started using his mother's anti-age creams, which had been the beginning of a lifetime pursuit of beauty. Now, he manipulated his body, as a matter of routine and had changed his name, so he could better fit into a certain image, that would be attractive to men.

In his own mind, he almost achieved his own idea of desirability, for a brief period in his teens, when he'd been anorexic. Unlike most boys, skinny didn't come natural to him, so he'd fixated on it, until weight loss had become an obsession. This image of himself had resonated and set a bar for his physical appearance and it was an ideal he had hunted ever since. That was what the daily "ugh" was about, when he saw his own reflection, the ongoing disappointment, that he no longer was the type ideal, he used to be. That he was no longer a dangerously skinny sixteen-year-old queer boy, that always caught the eye of older men. Older men still sought him out and hit on, but he worried about when he'd age out of their gaze. So, he kept himself up and kept working on himself, to keep their gaze and stay within their frame of desirability.

Like every morning, he started his routine by the bathroom sink, where he'd pluck, shave, cleanse and scrub himself for the better part of an hour. The whole time, he'd pay close attention to his every move in the mirror, controlling the process almost robotically. Then he'd fill his bathtub with ice cold water and bathe himself. It was hard for him to clean his body, because he hated to touch himself, he'd rather be touched by anyone else. His own touch reminded him of his mortality and worse, his endlessly humiliating humanity, but he forced himself through it, soaping himself in and cleaning himself off, with as little touching as he could get away with. Afterwards he'd lie in the freezing cold water, until his entire body felt numb. The purpose of the cold water was to tighten the skin and toughen up his spirit. There was both pleasure and pain associated with this ritual.

When he got out of the bathtub, the air would warm his frozen limps and he felt resurrected. A significant part of his bathing ritual was to stand up, leaning against the wall, covering his face with a towel, so everything went dark and he could spend a few minutes ignoring everything and everyone. He was like an ostrich, hiding its head in the sand. This was his safe place, the only place, where he could afford not to care about anything. Here, in the towel, the world did not exist. After a few minutes, the world would always call him out and he'd move on in his routine.

Dropping the towel, he went naked into the kitchen and made a cup of black coffee, that he brought back to his bedroom, to drink while he finished up.

He'd embalm himself in a myriad of anti-age serums and creams, before sitting down naked, in front of his bedroom makeup counter, to mask himself with concealer, foundation, powder and tint for his lashes and brows.

He would try his hardest to look like, he wasn't wearing any makeup at all. This wasn't about artistic or stylistic expression, but about creating an illusion of a better person, a prettier person. This attitude was indicative of his overall behavior. Everything he did had to be choreographed and 'made up'. To help him, there were two books one his makeup table, one was Dostojevsky's 'The Brothers Karamazov' and the other was Balzac's 'Nana'. They were there to remind him of who, he was trying to be and what kind of world he was trying to succeed in. It helped him daily, to prepare for the part he was playing.

As he applied his makeup, he slowly saw himself disappear and give way for the character he had invented. It was the character of Mishka Balzac.

He'd assumed the name Dmitri Balzac, when he'd first moved to the city, from his parents' house in a far away village, placed in the conservative and clean-cut Danish countryside.

Dmitri was chosen from his appreciation of the recklessness and passion of Dostojevsky's character Dmitri Karamazov. Like Dmitri Karamazov, Mishka also felt haunted by the devil and had a tendency to follow his whims, even when it was contrary to his goals. He also appreciated, the short hand of Dmitri was 'Mishka', which could sound a bit androgynous, almost feminine. Most of the men he met, liked him to be a bit effeminate. He'd learned they were more indulgent with him, if they felt he was under the protection of their masculinity and he happily played along, when it resulted in expensive presents or a cash reward. He'd chosen his last name because he was obsessed with Honoré de Balzac and partly for the vulgar homoerotic undertones of the name.

When his makeup was done, he carefully pomaded and brushed his dark curls.

Then, all there was left, was to dress the part, but he was in no rush. He could take his time in the mornings, he never had visitors then.

Unlike most of his friends, he didn't have a job or a study to hurry to, so time was different for him. Everyone else his age was always hurrying to meetings or lectures, so intent on being a specific place, at a specific time. Mishka's life was subsidized by men who took a fancy to him and he in turn, devoted his time and his bed to their patronage – that's how he saw it.

He used to study design, because he thought it would teach him more about beauty, but it wasn't for him. The whole scene was too… fixed. Everyone had to be a certain way, think certain things and do certain things. Certainty always made him feel uneasy, he considered it philosophical fraud. The only thing he felt he knew for sure was, that people could never escape their own perspectives. In most conversations, he found, people mostly spoke to have their own views confirmed and spread to others. People never really conversed because they never really listened. He had learned to listen and used it with his patrons. Mishka found, that most people would do anything, for those who listened and simulated interest in their perspective. His great tricks were simply vagueness and repetition. He kept his own statements vague and open to interpretation. This forced everyone else to carry the conversation and to decide what Mishka actually meant. Their interpretation of Mishka's statements, would mirror what they wanted from him, like agreement or opposition. When someone else said something, he'd simply repeat it back to them in other words. He'd yet to meet someone, who noticed they were talking to a parrot, usually, they felt heard, seen and appreciated, which usually moved them to generosity towards Mishka and sometimes even steady patronage.

To Mishka, the world was simple, opportunistic and banal.

His thoughts kept distracting him from the task at hand, getting dressed. But he could afford being distracted today. He only had one appointment. Mr. P was coming by later and he was trying to figure out, what part he should play for Mr. P today.

    Mr. P liked to play games, he had never even given Mishka his real name, although he had heard somewhere at a dark bar, that it was Petersen. Which seemed like an absurdly unromantic, common and forgettable name to hide behind the initial 'P'. It was so common, Mishka couldn't see the point of hiding the name at all. It wasn't as if it could make him easier to find. Not that Mishka's vanity would allow him to track someone down. Mishka didn't really know anything about Mr. P, other than his real last name and that he made his money from investments and investment consulting. Mishka didn't really know or cared, what that meant, but he knew it paid enough, for Mr. P to be his second most generous patron and that was worth the effort.

    Mishka had finally settled on an outfit. Mr. P had sounded bored and frustrated on the phone, when they set up the appointment, so he had chosen to dress for the occasion. He would dress to entertain and to see how far he could monetize on Mr. P's boredom with his 'normal life'.

    Mishka dressed in a white ruffled shirt, which he wore under a black Chanel-looking tweed pull-over, with tight charcoal satin pants, which he accessorized with a pinky ring with a big grey pearl set in white gold, a black velvet bow around his neck and black velvet loafers - no socks of course. Socks were always a hassle to take off elegantly. He often preferred tying actual bows, instead of wearing bow ties, since it made him look a bit younger and also made him look like he was giftwrapped. Both he and his patrons enjoyed these small symbols of objectification.

    How much time did he have left. He looked at the clock his great, great grandfather had made, which had been passed down to him and ceremoniously given to him, by his mother, when he'd moved away from home. It was a bit past two p.m., so he'd already spent four hours getting ready and he was expecting Mr. P at three p.m.

Usually, when he had patrons over at that time, he'd prepare a classic afternoon tea, which was just for show, since he knew, most patrons would immediately ask for a drink instead or go straight to the bedroom.

This time, he wouldn't even bother with the pretense of tea, it was too wholesome for the plot he had in mind. Instead he drank most of a half-bottle of champagne, to get in the right head space and get champagne breath. Then, he grabbed all the empty bottles of champagne, stacked neatly in the kitchen, and scattered them around his apartment along with some of his latest purchases and gifts, including the shopping bags they came in. He arranged it all very carefully, to make sure it all looked accidental and messy.

Then he put on some Django Reinhardt and arranged himself in his antique chaise longue, posing like an infantile dandy fatale, with his glass of champus in hand, surrounded by the scattered empty bottles, fashion goods and empty shopping bags.

In his mind, the whole tableau looked like a scene right out of a novel by Balzac – like he was Nana. He took a series of selfies, lying back in the chaise with one hand resting suggestively in his lap and posted the best ones to his Instagram accounts, both his public and his members only profile.

While he waited for Mr. P to arrive, he practiced the attitudes he'd throw and the remarks he'd make. He was going to push Mr. P's boundaries today, so he could see how far he could go with Mr. P and see, how much he meant to Mr. P. He would give in to Mr. P, but only after he'd wrung out something good from Mr. P's pockets. He didn't really know what he wanted to wring out of Mr. P, but it had to be something extraordinary to prove his worth and set a high price for his services.

When he'd first moved to the city, he was surprised how easily he could get a designer bag or an expensive suit, simply by being nice to grown up men. He knew they eventually all expected something in return, but their courtship was usually lucrative for him. From the first day, he'd become a fixture in the city's gay scene and in the bars of exclusive hotels, where he'd give his attention to anyone who gave him a complement and gift, which men kept giving to him.

There was something about his air, that gave his appearance a feel of insolence, mixed with general disappointment and an eternal quest for the next fun thing to do. Some people avoided him because of it, while it attracted others, because it made them think he had a secret, like he was better than the rest of the world, for some inexplicable reason. The truth was, that Mishka had grown up in a safe and comfortable world, ruled by good table manners, which made him surprised and titillated with the world's many opportunities and possibilities. Having always been effeminate and stereotypically queer, Mishka had been bullied and grown up without many fans or even friends. It had surprised him, when he reached his teens and started sneaking out at night, how many people found him fascinating and even attractive. People saw him and remembered him. Each time he'd gone out, he'd caused a stir. Without trying, Mishka was a polarizing figure.

He consciously used his fans to wring out the funds to create a gilded cage for him to inhabit, one that was halfway between the bourgeois comforts of his childhood and the decadent debaucheries of his current life. Something beautiful that set himself apart from everyone else and would keep him safe.

Mr. P was one of these fans and he mentally prepared for him, while he set the scene for a one-man performance to a one-member audience.

Chapter 2

Mishka could hear the heavy, deliberate steps of Mr. P in the hallway. He checked his reflection on his phone and settled into a reclined pose in the chaise, as Mr. P locked himself in. Many of his patrons had keys to the main lock of his front door. The keys were like a VIP pass to the patrons and it was convenient for Mishka. When they locked themselves in, it gave Mishka the opportunity to make a better, more stoic and dramatic impression, than opening the door himself. However, no one had the key to the safety lock he had installed. He let the safety lock be unlocked when he was prepared for visitors and locked it, when he wanted privacy. The keys he gave out to patrons was symbolic and the safety lock gave him control over their access to him – it was a matter of supply and demand, Mishka reasoned with himself.

Mr. P stood still in the hallway, apparently waiting to be greeted, but Mishka remained silent, it wasn't his line yet, Mishka waited for a queue from Mr. P.

Mr. P gave up first, gave an exhausted grunt and stomped into the living room, asking annoyed "Fix me a drink?"

Silently, Mishka handed his own champagne glass over to Mr. P.

Mr. P looked disapprovingly down on the glass and then at Mishka. Mishka knew Mr. P didn't drink champagne, it was too girly for him and he'd only ever drink out of Mishka's glass, if he'd snatched it from Mishka himself.

"Can you fix me a real drink?" Mr. P groaned.

"Oh, I can do all sorts of things. Isn't it clever of me." Mishka replied playfully.

"Are any of those things how to bartend?", Mr. P mumbled to himself, then adding more charmingly, once he'd looked Mishka up and down "... or don't you know anything useful?"

"Useful," Mishka laughed, "what a dirty, utilitarian word! Besides, I'm not sure what else I have," he said, emptying his glass.

Mr. P looked around the room, with all its empty bottles and various shopping bags and various designer products and said, "Yeah, I can see the problem," as he looked sternly at Mishka.

Mishka was thrilled that his tableau had made an impression on Mr. P, he knew it was in stark contrast to Mr. P's macho-yuppie lifestyle.

"Oh, don't be like that," Mishka said smilingly, as he moved up close to Mr. P, to play with his tie and then immediately retreated.

"You know I'm only trying to have a good time, a bit of fun." Mishka said this like it was a challenge, trying to sound both depraved and innocent.

Mr. P took a flask from the pocket of his conform and neutral suit jacket and took a big swig.

"Fun has nothing to do about knowledge, junior, it's just that we can't all live like you. Let daddy here explain," Mr. P said, pinching Mishka cheek, before he continued: "Some of us choose to be productive, you know, have to be productive enough to pay for... well, you."

As he talked, Mr. P got more and more annoyed, so he felt

he had to censor himself from saying the word 'whore' outright.

Mishka froze and intentionally stared vacantly into the air, until Mr. P got annoyed and shoved him.

"Sorry daddy, I simply forgot to listen. I think I may actually have had a little too much champus, to be honest." Mishka explained, sarcastically.

Again, Mr. P got irritated by all the empty bottles of fun, that he hadn't got to empty.

"Well, I haven't had nearly enough," Mr. P said taking another big swig of his flask and added, as calmly and charmingly as he could, failing to hide his aggravation "Why don't you look for something to drink, kiddo. Anything? And turn off that grandma music, can't you play something from this century?"

Mishka obeyed silently and smilingly. He ruffled through his half empty cabinets and even emptier fridge. He didn't keep much food in the apartment, especially not things that were ready to eat, only dry goods like dried chick peas or lentils. It would only tempt him, if there was food around him.

"Ah, perfection! Vodka!" he yelled joyfully.

"For fucks sake! How many times do I have to tell you, I don't drink vodka, it's for housewives trying to lose weight. I'm a man! I drink scotch!" Mr. P shouted in frustration.

Mishka knew Mr. P only drank scotch and he also knew why. It was part of Mr. P's never-ending performance of traditional masculinity. He was desperate to be part of the club of rich, powerful and bougie white men and therefore behaved like they behaved in movies. It was for that same reason, Mr. P called him things like 'good girl' or 'junior'. Mr. P always tried to feminize him in pronouns, so Mr. P could feel like more of a heteronormative man. Normality held a strange and special significance for Mr. P, a significance Mishka didn't understand and a significance Mr. P refused to be conscious of. Because Mishka didn't understand the appeal of normality, he dismissed it as something worthless and unambitious. However, Mr. P saw the value in fitting in, to be part of a group, especially a group of privilege, like that of the normative, white, straight male. Mr. P saw power in that!

"But? What about the music?" Mishka asked urgently, with a childish expression.

"What about it?" asked Mr. P, having forgotten he was the one, who asked to have it changed.

"You made a request for me to play something more... Modern." Mishka said, putting his nose to the clouds and rolling his eyes, as he spat out the last word and handed Mr. P a large glass of single malt.

Mr. P downed the whiskey in one gulp and exclaimed "Ahhh, get me another", handing Mishka the empty glass and adding: "Oh, you're always fretting about things that doesn't matter. Just turn it off, if you can't find something we both like". Mr. P's mood had improved significantly, now he had downed his whiskey and felt catered to.

Mishka froze, in half conscious terror, with the empty glass in his hand. "So, it'll just be quiet...?"

"Yeah, what's wrong with that?" Mr. P said with a distinctly neutral voice.

Mishka thought for a second and then replied, all bewildered: "Is that enjoyable?"

Mr. P smiled at the childlike terror of Mishka's reply, enjoying how little he recognized, why he was afraid of the quiet. Despite Mr. P's fight for normality, he was truly entertained by Mishka's little neurosis and eccentricities. It was Mr. P's own little party game to spot these eccentricities and discover their unconscious root. Mr. P did this to gain control of the relationship and get some ammunition against Mishka in case he should need it later. Despite both their true egocentrism, they spend most of their relationship studying the other and had quickly learned to know the other person better, than they knew themselves. Of course, they never expressed any of this and both believed themselves to know the other best. It was also unclear to themselves, exactly how much of their study of the other person had selfish motivations behind it, as they both told themselves, and how much was based on actual empathy.

Neither of them allowed for human emotion, they saw no value in it and this had become the basis of their relationship. Their relationship was a continual exchange of gratification of needs, based on mutual exploitation. They both knew this, it was their shared understanding, but neither would ever openly acknowledge it before the other. Because of this, their interactions were a series of parlor games, where they passively negotiated, how they could satisfactorily gratify each other's needs and at what cost. It was always an implicit negotiation, where both sought to get as much from the other as they could, at as little cost as the other would accept.

Mishka slowly strolled, with Mr. P's empty glass in hand, over to his Bluetooth speaker and turned off the music. Then, Mishka moved towards the kitchen and poured Mr. P another big serving of single malt whiskey.

Mishka brought it to Mr. P, with a vague smile on his face. He enjoyed having music and noise around him, because it provided him with distraction and set a scene for him to act upon. The noise was like a camouflage, a safe space, without it he felt exposed like small game on an open meadow. The quiet was always deafening to Mishka, it made him a bit paranoid and jumpy, like a hunter might suddenly appear out of nowhere and shoot him down.

He walked over to a chair, sat down and looked challengingly at Mr. P. "So, what now!" he said with a passive aggressive smile and an intense look in his eyes.

Mr. P nursed his whiskey and looked at Mishka with a crooked smile. Mr. P enjoyed the performance because he knew the silence bothered Mishka.

"Well, we can sit down together. Have a chat," Mr. P said.

"Please," Mishka replied, with an empty smile.

Instead, Mr. P sat down on the chaise, with his legs wide open, in that distinctive way, most cis-masculine men do.

"What could we talk about? The weather? The real estate market? Finance?" Mishka asked Mr. P.

Mr. P responded with a scoff and a boyish crooked smile. "Come on. You know that's not what I came here for," Mr. P said and moved down the chaise, to be closer to Mishka's chair, softly caressing his shoulder.

"Shoes, then?" Mishka asked, as he took off one his own and placed it on a side table.

"I like where this is going, take off some more," Mr. P teased.

"No, I'm not in the mood just now," Mishka said, as he rose from his seat and walked over to the window, staring at the view for a few seconds. He could feel Mr. P's hungry eyes on him all the time. They both knew this meant the negotiation had begun. Mr. P knew this meant he was getting closer to getting his way and his pants was already getting tighter by the thought of it.

What did he want from Mr. P? This was on both their minds, what was the price for Mr. P this time?

Mishka dramatically turned around and faced Mr. P, still standing at the window. "Maybe you could lend me some extra money, for some more modern music? You know, to expand my musical palette and all that."

Mr. P looked at him with a mixture of surprise, humor and distrust. Mr. P viewed Mishka like a greedy child, that had to be sated enough to be agreeable, but also had to be paced.

Mishka lit a pink Sobranie cocktail cigarette and looked challengingly at Mr. P, once again. He knew Mr. P loved it when he smoked. In fact, Mishka had only started smoking at Mr. P's insistence. At first, Mishka had refused, because he worried how the smoking would damage his looks, but at last Mr. P had worn him down, one drunken night and before he knew it, it had become a habit.

Mr. P still hadn't answered the question about money for records, so Mishka moved on.

"You know, it really is too bad," Mishka said, taking a long drag of his cigarette.

Mr. P didn't answer, he knew Mishka was fishing for something and he enjoyed letting Mishka improvise and force him to steer the interaction.

"… It's too bad, that I never remember that you drink whiskey…" Mishka gloated, but Mr. P still just looked back at him, with no expression at all.

"… Perhaps you should start sending cases of it over here, so it's always ready for you. You know, sort of like a *subscription*, darling" Mishka said the word 'subscription' with enthusiasm, while he did a little jump and fanned his hands out, like it was a stroke of genius.

"Fine," Mr. P said, putting his now empty glass on a side table, waiting to see if there was more on Mishka's mind.

When Mishka remained silent, Mr. P hoped the matter was closed. He got up, moved towards Mishka, got up behind him and then wrapped his hands around Mishka's waist, caressing Mishka's body and laid his head on Mishka's shoulders.

"Could I have a case every week? I think I've gotten quite a taste for it myself," Mishka said, sniffing the whiskey on Mr. P breath.

Mr. P laughed at the obvious play here and replied: "A taste, you've been drowning in it, since I met you." Mr. P kissed him again, roguishly. "Sure," Mr. P added. "We can make it every week, as long as you save some for me." He started kissing Mishka's neck from all sides, sliding his fingers through Mishka's hair.

This boldened Mishka. He sometimes asked for something small of his patrons, before asking for something bigger. It was his way of testing the waters. He searched his mind for something big he could ask for, something that could seem just a bit apropos, but still be an obvious ask.

"You know, drinking is often a sign of boredom," he said, unaffected by Mr. P's kisses and caresses.

Mr. P stopped his kisses, recognizing that the negotiation wasn't over and raised his head up to listen. Mr. P was waiting to know, where Mishka was heading with this comment. Mr. P had long since learned to wait to answer, until he actually knew what he was being asked.

Mishka broke the silence, explaining: "Maybe you could give me something to entertain me, between your visits. Then, maybe I could keep my hands off your whiskey."

Mr. P scoffed. "Have you tried cleaning up". Mr. P smiled at his own joke and they both surveyed the room.

"Well, this is what I mean," Mishka said firmly and turned around, to return Mr. P's caresses. "I get sooo booored between your visits. You really should pity me! Woe is me, I tell you! I simply *had* to party to keep from *jumping* in a moat!" Mishka added, putting on a slight pout, trying to sound spoiled and silly.

This was more pretentiousness than Mr. P could bear: "What? You're too damn much, Mishka," he laughed.

"Like Joan Crawford," Mishka cheered.

Still laughing, Mr. P shook his head, not understanding the reference.

Mishka returned Mr. P's laugh and defended himself in jest: "I'm the real victim, the victim of my own generous, social spirit, I shouldn't be punished for that, I should be rewarded... preferably with a pair of Ferregamos and maybe even a ring, a great big shiny one from Georg Jensen or Bulgari?"

Mr. P was in a good mood now and inclined to grant Mishka his wishes, but he knew, this would just lead to bigger and bigger requests later.

"You greedy child. I'll get you the shoes and we'll see about the ring some other time," Mr. P said, still laughing.

"FINE!" Mishka shouted, tossing both his arms in the air. "But I still want the ring another time and it better be at *least* a carat worth of neatly stacked carbon atoms," he added, emphasizing the word 'least'.

Mr. P grabbed Mishka's head and held it under his arm, as he roughly rustled Mishka's hair, as he laughed. "You'll get what I give and you'll like it."

To stop it, Mishka grabbed Mr. P's groin and pulled his head out from under Mr. P's arm.

Mr. P just laughed, feeling the negotiation had come to an end and he could claim, what he felt it had bought him. So, he quickly grabbed Mishka and pushed his tongue down Mishka's throat, before Mishka could ask for more goods. Mr. P's hands were moving all over Mishka's body, grabbing every limb hard, as his hands encountered them. Mr. P forced Mishka into his bedroom and threw him down on the bed, so hard Mishka feared it would break. Instead, the heavy motion caused the madras to flex up and down, like a trampoline. Mr. P had that intense, almost psychotic look he always got, right before sex. It meant Mr. P could no longer be reached by the outside world, he had retreated into himself, as he indulged in the sexual proclivities he was ashamed of having.

Sex with Mr. P was like psychoanalyzing him. Mr. P was intentionally rough and inconsiderate, bordering on ruthless. It had felt unsafe at first, but now it had become routine for Mishka. Mishka knew it was part of Mr. P's performance of the straight, white male. Mr. P felt ashamed of not being heteronormative, he habitually carried out his homosexual urges with younger men, he paid and was intentionally rough with them, to explain away his homosexuality as something he just did for entertainment, to try it. It was a way for Mr. P to try to retain control over his own self-concept and social identity and Mishka knew that. But there were times, right before and right after Mr. P orgasmed, when he forgot himself and he would be sweet and tender with Mishka. It had been hard the first time, when he didn't know Mr. P would ease up exponentially as he came closer to climax. Mr. P would always start by kissing him and caressing him, giving him harder and harder kisses and tightening his grip. Then Mr. P would grab Mishka's head with both hands and force Mishka to his cock. Holding Mishka's head fast by his hair or by his ears, while he forced his cock in and out of Mishka's mouth, slapping Mishka, when he did something wrong or just to be rough. Other times he would pin Mishka down over a piece of furniture, placing his left hand hard on the middle of Mishka's back to forcefully hold him down and using his right hand to first rip off Mishka's clothing, secondly to force his cock into Mishka's ass and then place it under Mishka's right hip, to steer his ass, while the tempo increased, then just as the tempo reached the highest, Mr. P would ease up his grip, let the tempo go down, use more rhythm in his movements and start to softly cuddle Mishka, while he panted out genuine compliments. It was always the same with Mr. P and Mishka had come into the habit of it, he'd even come to enjoy it and take pleasure in it.

Most of his patrons, by far, were rough, in the same way as Mr. P, some were soft from start to finish, but only Mr. P took Mishka in this exact way. That was one thing Mishka had learned from his patrons, sex was not as varied, as most people thought.

As Mishka lay on his stomach groaning, he thought about the weekly cases of whiskey and browsed Ferragamo shoes in his mind, trying to choose the style he'd get, when they were finished. Mr. P was gasping and trusting harder, until he collapsed down on Mishka, in a giant moan and softly whispered, "You're so beautiful," into Mishka's ear.

When Mr. P had finished they were both exhausted by their physical and emotional performances, so they fell asleep in the bed, Mishka sleeping on his left side, in the fetal position, turning away from Mr. P.

A few hours later, Mishka was awakened by a strange tickling sensation on the right side of his torso. He drowsily opened his eyes, to see Mr. P wiping his nose up from Mishka hip to his ribs, while making a snorting noise.

"Wha-what are you doing?" Mishka asked half asleep, with little interest.

Mr. P tilted his head to meet Mishka's gaze, now wiping his nose with his fingers, still snorting.

"Want some?" Mr. P asked, offering up a small silver pill box, holding white powder.

"Coke? I heard of this model, who did so much coke, she damaged her nose. Completely lost that thing, that separates the nostrils. She looks terrible... No one wants her now." Mishka said matter-of-fact, mostly for his own ears and lay his head down, to go back to sleep.

"Suit yourself," Mr. P said, drizzling some more coke over Mishka's torso, in a long, sloppy line and snorted the whole thing.

Inside, Mishka was shocked by Mr. P's behavior, but he didn't know what to do about it. It seemed very middle class to be so shocked by someone doing cocaine of him, but he was middle class, no matter how hard he tried to escape it.

"Please don't," Mishka pleaded, as Mr. P drizzled yet another line of coke on Mishka's body.

"I thought I had the night?" Mr. P asked bewildered, still hutched in the same position, as when he was snorting coke of Mishka.

Mishka recognized this attitude. Most of his patrons really viewed him as an object, which he rather liked, what he didn't like, was the fact that they thought they owned him and could do what they wanted, without silly things like consent.

Mishka always tried to shut down these acts of implied ownership and tonight was no different. He got up from the bed, paced over to a side chair and put on the dressing gown, that was draped over it, then turned around in a swift movement.

"Well, you don't!" Mishka said, determined, as he collected Mr. P's clothes. Mr. P stretched himself out on the bed, flexing his muscles and gave a tired, frustrated sigh.

"But what about the ring," Mr. P haggled.

Mishka started to realize the precariousness of his position and the danger of being so standoff-ish to one of his favorite patrons. He changed tactic. Mishka lay down on the bed next to Mr. P, caressing his face.

"You're good man," Mishka said, touching Mr. P's muscles, to make him feel more masculine.

"I'm sorry, darling. Anyway, I haven't gotten a ring yet, bring it to me next time and we can continue the night then." Mishka added.

Mr. P was perplexed by the sudden change in moods, frowned his eyebrows and inspected Mishka's face. Then, like he remembered Mishka couldn't be trusted, he relaxed his face and chuckled. As a response, Mr. P grabbed Mishka by his hair and forced his head down to his penis. Mishka knew, this was an olive branch, so he opened his mouth to receive Mr. P's cock and sucked it the way he knew Mr. P liked it.

"That's my good little girl," Mr. P moaned repeatedly, until he let out his final groan.

Afterwards, Mr. P was satisfied and more docile.

As Mishka went to the bathroom to use some mouth wash and fix his makeup, before he said goodbye, Mr. P fixed Mishka's allowance and put it on the bedside table. Mishka always made sure he looked good at the start and end of every visit of each of his patrons, he saw a lot of power in first and last impressions.

When he came out of the bathroom, Mr. P was almost done putting on his drab suit. Mishka leaned in the doorway of the bedroom and saw Mr. P getting ready to leave, scanning the room for any items he may have left behind, making sure he hadn't forgotten anything and repeatedly checking if he still had his wallet. Mr. P always seemed anxious not to leave anything behind, a habit which made Mishka feel closer to Mr. P. They were bound together by their mutual understanding and mistrust. They saw the worst in each other and still enjoyed each other's company.

Having finished dressing, Mr. P gave the bedroom a fifth and final scan and that's when he noticed Mishka. In his postcoital mood, he gave Mishka a crooked smile and Mishka smiled back.

"I'm gonna head out," Mr. P explained.

"Really?" Mishka said ambiguously, in the hope it would haunt Mr. P, not knowing if it made him happy or sad.

"Yeah, but let's see each other soon. I'll take you out to dinner. Give you that ring," Mr. P. said, giving Mishka a quick kiss on the lips, as he walked out of the bedroom, heading for the door.

This gave Mishka some pause, it seemed too romantic for Mr. P, he was always trying to distance himself emotionally. Not knowing what was actually being said, Mishka didn't reply, but herded Mr. P to the door.

When they stood in the doorway Mr. P looked at him, with frowned eyebrows, by the lack of response.

"Unless you don't want the ring anymore?" Mr. P

threatened.

Now, he knew he'd hurt Mr. P by his unresponsiveness, but he could use that, so he hesitantly answered.

"Dinner sounds lovely, It'd be great, if I'm not too busy. Text me the details."

"Hmm," Mr. P grunted, giving Mishka a long stare, as he walked down the corridor.

When Mr. P was out of sight, Mishka closed the door and put on the safety lock, while he unconsciously shook his head, as he thought about how fussy these patrons were. Either they felt Mishka was clingy or too emotionally unavailable. It was an impossible balance, but he knew it was better for him to be distant and unavailable, then obviously interested. He'd learned that with his first few patrons. When he was unavailable, they got possessive and worked harder to prove to themselves, that Mishka 'belonged' to them, which meant more attention and better gifts. When they felt certain Mishka was theirs or they thought they owned Mishka outright, they'd usually dump him for someone else.

It all seemed so simplistic and juvenile to him, despite they fact, that these patrons were sometimes sixty years his senior.

Mishka enjoyed being alone. He jumped into the shower, thoroughly cleaning his body and his ass, so he no longer smelled of Mr. P or his cum. He didn't clean his face or hair, since he didn't want to reapply his makeup or style his hair again. He already spent a lot on hair and skincare products, he didn't have the money or time to reapply every time he was fucked. When he got out of the shower, he put on deodorant and lots of perfume, to make him smell completely clean and erase every whiff of humanity. He hated smelling like a person, he preferred the artisanal smell of designer scents, preferably leathery, musky ones, that smelled a bit of sex.

He felt spent, still feeling Mr. P's harsh grasps and his rough penetrations, so he put on a fresh kimono and went into the living room to lie lazily on the chaise. He lied like a cat, enjoying the feel of the kimono against his naked skin.

Outside the window the sun was beginning to go down, which meant the whole séance with Mr. P must have been at least four hours.

But it was over now.

Finally, he was alone. He could only ever be himself, when he was alone, when he was put in any social context, no matter how informal, he couldn't help but acting out a version of himself, that he felt the others wanted. He always played a role. This caused him to often isolate himself, since being with others invariably became work. It was work to pretend to be something, for everyone else.

He stretched out his body and massaged his temples, while giving out a slow, unconscious growl. His stomach was growling too. He hadn't eaten anything all day, but because he'd been occupied, he hadn't consciously abstained from food, but now, when there was nothing taking up his thoughts, he felt he was starving. Eating was a serious and dangerous undertaking for him, which required long deliberation over the pros and cons. Eating something would give his body some peace and make it ache a little less, but it would trouble his mind and make him fatter, less desirable. Daily, he would negotiate eating in a long internal discussion, which would most often end with him drowning his hunger in coffee and cigarettes.

For the moment his deliberations were interrupted by the

sound of someone at his front door. Someone was trying to unlock the door. He hoped it wasn't Mr. P again, he didn't have the energy to deal with him again.

At this moment, all he wanted was to be alone. So much so, that he felt almost personally attacked, by the intrusion of a visitor.

He listened for any sign of who it could be. The intruder got more and more heavy handed with the door and suddenly kicked it.

He lay stiff, motionless, and completely quiet in the chaise.

Some recognizable murmurs came from the other side of the door, which Mishka recognized.

He gave a quiet sigh of relief and relaxed. Thank God, it wasn't Mr. P, but Mervin.

Chapter 3

Mishka couldn't be bothered with any more patrons tonight. He needed to feel free, so he hoped that Mervin would give up and go away, if he pretended not to be home. Mishka often locked the safety lock and pretended not to be home, either because he was already with a patron or he didn't have the patience to put up with anyone.

Today, this tactic didn't work. Mervin kept banging the door. If he didn't let him in, the neighbors would be bound to complain and he was already on thin ice with them, because of his constant music and guests coming and going at all hours. He sighed irritably and went to let Mervin in.

Mervin looked stunned, when the door opened, like it was something that defied belief, then he saw Mishka and Mervin just stood glaring, with a stupefied smile.

Mervin was a plump, but elegant gentleman of about seventy or so. Mervin had worked as a publishing executive, but now lived off some obscure investments, that apparently were very lucrative. Mervin was nearly always dressed in the same uniform, a starched white dress shirt, with gold cufflinks and studs, a pastel-colored bowtie, grey flannel trousers, black oxfords and a suit jacket in either tweed or pinstripes. Only on special evenings would he defer from his uniform, by wearing a neutral, black smoking.

Mishka always thought Mervin looked like Hercule Poirot, but with a full beard. It was this imagined similarity, that had endeared Mervin to him, at first sight.

"Well, come in, hurry," Mishka snapped and grabbed Mervin's arm to drag him in.

Despite Mishka's desire to lead a life of scandal and debauchery, he was so markedly middle class, that he instinctively worried about what the neighbors thought and felt uneasy whenever something approached a 'scene'.

Mervin was dragged in and Mishka carefully closed the door behind him, checking that none of the neighbors were keeping watch in the hallway.

Now, that they were alone, Mishka had the serenity to put on his usual conditionally accommodating air.

"We don't have an appointment today, do we, you cad?" Mishka said laughing at Mervin, then furrowed his brows and asked "Or did I forget something?".

Mervin was obviously drunk and Mishka's words didn't seem to land on Mervin. Instead, Mervin was pacing around the living room, like he was looking for something.

Mervin paced around, paranoidly looking about himself and trying to articulate something: "I, I don't know, I suppose it depends…" Mervin said pointing at the wall facing the street. "I was just, uhm enjoying some brandy and a cigar and I thought to come by… as it were."

Then Mishka noticed, Mervin was holding an empty brandy glass and a lit cigar. Mishka stood still, watching the scene with a stoic suspiciousness, while he was waiting for someone to do something about it. Then, remembering it was just him and Mervin there, he came to Mervin's aid.

"I see, but your brandy is all gone, old boy. Did you come here for a top off? I'm afraid I don't have brandy. How about moving on to scotch?" Mishka asked patiently.

The question had the desired effect. Mervin noticed the glass and his cigar. Confused, Mervin started apologizing "Oh dear, I'll be hearing about that from the club. Blast it, the cigar. I'm getting ash everywhere, aren't I. Please, an ashtray."

Mishka was amused and couldn't help laughing. It seemed strange to him, that a man who was usually so responsible and proper, could also behave so silly and undignified. He got up close to Mervin to help him. In his drunken state, Mervin took this as an invitation for intimacy and he started kissing Mishka, with wet loud kisses. Mishka flinched and lovingly took Mervin's arm and led him to an armchair in the corner of the living room. Mishka quickly fetched a crystal ashtray and placed it on the side table next to Mervin. Mervin was breathing heavily in Mishka's proximity, his breath wafted fumes of cigar and alcohol into Mishka's face.

With Mervin seated, Mishka placed himself in the windowsill a few feet away, lit a cigarette and observed Mervin.

Mishka waited for the situation to develop to a critical point or a queue for his line. Mervin just sat there, smoking his cigar, trying to get hold of himself, as Mishka soundlessly went through three cigarettes.

Suddenly, Mervin realized Mishka was there, looking at him. Mervin slowly raised his head, to meet Mishka's gaze. Mishka was looking at him with wondrous eyes and pouted lips, as he posed up against the window sill, smoking out the window.

Neither of them spoke, but Mishka had a long internal dialogue, contemplating what Mervin actually wanted, why had Mervin come and what he could do. Was there anything to be gained here?

Then, as if Mervin sensed his internal discussion, Mervin stammered out: "I brought money!"

Mishka raised his eyebrows and nodded by the brazen mention of money, then he demonstratively put out his cigarette. It was very unlike Mervin to be direct; he was usually more tactful. Mervin was all old school class, like an old Hollywood movie character, behaving like a David Niven character.

Mervin added, stammering: "... P-please, let me reimburse you for any possible damages... It's really the least I can do."

Mishka sighed instead of answering and walked over to Mervin and brushed Mervin's hair, with his fingers. Mervin looked up, like a small child might look at their mother. That gentle look hit a nerve with Mishka, he had an intense feeling he didn't recognize, but he knew he didn't like it. Mishka took Mervin's cigar from his lips, took a few tokes and returned the cigar to Mervin's lips. All the while fondling Mervin's hair with the other hand. Mervin never lost eye contact with Mishka.

"Very nice," Mishka said calmingly, but he couldn't help shivering ever so slightly at Mervin's persistent stare.

There was dead calm in the apartment, which was alien to Mishka, there was usually music playing and he was always occupied with something. The silence became deafening to both of them, as they stared into each other's eyes, both contemplating what they could gain from this moment.

"So nice of you to stop by, were you in the neighborhood?" Mishka asked, mainly to move events along.

"Not so much, no. I was out to dinner with the board, at

the club, we were well served and I wanted the night to continue," Mervin stammered. Mishka tilted his head, let out a childish giggle and reproached Mervin "That's so sweet, you're such a dear. But I'd prefer you'd call before dropping by, when we don't have an appointment."

Without a word, Mervin took out his pocketbook and emptied it for bills, which he casually dropped in the ashtray. Then he grabbed Mishka and dragged him closer to the chair, letting his hands inspect Mishka's young and fresh body.

Meanwhile Mishka tried counting the bills with his eyes, making sure the bills didn't catch fire. It was clearly much more, than he usually got. Mishka was in no mood for this, so he just stood there, letting it happen, as he retreated into himself and tried to disassociate.

Mervin slid the kimono of Mishka and let his hands wander all over Mishka's naked body, trying to excite Mishka, but Mishka remained unexcited and flaccid.

In response, Mishka kneeled before him, unbuttoned Mervin's pants and teased Mervin's semi-hard dick with his tongue, until it got hard. Mishka started stroking and petting it with both hands, while he licked his balls. Mishka continually increased the tempo of his hands, while he kissed, licked and sucked Mervin's balls less and less. Mishka was trying to finish this, as fast as he could. To help himself, he tried thinking about all the things he could buy, with the money Mervin had dropped in the ashtray.

Mervin's breath was getting heavier and heavier and his grunts louder. Mishka waited until he could hear Mervin wasn't far from an orgasm to suck his cock. He sucked Mervin off as hard and intensely as he could, while bumping his forehead into Mervin's hard, round belly. Within a minute or two, Mervin came in his mouth. 'Christ!' Mishka thought to himself, noticing that even Mervin's cum tasted like brandy. It was a big load, it had obviously built up. Mervin probably hadn't had any release, since he was with Mishka five days ago.

Mishka sucked and swallowed until he was sure Mervin was done, then he got up from his knees. He stared down at Mervin, who lay in the chair, with his old, now limp, penis hanging out, grunting slightly, as he came to. Mishka quickly put on his kimono and fled to the bathroom, to wash out his mouth and brush his teeth. When Mishka got back, Mervin was standing by the window, finishing up a conversation on the phone.

"I've just called the car, he'll be here in a minute, then I'll get out of your hair," Mervin informed him.

Mishka answered with a nod and a demure smile, trying not to let it show, he was happy Mervin was going.

It was so funny to him, that Mervin never differentiated between his driver and his car, they were one to Mervin. He wondered if Mervin knew the name of his driver, but then again, he couldn't remember Mervin's real name and he didn't want to, so who was he to judge.

Names humanize us. Just like it's difficult to roast a chicken, you've named when it was alive, it was difficult for Mishka, to exploit people, he'd learned the name of, so he rarely retained anyone's name. Instead, he gave them nicknames, often just calling them by their title, just like Mervin did with his driver.

As they waited for the driver, Mishka felt awkward and didn't know what to do, so he just kept smiling stiffly and giving out small unconscious laughs, whenever they made eye contact.

The awkwardness was quickly interrupted by the door buzzing.

"That'll be him, the car," Mervin said, putting the whiskey down on the windowsill and walking over to the door.

"It was nice tonight," Mervin said, smiling. "Anyway, I better be off," and with that, Mervin slipped out the door.

Chapter 4

Alone at last.

Mervin was out the door and somebody else's problem now and he was free not to think about Mervin or any of them. Now, he could focus on himself. In fact, he couldn't even be bothered to count the money tonight. Finances would have to wait.

Mishka's stomach was rumbling again and it led him into the kitchen. He hadn't eaten all day, but how many calories had he had. He visualized everything he had consumed during the day, as he did every day. He'd had five glasses of water at 0 calories. A cup of black coffee while he dressed at 2 calories.

Then the half bottle of champagne, which was equal to three glasses of champagne at 95 calories a glass, which meant... how did the 9-table go again... 9, 18, 27, okay so 270 calories, plus 5 x 3, 15, so 285 calories of champagne.

He'd also had a whiskey with Mervin, which had probably been a triple shot, so roughly another 330 calories, so 285 + 330, which was... 285 + 15 = 330 − 15, so 300 + 315, + the 2 calories for the coffee, which he had consumed 617 calories today.

So, if he ate an apple, at approximately 95 calories, it would be around 712 calories for the day... that was okay. It wasn't easy to stay hungry, to stay unsated.

He tried to stay between 500 to 1000 calories a day, to keep skinny enough, that he could accept, when his patron took him out to dinner, which happened about two to five times a month. Most of his calories were from booze, which he had learned made it easier not to eat.

The less he ate, the rarer he actually felt hungry. When he went an entire week without eating solid food, his body wouldn't get sick until he began to eat again. Like his body rejected food, didn't recognize it, like a failed organ transplant. To him, starvation was like mounting climbing or diving, he'd train for it, trying to acclimatize to go longer and longer stretches, without getting sick. With each fast he felt he came closer to something impressive, something divine. Fasting made him feel elevated.

He ate the apple, slowly and carefully, since he knew how sick he'd be, if he ate too fast. At the same time, he tried to abstract himself from the sensory experience of eating. He didn't want to be reminded how pleasurable eating could be. He was afraid if he did remember, he wouldn't have the strength to starve himself any longer, which seemed like the only natural thing to do. Starving was an imperative to him. He ***had*** to stop eating, he ***had*** to slim down.

To abstract himself from his apple, he concentrated on what he could see, inspecting his surroundings. He felt proud as he saw the empty food cabinets, the full wine fridge, the full bar cart and all the beautiful porcelain, silverware and other bourgeois luxuries.

By the time he'd finished his apple, he was deep in thought. He contemplated what treatment he would do tonight.

"A milk bath! Like Cleopatra," he whispered out to the empty room. That's what he'd do, take a milk bath! The thought energized him. He swiftly jumped to the refrigerator and took out three cartons of milk and went to the bathroom.

He ran the water in the bathtub until it was freezing, then let it fill the tub, as he poured the three cartons of milk into the water. He got some ice cubes and put them in the tub as well. He rinsed off his makeup by the sink and rubbed his face and body with almond oil before getting into the freezing tub. It was a slow and gradual process, to submerge himself in the freezing, milky water. He had to let the cold grip him bit by bit, first one foot into the water, then the other, then slowly dap himself with the cold milky water, until his body was cold enough for him to lie down in the tub, without his body going into shock from the intense cold. Laying there, the coldness numbed him and he occasionally dipped his head in the milky water.

Using his hands, he carefully washed himself all over, to get the benefits of the cold water and the milk, also reducing the greasiness of the almond oil. The cold was meant to tighten his skin, the milkfat was for moisture, the milk acid to gently peel his skin and the almond oil to soften it. He lay there, meditating and primping until he was cold to the bone, then he got out of the water, being warmed by the room temperature air. He felt such ease during his various nighttime rituals. When the day was behind him, there was nothing he had to do and he had time to himself. Night was generally more enjoyable to him, than mornings.

He scrubbed himself with a clean towel, drying up and taking the rest of the oil off him, leaving his skin fresh, clean and soft.

He put on his kimono, brushed his hair back and took measure of himself in the bathroom mirror.

He really wasn't too bad. His face had clean lines and straight features. The eyes had heavy lids and lashes. His eyebrows did an almost Joan Crawford like bow. His hair was dark and there was plenty of it, even if his hairline had always been a bit too high. He hated his ears though, they looked like they belonged to a chimpanzee, but people didn't seem to mind. In his experience, most patrons appreciated little imperfections like that.

Though he was constantly starving, his reflection was never thin enough, there were always thinner boys out there, prettier boys. He felt he had to compete and it made him anxious.

After brushing his hair, he summed up necessary changes; lose weight, exercise his jaw line, ass, legs and stomach, get supplements to strengthen hair and skin, whiten his skin even more and maybe get an eyelash curler. He was always adding things to his never-ending list of self-improvements, every time he got a compliment, critique, felt less than perfect or caught a glimpse of himself in any reflective surface. His thoughts were always working against him, coming with more and more things that were wrong with him and needed to be dealt with, to be changed. It deprived him of basic human requirements, like eating, resting, emotions.

Booze provided him with a release and he often took a glass of hard liquor, to numb his thoughts and help him sleep at night. Tonight he poured himself a shot of Mr. P's single malt, took a few mild pain killers, put on some Billie Holiday and lied down on his bed, sipped his whiskey and disappeared into the lyrics of 'You Let Me Down'. He played the song over and over again, while finishing his whiskey and he dropped into a whiskey and drug induced sleep. Now he was up to 820 calories.

Chapter 5

"No! No, no!" Mishka mumbled as he woke up.

Without being aware of it himself, he always said "no", right before he woke up. It was quite poetic in a way, since "no" was the first word he had learned as a child. He had hated the way people always fussed and petted him, as a child, so it made sense, that setting boundaries was the first thing he had learned to express. He felt spent.

In his hand, he was still holding the whiskey glass from the night before and Billy Holiday was still playing.

He got up, put the glass on the bedside table and turned off the music. Then he went to the bathroom, splashed some cold water in his face and drank eagerly from the faucet. His breath stank. He flossed and brushed his teeth and went back to the bedroom. Had he finished his glass of whiskey before he fell asleep? He sniffed his sheets, but they didn't smell like whiskey, but of Mr. P's sweat and cum. There didn't seem to be any whiskey stains, so it was probably fine, he must have drunk it all. The sheets should probably be washed anyway – he'd do it later.

He checked the time on his phone; it was five a.m., then checked his calendar; no appointments today. 'Oh, thank God,' he thought and went back to sleep.

He woke four hours later very abruptly and jumped out of bed. He was suddenly wide awake. He went to the kitchen and put on the kettle. As he waited for the water to boil, he drank glass after glass of water, while downing pain killers and various supplements for his skin, hair, appetite suppressants etc. Then he clenched and released his buttocks 100 times, did 100 chin crunches and started on 100 sit ups. He counted out loud, as he did his exercises, careful to do each exercise 100 times exactly. The kettle started whistling when he'd reached 78, but he ignored it until he'd reached the 100.

He made his coffee and arranged a tray, with a French press pot, skimmed milk, a gilded cup with saucer and a glass of water, then took the tray to the bedroom.

It was a warm morning, so he dropped the kimono he'd slept in, dapped on some of his favorite cologne, put on some music, a playlist of assorted Maria Callas performances and took his tray with him to bed.

He half lay, half sat in the bed, sipping his coffee and enjoying the music and his own nakedness.

The strong coffee energized him and made him jumpy, which he rather liked. He fidgeted and kept resituating himself in bed, which nearly caused several accidents, as the tray and all its content bounced up and down, every time Mishka shifted his body. The reason he drank French press coffee was because of the high caffeine content, which he'd read in several lifestyle magazines would boost his metabolism and help burn fat. It also helped to lessen his hunger and gave him the energy he wasn't getting from food. Usually he drank up to two to three liters of coffee a day, leaving him almost frantic with energy.

In his jumpiness, he looked for something more concrete to focus on then music and his fifth cup of coffee. He remembered the money Mervin had left last night and how he hadn't counted it yet. The thought made him rush out of bed and he skipped naked into the living room, where he snatched the dusty cash from the ashtray and started counting the bills: 500, 100, 100, 200, 100, 1000, 500, 200, 1000, 100, 1000, 1000, 200, 1000.' He slowly did the math in his mind, 7000 Danish kroner in cash... Mervin usually didn't leave more than 2000-3000 Danish kroner a visit. Mishka felt uneasy about this generosity, especially because Mervin had done it, without trying to harvest praise or gain some special 'service', like that time he tried to persuade Mishka into a threesome with some cheap and ghastly girl. In the end Mishka had done it for 10,000 but he'd hated it and wasn't going to do it again. In group sex, he'd learned, you had to compete for attention and adoration and he didn't care for that – too risky.

What could this money mean? Mishka was getting paranoid...

As he saw it, there were three possible reasons for the extra cash.

Option one; this was Mervin's way of saying goodbye and the money was a sort of severance package, to pacify Mishka into not making a fuss or telling Mrs. Mervin and that's why he hadn't mentioned the extra cash, because he wanted to leave, before Mishka found out and guessed what it was about.

Option two; Mervin was so drunk he didn't actually know, how much cash he'd left, but thought it was the regular amount.

Option three; the extra money was given to him out of gratitude, because Mervin was embarrassed, that he'd come by while he was soused and without an appointment.

The last option sounded almost too good to be true, so it probably was. Option one seemed very convoluted, but it was possible, if so he'd receive a note or something or someone would come and kick him out of the appointment, which was legally Mervin's.

So, it must be option number two, he got the extra cash out of sheer neglectful luck, unless there was a worse option, that he hadn't even thought of...

Either way, he probably shouldn't spend any of the money, until he knew he hadn't lost Mervin's patronage. He sighed deeply, annoyed by the ambiguity of Mervin's sudden generosity.

What he needed now was a distraction. Something to clear his mind. Instinctively he looked for his phone. Where was it, the little sneak. He never could find things. Oh, he must have left it in the bedroom, when he put on music.

He went into the bedroom, found his phone and lied down on the bed. He checked Instagram, scrolling through his feed to find something entertaining, something to strive for. He looked detached and disinterested at myriads of selfies of fashionistas with hyped teas or coffees, at events, shopping or on vacation. Each selfie looked curiously like the last, some faces he recognized from the night life, some he didn't, but all of them bored him in their commonplaceness and similarity.

In an attempt to see something new, he switched to search on Instagram and scanned the various images until he found something interesting; the top half of a naked man in an outdoor shower, on the terrace of a high-end rural country estate. The man in the picture had the kind of body, where you're not quite sure how much is muscle and how much is fat. He just looked big, as did the house and the surrounding grounds.

The caption read: 'Make bank, spend bank, wash and repeat'.

This maxim excited Mishka, even more than the man's bulgy appearance. He inspected the picture more closely. The house, the terrace and the plants in the picture were all very well kept, which likely meant there was a household staff in his budget. The man had streaks of silver on both his facial and body hair.

This was the type of man Mishka had always dreamed of and he could feel the blood rushing from his head, slowly hardening his penis.

Mishka wondered how old the man was, he guessed around forty-five. He went to his profile. There was no clue in his bio, so he scrolled down locking for clues and found a picture, that was obviously a birthday party. Fifty-two, he was fifty-two! At this news Mishka's penis got a little harder and he was now close to being fully erect. He went back to the original picture and started touching himself softly and slowly, while he inspected every inch of the man's body and estimated the cost of the house in the background. He was almost built like a Scottish pole thrower, with a big frame, that emulated strength and an excess of both food consumption and exercise.

While Mishka was still touching himself, he looked through the myriads of pictures of the man on his Instagram profile. This man was obviously a narcissist, obsessed with himself and his lifestyle, posting all aspects of his life. Mishka swallowed all the information and images on the man's profile, all the while Mishka got more and more excited and stroked his penis increasingly harder and faster. Apparently, the man was an American hedge fund manager. There was also a post that referenced an article about him in some business magazine. Mishka started moaning, as he got rougher with himself. He went further to read the article and then searched for the guy's net worth, which he found out was estimated to almost eleven million USD. Mishka's penis got wet with pre-sperm. Then he went back to the first Instagram picture he saw of him, turned to his back and held the picture up over his head. Mishka touched himself ferociously as he pictured a life together with this man and his eleven million. He thought of days spent shopping with this man's credit cards, being at his side at fancy restaurants and nights spent underneath the man's sweaty and bulgy body, thrusting itself in and out of him. It was with these materialistic dreams of wealth and patronization, that Mishka lost in himself in an orgasm and ejaculated all over his own stomach.

Mishka let his phone drop down in bed next to him, rested his body and let his penis grow limp, while he tried to catch his breath.

The dream was over.

Mishka grabbed his phone and took a selfie, showing his flushed face and his cum stained upper body, which he posted on Snap Chat and his Instagram only fans profile, with the caption: 'Missing daddy'. It didn't make sense, but he hoped the hedge fund manager guy would see his selfie somehow and masturbate to him as well.

Semen was a good anti-ager, he remembered, as he looked down and saw his cum-soaked stomach. Mishka wiped the cum of his stomach with his hands and smeared it all over his face.

He'd read that sperm was an effective way to prevent lines and wrinkles. So, he figured he might as well use it, when the chance arose. He cleaned his hands with an antibacterial wet wipe, from his nightstand, then he grabbed his phone to see what he looked like. It was probably hot to some, he thought and took and posted another selfie on Snap Chat, showing his tussled hair and cum-wetted face. This time with the tagline 'trouble tastes good'.

Carefully he got up and went to the bathroom to rinse off his excitement and then commenced his usual, extensive, bath routine.

After the shower, followed his comprehensive grooming routine, after which he walked around his bedroom naked, trying to pick out an outfit, but he felt unmotivated to be anything today. There was only one thing to do, he simply had to go to the botanical gardens.

He had adopted these imperatives from Evelyn Waugh's character Sebastian Flyte and made a habit of them. Turning his wishes into imperatives had become useful to Mishka, both in his private life and in his dealings with older men. It was impressive to Mishka, how easy life was, when you simply took choice out of the equation. If you felt like going to the botanical gardens, then it meant you HAD to go to the botanical gardens. If you felt a patron should take you out to dinner at D'Angleterre or buy you a new suit, then he HAD to do so. Most of his patrons were rather obliging, when it came to Mishka imperatives, since they themselves were ambitious men, who understood demanding appetites. They also appreciated that Mishka's imperatives were trifling in their eyes.

The idea of walking in the botanical gardens cheered him up and gave him some focus.

Determined, he went to his closet and quickly picked out a pair of charcoal, pin striped, cropped trousers, an olive-green mock turtleneck sweater, that fell oversized, like a parachute, over Mishka's starved body and a pair of black alligator loafers. For some reason, the outfit reminded him of Audrey Hepburn as Holly Golightly, which made him laugh. To enhance the experience and the reference he topped off the look with the Oliver Goldsmith sunglasses, that Audrey Hepburn had worn in the movie.

He grabbed his keys, phone and pocketbook and threw them in a clutch and went out the door.

The weather was mild, but the sun was shining. Mishka smiled to himself, it was the perfect day to walk in a garden.

It was five kilometers to the botanical gardens and Mishka walked eagerly the whole way, so he could get some exercise, while he smoked a cigarette to dull his hunger.

As he walked, he noticed people taking notice of him, staring at him and some even stopping in their tracks to take sight of him, as he swiftly stomped pass them. For some people looking wasn't enough, they had to pass commentary. The word 'queer' was angrily thrown at him, from the open window of a passing car. This is how it usually was, when Mishka went outside and he hated it. The fact was, that Mishka looked so terribly out of place in the common streets and it caught people's attention. It made people view and treat him like a misplaced object. Some people simply wondered how he'd gotten there, others viewed him as a rare find and then there were those, who saw him as something suspicious and dangerous, that had to be exterminated.

For Mishka, walking in the streets was a manic experience, where he unintentionally disrupted the world and divided everyone into groups of supporters, admirers and haters.

It was different when he went out with someone, like one of his boyfriends, then the disapproving looks were rare. Being with other men, seemed to validate Mishka in the eyes of the masses or at least place him in a place beyond their critique. Mishka sometimes wondered why that was, but he always got distracted by something or other, before he could reach a conclusion.

Not knowing how to deal with the world, he simply ignored it and hid behind his sunglasses. Sunglasses had become a staple part of his armor when he ventured outside in public. The sunglasses provided him with a sense of protection and separation from the gawking masses. Though he realized the irony, that the armor he used to protect himself from the masses, was part of what made him conspicuous to the normative majority. He hated the majority of 'ordinary people', with their complete lack of imagination, lack of manners, lack of style and their base uniformity.

It wasn't all bad though, he always got a few looks of appreciation or attraction and even some compliments.

As he reached the gate of the botanical gardens, he paused for a moment to give the situation an air of gravity. The botanical gardens were one of his holy places, so he made small gestures to honor it and entered with serenity, like a true believer might do at their place of worship.

He strolled slowly around in the garden, taking small, deliberate steps to keep from dirtying his shoes and to take it all in. The botanical gardens were holy to him because he saw it as a place of delicately constructed beauty, with the carefully pruned flowers and trees, that had been planted and arranged so neatly. Unlike wild nature, a park grew out of planning and continuous care and was made for the pleasure of civilized people. He liked that, he empathized with each flower, bush and tree in the gardens.

Out in the wild forests and heaths, plants grew despite civilization, in a wild Darwinian competition for life, for the sake of living. Mishka hated the wild, simply because it was uncivilized, untamed and because it was impossible to engage with it in elegant outfits. He saw wild nature as filth, waiting to dirty the shoes and trousers of anyone who ventured into it.

Mishka bowed down and slipped off his sunglasses to inspect a bush of dark ruby flowers. The sign read "Nerium Oleander Rubis". He'd read somewhere, that oleanders were extremely poisonous, that even honey made from oleander pollen could kill you. He inspected the flowers again. Suddenly they seemed rather impressive, being both delicate and deadly at the same time. Mishka fell into meditation, staring at the red oleanders and only came to, when he felt someone staring. He looked around to see who was watching him. It was a handsome man in some sort of uniform, pulling weeds in a flower bed close by, so he was most likely a gardener working for the gardens. The man was smiling crookedly and looked persistently at Mishka, with a curious stare. Mishka gave the gardener a meek smile and quickly diverted his eyes. Mishka gave the oleanders one last look, as he paced away. He could have sworn the oleanders had an almost menacing look in their blushed petals.

As Mishka was strolling along the path, getting further and further away from the handsome man, he was a bit unsettled by the man's unabashed stare. Mishka looked discretely back. Was he still staring? No, he was focused on the flowers and weeds again! Mishka observed the gardener flexing his arms, as he pulled up weeds and the curve of his ass, as he bent down.

He was very handsome!

And strong!

What *does* a gardener make a year?

Maybe he was a botanist, not a gardener, maybe that was better?

Mishka mused whether he should go back and start a conversation with him. Maybe he could be happy with a botanist? He certainly wasn't happy now.

Maybe he could date the botanist, they could become boyfriends and spend their time cooking for each other and watch movies together, then eventually move in together in a small apartment or maybe a small house in the suburbs and get a cat or something? Wasn't that what people did? Could he really do it, switch out champagne for Netflix and chill? What would he wear? A velvet smoking jacket was probably too formal for that kind of casual, domesticated bliss... maybe they would be that kind of couple, that left the door open to the bathroom? No, he could never be comfortable with that, in fact, none of it sounded like him. Did other people find happiness in that sort of docile lifestyle? Anyway, he wasn't trying to be happy, had never tried it, he tried to be beautiful and that's why the man looked at him. Happiness is too fleeting, like in Voltaire's Candide! Everyday routines could turn any happiness into tediousness.

Besides, being in a real relationship like that would mean compromises and giving up individual freedom and for what, what did you get in return?

He remembered how his mother used to tell him, he'd never be happy. The first time she'd said it, he was taken aback. They had been sitting in each their sofa in the living room of his parents' house, reading each their own book and his mother's statement had seemed so out of context. Then, he'd asked for an explanation and she'd reasoned, that to be happy meant being contend with the way things were and he always wanted something more or something different, then what he had and so, he would never be happy. In shock he hadn't responded, but just turned his attention back to the book he'd been reading. His mother had often repeated it since and each time he had avoided responding.

Maybe that was what the gardener was, something different?

Mishka was almost at the café in the botanical gardens and decided to sit down for tea.

A waitress came, took his order and came back with his pot of tea, but when he reached for the cup, he suddenly saw bruises all around his wrist.

Mr. P had been too rough last night! Or did it happen with Mervin when he'd tried lifting him up? He wondered if the waitress had noticed the bruises, he hoped she hadn't. What would she think of it, if she had, what did she make of him?

Thank God he didn't have any appointments today.

Over his tea he pondered about his patron's relationship with bruising. He'd noticed that patrons didn't like to see bruises caused by other men, but they didn't seem to mind if they'd left the marks themselves. Some of them almost seemed proud to see the marks they had left on him. It probably gave them a feeling of power and potency, that helped them feel masculine enough for the society they lived in. Maybe it enhanced the feeling of possession, they usually felt for him, the same way farmers marked their livestock, like Edelweiss ponies.

He had almost finished the whole pot of tea and had succeeded in ignoring the complimentary butter cookies, when he noticed the gardener was walking past. Mishka fled to the bathroom, where he took some concealer from his bag and began covering up the bruises on his wrist. How far did the bruising go? He took off his sunglasses so he could inspect and effectively apply the concealer. It was mostly his right wrist and some around his left elbow, not too bad. He washed concealer off his fingers, put on his sunglasses and went back out.

Instead of returning to his table, Mishka paid his bill at the bar counter, so he could hurry away, without meeting the gardener again. As he was paying, he noticed the waitress inspecting him, with a patient smile. Had she noticed the bruises? Did he really deserve pity from a waitress? Between the waitress and the gardener, Mishka felt hunted and judged, so he hurried out of the café and rushed through the gardens, until he was back out on the streets.

What now? What time was it? 5.10 p.m., had he really been in the gardens that long?

He walked lazily towards the city center. His stomach growled and he answered it by lighting a cigarette.

Unsure of where he should go, he walked aimlessly through the streets.

Clouds were gathering and it was getting dark, yet he kept his sunglasses on, to avoid eye contact with the passersby. People were still staring at him, as he walked by and it made him feel self-conscious and unsure of what he should do with his hands, so he lit cigarette after cigarette to keep himself busy and hid behind his dark sunglasses.

He walked for a few hours, without direction, zigzagging through midtown, until it started to drizzle. One of his favorite hotel bars was nearby and so he decided to go there. He felt safe there.

When he entered the hotel, the concierge smiled disinterested at him.

Mishka was often here, so the concierge knew him by looks and knew his type. Boys and girls like Mishka brought business to these exclusive hotels and the concierges all knew this, but they also saw them as types that were best left to their own devices. Mishka went to the bathroom to dry off with a towel and then proceeded to the bar. Unlike the concierges, the bartenders were always very attentive to types like Mishka, since they drank like fish, usually tipped well and inspired big orders from the more affluent guests.

Mishka sat down in a plush velvet sofa and dried himself off, as a waiter appeared.

"Hey beautiful, good to see you. What can I get you tonight?"

Mishka was startled "Oh, hello Albert. I didn't know you were working here, I thought you were still at Retro Bar?"

"Nah, I started here like a month ago. It's great, higher salary and bigger tips. I'm seeing a guy now, a Brazilian guy named Joao, who studies art. So, yeah, things are good. You're up to your old tricks, I assume. What can I get you?" Albert answered and asked casually.

"Yes, you know me, having fun. A bloody mary, please." Mishka answered, disheartened that Albert had a new boyfriend.

"Coming right up," Albert replied, as he winked and walked away.

Mishka always felt a little awkward around Albert.

When Mishka was new in town, he had often come to Retro Bar to meet people. On the night he first saw Albert working in the bar, Mishka had gotten way too drunk, drinking alone at the bar counter and he'd started flirting with Albert. At the end of that night Mishka had run up a big bill and Albert had offered to foot the bill, if Mishka went home with him and in his loneliness, poverty and vanity, Mishka had readily agreed. But they'd rarely seen each other since, except when they'd bumped into each other by chance or for a late-night hook up. It had never really turned into a real relationship because they were a bad match. Albert was so content with a life in a small, rundown apartment in the further outskirts of the city, living a life of bartending for pennies and partying between shifts. Mishka didn't fit into that life, just like Albert didn't fit into Mishka's ambitions. They were friendly though, because Albert had never seemed to have a problem with Mishka's way of life. Sometimes Albert had even asked Mishka to entertain certain men he knew, from the bars he worked at.

Albert silently served Mishka his bloody mary, with a wink and lusty smile, quickly retreating behind his bar counter.

As Mishka sipped his drink and occasionally took a careful bite of his celery, he logged the 140 calories away in his mind. The drink helped him, he felt less faint and could concentrate on other things, than his growling stomach, so the calories were well spent.

His eyes scanned the room. The place was pretty empty. It was just about seven p.m. so most people were thinking about dinner, not drinks.

He loved the enormity of the big hall and the high ceiling, not to mention the richness of the furnishings and the quiet atmosphere. That was the main reason he frequented hotel bars, they were always spacious, grandiose and calm.

The other reason he went to hotel bars was of course the abundance of bored, rich men, that were usually quite easy to catch. All you had to do there, was sit back, look young and wait for someone to stare at you or send over a drink. In places like this, the older men often took initiative, so it was easy money.

Mishka finished his bloody mary and had Albert bring him a dry martini. The alcohol was getting to him and made him feel at ease.

And so Mishka sat meditating over his drink and enjoying his surroundings, just waiting for something to happen. A few hours went by like that, with Mishka doing his best to ignore the other guests, that were coming in for pre- or post-dinner drinks or starting a night out.

After a while, one of the bartenders dimmed the lights and turned up the music. Mishka knew that meant it was around nine p.m. and it would soon start to get even busier.

Shortly after, a tall, grey-haired man appeared at the seating arrangement, where Mishka was sitting. "What are you doing all alone," he asked Mishka.

"Drinking," Mishka replied, while taking a long, drawn out sip of his martini, pointedly staring at the man the whole time, both to create tension and give himself time to take stock of the man.

The man was dressed all in black, wearing a black shirt under a black wool crepe suit, possibly Armani, with well-polished black oxfords. His hair was varying shades of grey, cut and styled in a classic pompadour.

"But it's no good drinking alone. Hasn't anyone ever told you that?" the man teased. "Allow me to join you," the man added, as he quickly sat down next to Mishka, before he could reply.

He was clearly a man used to getting his way, that was evident from his direct and uncreative manner. But in Mishka's experience, most rich men were like that.

"How kind of you," Mishka said tepidly, downing the last drops of his drink, before adding; "but I've already finished off my martini."

The man sat grinning like a Cheshire cat, clearly amused by Mishka's small gesture of resistance.

"Luckily, I know a cure for that," the man said, raising his hand to signal the bartender and immediately Albert brought a bottle of champagne and two glasses, without any words exchanged between either party. Clearly, this was a matter of routine, well-known to the staff through countless repetitions and by the clichéd nature of the move.

"What makes you think I'd sit here and drink with you? A complete stranger. My mother warned me about those!" Mishka asked, trying to fain indignance. He'd learned that men like that, who are used to getting their way, didn't value anything they got easily – another cliché, but a true one.

The man let out a few laughs, while he filled up both glasses and replied, "Two reasons. One, because that's exactly the sort of thing you do and two, I bet we won't be estranged for long. Here's your drink, cheers."

He handed Mishka a glass, clinked his own glass into it and drank his champagne in one big gulp. Mishka sat motionless and stared, with furrowed brows, trying to figure out if this 'scene study' was good or bad.

"What's the matter, you don't like champagne? I'll get you something else if you like... Say something!" the man asked hastily.

"No, no, I adore it. I'm just trying to figure you out," Mishka said softly and sipped his champagne.

"Oh," the man chuckled, "that's all. That is not so difficult. I'm Phillip Jaeger. I've noticed you before and I've heard good things. When I saw you alone tonight, I thought we should meet. You still go by Mishka, right?"

"Yes," Mishka replied hesitantly, still waiting for a clue, as to whether this meeting was a good opportunity.

For a few minutes they just stared at each other. Mishka let out a small 'hmpf' and shifted his attention to his champagne. He could feel Phillip was still staring at him and that pleased him.

Phillip moved closer and asked: "What do you like?"

"Oh, I like lots of things," Mishka answered vaguely, still concentrating on his champagne. Mishka had learned, that it was good policy never to answer direct questions or say anything of note. If he left enough room for interpretation, people tended to turn him into exactly what they wanted him to be.

"I bet you do," Phillip said with a smirk.

"Do you? Isn't that terribly boring?" Mishka asked.

"What?" Phillip asked as he moved even closer, enjoying the suspense.

"Betting? You keep betting on things. Betting we won't stay estranged, betting I like lots of things," Mishka clarified.

Phillip laughed. "No, no. Not anymore."

"So, you did. What made you stop?" Mishka said in surprise. He hadn't expected an actual answer.

"A lot of money and a little responsibility," Phillip sighed.

"You lost too much and felt guilty, you mean?" Mishka

asked, as he emptied his champagne glass and refilled both their glasses.

"It was more about the line of command. I had fun gambling my father's money. If I lost his money, I hadn't lost anything myself, but if I won gambling his money, I'd earned my own. There's no risk in risking someone else's capital. When he died, I took over the money and I stopped gambling. Now, I invest instead, which is close to the same thing, but not quite," Phillip explained, as if Mishka was somehow completely aware of Phillips personal and financial history. Mishka was warming to Phillip, he reminded him of Omar Shariff in Funny Girl.

"Except for betting on me and my answers. Or is that an investment too?" Mishka said, while downing his second glass of champagne.

"We'll see. Betting is a recreational sport, investment is asset acquirement. I guess it depends if it's fun or work," Phillip said as he refilled Mishka empty glass.

"Does it have to be either or? Can't it be both?" Mishka asked, with wide staring eyes, as he slurped some more champagne.

Phillip just sat there, staring and smiling again, self-assured, until he broke the silence. "What do you want, Mishka?"

A direct question. Mishka sat still and posed like a statue, as he tried to think of a fun evasive answer. It had already taken too long, not to sound like a line, so he knew it had to sound revealing.

Phillip repeated himself, adding to the tension. "What do you want? Do you know?"

Suddenly Mishka perked up, smiled and slowly answered,

"More! I just want more!"

Phillip smile widened. "You're greedy boy, aren't you Mishka!"

Without confirming or denying, Mishka returned the judgement and asked, "What are you?"

"A man with enough to take care of an odd greedy child or two. Enough to satisfy you, if you satisfy me." Phillip said, with an intensity in his voice, that sounded mildly threatening.

Mishka swallowed the last of his champagne, then downed Phillips and said, "Let's put it to a test".

Phillip signaled to the bartenders and said, "See, I won. I said we wouldn't keep being strangers". Just then Albert came up.

"Yes, sir?" Albert said.

"Will you prepare another room, just for tonight and bill the champagne to the room," Phillip instructed.

Mishka couldn't help noticing the wording; 'another room' and 'just for tonight'. Obviously, Phillip did this all the time, most likely consecutively and sometimes spent more than one night at a time, with the boys he picked up in the bar.

Albert returned a second later with a key, winking to Mishka, as he handed the key to Phillip. It usually interested Albert, when Mishka got picked up, but Mishka had yet to figure out, if Albert's interest was out of jealousy or entertainment.

In the hotel room Phillip moved fast. Without a word, he removed Mishka's clothes until he was in his underwear, then tossed him on the bed and started undressing himself, while Mishka watched. As he took off his pants, Phillip grabbed his pocketbook and counted out "1000-2000-3000-4000-5000-6000-7000-8000-9000-10,000 kroner" and put the banknotes on a side table. Mishka couldn't help touching himself, as Phillip counted out the money. The most Mishka had ever made from a one-nightstand was 6,000 kroner, usually he only got between 2,000 to 4,000 from a first-time thing. When Phillip dropped triple his usual rate on the side table, Mishka wetted his underpants with pre-sperm and unconsciously let out a moan.

Phillip no longer smiled but looked very serious and had completely dropped the jovial and gentle manner he had displayed at the bar. Moving over to the bed, Phillip grabbed Mishka by his hair and skull-fucked Mishka, with the words: "Show daddy you're worth it".

Mishka's nose was flattened against Phillip's stomach and Mishka was struggling to breathe. He couldn't help thinking, that it was like swimming in choppy waters, where the crashing waves suddenly takes you under and you struggle to find the rhythm and match your breath to it, so you don't drown. It was hard for him to find the rhythm with Phillip, so it was a relief when he tasted cum and Phillip let go of his grasp. Mishka swallowed and gasped for air, while Phillip stroked his penis to keep it hard. Just when Mishka had caught his breath, Phillip instructed him to lie down on his back. Mishka sucked in his stomach, lied down on his upper torso, stretching out his arms and spreading his legs, while he tried making his shortness of breath sound seductive.

"I'm ready for you, daddy. Give it to me," Mishka said, as he glanced up at Phillip's face.

Phillip smiled, not the smile from the bar, but a different, uncontrolled smile. As Phillip got up on the bed and moved closer, Mishka nodded to him, while he hoped Phillip would be gentler now. Phillip wasn't. As soon as Phillip had positioned himself, wrapping Mishka's legs around him, he pulled Mishka in by his hips. In the same moment, Phillip quickly thrusted himself dry into Mishka and forced a pillow over Mishka's head. The pillow muffled Mishka's screams, as Phillip tore Mishka's anus. It felt like an iron rod was mechanically tearing him up from the inside. Mishka could feel liquid leaking out of him, as Phillip pulled himself in and out of Mishka. Mishka hoped it was cum or at least blood and not fecal matter.

Mishka tried to keep as quiet as possible, but Phillip just got rougher and rougher, until Mishka was crying into the pillow and couldn't help but whimper.

"Yeah, there we go. Don't worry boy. Daddy is almost done," Phillip consoled, as he made his last hyperactive and deep thrusts, letting out a howl, as he finally came in Mishka. When Phillip pulled himself out, he spanked Mishka's ass and said, "That's it. You earned it. You earned it, boy."

Mishka lay flat and motionless on the bed, hugging the wet pillow, that had covered his face.

"Was I? You liked it?" Mishka asked, weeping and seeking reassurance.

Phillip was already getting dressed. Once again, he had the same charming smile, from the bar. "Yes, immensely. In fact…" Phillip said, as he reached for his pocketbook. "Have another… 500. We should do this again, sometime. Here's my card." He left both on the same side table, he'd put the 10.000 and finished dressing.

Mishka had gathered himself and sat at the foot of the bed, draped in a sheet. "Do you like me," Mishka asked, "Do you think I'm beautiful?"

Phillip scoffed. "Why else do you think I did, what I just

did. I wanted you and I'll want you again. But now I have to go. You have the room until noon tomorrow. I'll settle the bill before I go."

Left to himself, Mishka checked the sheets. They were drenched in blood and a little fecal matter, which filled the room with a rotting iron-smell. He draped the sheets to cover it and took a shirtless selfie, posting it with the caption "Indulge" and tagged the hotel as location. Then he raided the minibar for booze, drew himself a bath and drank the little bottles in the tub. When he got out of the tub, he put on the hotel robe and drank the last of the little bottles, while he stood looking out over the city, from the window. He didn't get dressed, before he'd robbed the mini bar of its last alcoholic beverage. Then he carefully collected his belongings, including the money from Phillip, drunkenly stumbled out of the room and took a cab home.

Chapter 6

With the money he'd gotten from Mervin and Phillip, he could afford a few spare days to himself, without any patrons. Mishka spent his time alone with his books and old Hollywood movies, emerging himself in stories of promiscuous figures, that had spell bound the world. After two days of gathering inspiration for his social identity and personal brand, he decided to go shopping.

He showered, lathered, creamed, patted, brushed and puffed, until he looked like he wanted. Then he quickly dressed in a sailor striped t-shirt, worn under a textured grey suit, which he styled with oversize tortoise sunglasses, a large golden brooch and a series of yellow gold rings, with various stones, of various quality. Variety in quality of dress was the hallmark for boys like Mishka, when you lived off the inconsistent generosity of others, the quality of their gifts would always fluctuate. Not being able to foresee the future, Mishka kept everything and wore what he liked, when he liked. Mishka's apartment and particularly his closet, was not unlike a theatre storage space – filled to the brim with treasures, some of significant value, stacked next to worthless splashy items.

Today, he could afford to splurge and buy things for himself. It had been a while since he'd gone shopping and he was looking forward to it. Most of what he owned was gifted from his patrons, which he'd gotten by hinting or directly bargaining. As a result, most of his possessions were a weak reflection of the things he really wanted, either because the patrons misunderstood his hints or they simply bought him, what they wanted him to have. This was another piece of freedom he gave up for his patron's patronage. Mishka's own tastes were regularly demoted or replaced by the taste of his patrons.

His vast collection of sailor striped t-shirts were gifted from Mr. P, together with several complete sailors' outfits. The grey suit had been a gift from Mervin. The rings were from a string of different former lovers, who had since abandoned Mishka and the brooch was passed down to him, by his grandmother. All of these things reflected other people's tastes, much more than they reflected Mishka's style. He styled them together, in an attempt to create a multifaceted image, that would speak to his patrons' collective desires.

It was rare for him to have enough money to go shopping alone and be able to choose the things that he truly wanted to have, without needing the approval of an accompanying patron. This feeling of independence made him feel strong, autonomous and giddy.

As he put on a pair of fringed, black loafers and stepped out of his door to hail a cab, he heard Yma Sumac's Gopher play in his mind.

As he arrived at his favorite department store, his excitement grew and he stormed the store, like a soldier going into battle. Forcefully pushing the big swing doors open, he walked forcefully and authoritatively through the labyrinths of shops and displays. This was one of his domains and he treated it with some pretense of ownership.

He rushed up to an area of Tom Ford and dramatically

removed his shades, before he started seizing items off the racks and shelves.

A salesperson quickly came forward: "Can I be of any assistance, sir."

Without looking, Mishka answered, "Hold this, please," and dumped all his loot in the salesclerk's arms. Confused, the salesclerk followed Mishka, as Mishka threw more and more things in the arms of the salesclerk. Mishka carefully weighed the potential of each single item in the store, considering what type of person it would make him and who it could help him attract.

As he held up each piece of clothing, the salesclerk interrupted Mishka's thoughts, with facts about that style, the popularity of the item, which celebrities had been spotted in it and so forth. Mishka purposely shut out each comment and instead just asked for the smallest size.

After almost an hour of fine combing the store, Mishka installed himself in a dressing room.

As he tried on the clothes, Mishka tried to see himself through the eyes of his patrons. What would they think of him in this shirt or those trousers? He looked for something, that could attract and fascinate his target audience of rich and indulgent men, whose admiration and generosity he wanted. Mishka dreamed of a tycoon in a fancy suit, who would give him enough money, that Mishka no longer had to worry about the future or speculate the rise and fall of his patron's generosity. It was a magical, imaginary future, which he didn't know how to secure, other than to look his best, adapt to the fantasies of his individual patrons and to play the field.

In the dressing room he tried on one item at a time, documenting each costume change and posting the best pictures on social media. Based on the pictures, he speculated which pictures would get the most lurid comments and he picked out items to buy accordingly.

He picked a variety of tight fitted evening wear, that made him look like the cross between a young gentleman and an oversexed club kid. It pleased him. He knew most of his patrons would love the idea of a high-end teenage boy toy and he really looked the part. The reason Mishka liked Tom Ford wasn't so much for the style, as to associate himself with the company's aggressive sexual advertising. To Mishka, sex was a branding tool, not an act. The sexual aggressive connotations to Tom Ford helped Mishka attract patrons, who usually wouldn't hit on him, if he didn't dress to signal sex and projected stereotypical homosexuality.

On his way from the dressing room to the cash register, Mishka greedily grabbed four shoes, a scarf, two sunglasses and three bags and dumped it all at the register, with the clothes he'd selected in the dressing room.

With forced politeness, the salesclerk asked, "Wouldn't you like to try on the shoes?"

Mishka stared blankly back at the salesclerk in response.

"See how they feel, if they're comfortable," the salesclerk carefully expanded.

Mishka smiled. "Oh, darling. Who really cares? It's the look, not the feel, I'm buying."

The salesclerk laughed nervously and gave up on further conversation.

As the salesclerk beeped and packed all the items, Mishka looked at the other people in the store. Most of them were watching him too and it made him feel exposed and awkward. He always made a spectacle of himself and people always took notice. Mishka put on his sunglasses and tried to avoid the gaze of the other shoppers.

It was always awkward for Mishka to pay for big purchases like this and the salesclerk never hid their surprise, when Mishka handed over wads of cash, instead of a credit card.

Mishka looked the salesclerk straight in the eyes and wondered if they'd guessed, why Mishka paid in cash and how Mishka earned his money or if they'd gotten the wrong idea.

Under Mishka's watchful gaze the salesclerk woke up and finalized the purchase. Despite the awkward moment with the salesclerk, Mishka was in high spirits. He strutted confidently out of the store, struggling to manage all the shopping bags.

Out on the sidewalk, he saw an old friend from design school, walking by. It was Julie. They'd spent a lot of time together, when they'd studied design together, but they had drifted apart, since he'd left school. He followed her with his eyes and she looked back. They shared a smile and approached each other.

"Hey Julie. It's been such a long time," Mishka said, trying to give her a hug, but failed, since the bags awkwardly got in the way.

"Too long. Great to see you. We really should see more to each other. I never see you anymore," Julie amicably chirped, as she curiously inspected him, up and down.

"You wouldn't happen to have time for a coffee now, do you? There's a nice bakery right around the corner, we could go to?" Mishka dared her.

Julie readily agreed and they went to the nearby bakery, ordering coffee and cakes. But as they sat there across from each other, all smiles, they couldn't help but feel how much time had wrecked their friendship. As fellow students they had gossiped constantly about everything, always laughing and filling the air with noise. Now, they sat and stared awkwardly at each other, with stiff, forced smiles on their makeup-ed faces.

Finding nothing original to say, Mishka started in on the boilerplate pleasantries.

"So, how you've been? You must be nearly finished with your bachelor's degree?"

"I'm great. Yeah, nearly finished. I'm writing my thesis now, on sustainability implementation in fast fashion and I'm working part time for the council of sustainable fashion. Oh, and I… uh, I met a guy and we've dated for about a year now and we're thinking about moving in together," Julie answered, sounding very grown up to the both of them.

Mishka had no idea, what to say. He felt the rift between them was bigger than ever. Julie had been upset, when Mishka left school, she had opposed to him changing his name and she had been adamantly against his boyfriends and patrons. He knew she had meant well, but she made him feel judged and so he simply stopped responding to her texts and Snap Chats. It wasn't his intention to end communication between them, but he needed time to heal, from the last time they had spoken. She had implored him to change, calling him names and crying. He had refused to dump his boyfriends and be an ordinary student. Now, they hadn't spoken in a little over a year and he didn't know how to fix it.

As Mishka struggled to find a response, Julie was inspecting his bags. She quickly estimated that it had cost more money, than someone their age would usually have to spend.

Looking at the many bags, Julie worried about how,

Mishka could afford such things.

Julie looked up and looked Mishka straight in his eyes. Mishka was alarmed by the serious expression in her face.

"Are you still doing the thing?" Julie timidly asked, with a purposefully blank expression on her face, only batting her big cat eyes.

Mishka looked perplexed.

"You know the thing? Are you being careful?" Julie added.

Mishka knew what she had meant, but it scared and angered him, that she would ask. He was afraid it would just reopen old wounds and repeat their last falling out.

"Oh," Mishka exclaimed, trying to laugh off his feelings. "Yes, indeed. I'm well looked after, but I'm thinking of settling down. Find someone and…"

"I wished you'd stop doing it," Julie interrupted, continuing: "I worry about you. Sometimes I think about you and I worry."

Mishka rolled his eyes. "Why, unlike Holly the field has been good to me, both socially and economically."

"Holly?" Julie asked annoyed and slightly angry. She had hated it, when Mishka did that. He retreated into his vast contextual knowledge, changing a serious, and in her mind necessary, conversation into a pretentious talk of literary and cinematic references.

Mishka dramatically drew back, putting on a faked look of dismay. "Why, Holly Golightly, baby…Breakfast at Tiffany's… The movie! It's a classic!" Mishka laughed at his own little sketch.

"It's not funny. Life's not a movie, you should take your life more serious." Julie lectured him. He hated being lectured to.

Mishka put away his jovial face and became serious. "I'm quite serious, Julie, whatever you may think. Just because my life looks different than yours, doesn't mean it's wrong. My life may worry you, but that's because you're too scared of life, because it's chaotic and brutal. So, you hide. At school you hid in your dreams, then in your ordinary little job and now in your little normative relationship. Yeah, I saw the fucking Facebook updates. But chaos and brutality can still find you, you can't hide from it. You might as well just go for things head on and be honest with yourself. Don't tell me, there isn't a transactional aspect of your relationship, arguing about who will cook or do the dishes and so on, dividing and bargaining, about who performs various chores. It's the same with me and my patrons. We divide and bargain. They pay my bills and give me presents and I play out some of their fantasies, just like your boyfriend might cook for you, if you do the dishes. It's all transactional. At least I do it on my own terms, not hiding behind and not conforming to some abstract idea of normality."

Julie hid her face in her hands and sighed. "You always do this," she sneered. "You explain away your bad behavior and rationalize everything, but you know it's weird, what you're doing. It can't go on."

"And you're always so dramatic, when you don't get your way, Julie. You always needed to be in control, to be the center of attention and to judge others. It has nothing to do with me. You just want to feel superior, so you judge people and stumble in the dark for some moral high ground." Mishka sneered, his voice sounding increasingly angrier.

"You know, I can't do this. I'm going," Julie said in a tired voice, as she picked up her things and put on her coat. Mishka straightened his back and sat straight up, like he was bolted to the chair, without saying a word.

When Julie reached the door, she turned around and calmly said, "I hope, that you one day wake up and realize, you could be more." Then she rushed out of the door, leaving Mishka to himself. Without looking, Mishka felt everyone's eyes staring at him. In response, Mishka sat proudly and slowly ate his cake and drank his coffee, before he paid the check, collected his shopping bags and walked out of the bakery, with his nose in the air.

Out on the streets the sky had turned grey and there were no available cabs in sight. Mishka was frustrated with Julie, so he decided to walk home. He always cleared his thoughts on a nice, long walk. There was something about concentrating on nothing more than moving forward, that cleared the mind and helped him gather himself. He walked fast paced, not minding the heavy weight of his shopping bags. As he walked, he put on his headphones and listened to Henry Mancini. With music in his ears and sunglasses on his face, he felt very safe, as he maneuvered between people on the street.

On his walk he reached the same conclusions, that he had said to Julie at the bakery. She wanted control over him and she wanted him to live like her. Her plea to him had nothing to do with him, but to do with her and her need for control and to have her life choices reflected in those around her.

It bothered him, that he had so definitely lost a friend, that used to be a close confidant, but he was glad there was an end to the matter. Now he knew, they were through and their friendship no longer lingered in a comatose state – it was dead.

By the time he reached home, his arms were completely

numb, his stomach was growling, and his feet were bleeding. As soon as he entered his apartment, he dumped his shopping bags, took off his shoes and poured himself a drink.

As he lit a cigarette, he wondered how many calories had been in the cake, he'd eaten at the bakery. He guessed somewhere around 500 calories. Figuring in the calories from the frothy coffee and the drink he was drinking now, plus the pot of coffee he'd drunk as breakfast… hm. He was probably up to about 800 calories for the day. That was too much, there was no room for dinner, no matter how much his stomach rumbled. He hungrily took a long drag of the cigarette, finished his drink and went to bed.

Chapter 7

Mishka had invited Jason over, that night. Jason was an engineer, of some sort, but was otherwise very different to his other patrons. He'd met Jason one night, years ago, when he'd been out partying, like so many nights before. Mishka had been dancing by himself, enjoying the buzz of some pills a stranger had offered him in the line to the restroom and he'd been drinking heavily. The night was all a blur to Mishka, but he remembered when he woke up in Jason's apartment and Jason had made him breakfast and asked him to be more careful. Just like that, their relationship was cemented and Jason became Mishka unofficial guardian. Jason protected Mishka in an almost fatherly way, even though they were nearer in age, than Mishka was to his other patrons.

Mishka loved how stable Jason was, he always knew where he stood with Jason and he could relax in his company. All he needed to do to get Jason over was text him a question mark. Without fail, Jason would reply with an exact time and place for them to meet, most often at Mishka's apartment, so Jason could check up on him.

Today Jason would come to Mishka's apartment straight after work.

Mishka spent the whole day preparing for Jason's arrival, trying on clothes and makeup looks, while Mae West played in the background. Each look he tested on his Instagram, posting selfies continuously, after each minute change. Based on his selfies engagement rate, he ended up with waved combed back hair, a la the 1920s, darkened eyelids and a white powdered face. He dressed in an oversize silver lamé t-shirt, paired with black pants and black velvet loafers.

With the support of random followers' likes, he was happy with his look for the day. Even though he was all alone, he felt like the life of the party.

In his cheeriness, he changed the music to Cole Porter, poured himself a glass of champagne and took a turn around his flat. He half-danced through his few rooms, admiring all the things he'd amassed in them. Occasionally he'd stop to review some particular item, reminiscing about how he'd gotten it, who'd paid for it and what they'd made him do for it. As he counted the amount of money he'd gone through, of other people's money, his life gained tremendous value in his own eyes. He was poor, but he'd spent several fortunes on his lifestyle. He relished, that he was able to get men to buy him these things. All these men had invested such resources and undergone such fuss to be with him, which meant he had value.

Just then, there was a series of loud knocks and bangs at the door and in popped Jason.

"Hey gorgeous," Jason shouted enthusiastically. "Can you help with the bags?"

Mishka moved slowly towards the door and saw Jason carrying grocery bags with his arms and feet. It looked ridiculous and Mishka couldn't help but laugh. Jason laughed giddily too, as he pleaded Mishka to help him: "Don't just laugh at me, help me dammit."

Mishka reluctantly put down his glass and came to Jason's aid.

"What on earth have you done? What do we need all this

for?" Mishka asked in genuine wonder.

"I don't need it, you do. You never have any food. It's annoying. You never have anything to offer, when I come by. Anyway, you need to eat something, at least once in a while!" Jason playfully scolded him, as they both made their way to the kitchen.

Mishka put down the bags he carried and left Jason to stock the fridge by himself. Instead of helping Jason, Mishka took out two fresh glasses and poured some champagne. He'd already forgotten the glass he'd put down to help Jason.

"There's just something so depressingly ordinary about grocery shopping. Who really cares about eggs and milk? It hardly seems worth the trouble... or the money. I prefer to buy something spectacular, like a Tom Ford suit, some jewelry or an old bottle of something fun," Mishka mused, as he handed Jason a glass of champagne.

"The last thing you need is more stuff or another drink. You need sustenance," Jason said teasingly, as he waved a loaf of bread for emphasis.

Mishka posed by the kitchen table, champagne in hand, as he stroked his clothes and said: "Oh, this is all the sustenance I need," punctuating the sentence by sipping his champagne.

Jason laughed and answered: "You're a silly boy!"

Mishka stood up straight and firmly said: "It's not like you're that much more grown up than I am."

Jason laughed at Mishka's sudden burst of seriousness and defended his position. "If you were 100 years old, you'd still be a silly boy. You'll never grow up or take responsibility for anything."

"I'm not sure I am responsible for anything," Mishka said in a philosophical tone. "I didn't... I mean, I don't... Actually,

I don't know what I mean. But you're being a bore, that's not why I asked you to come," Mishka said full of forced indignation, as he pointedly turned away from Jason and sipped his drink.

Jason was amused. He put down the groceries and crept up behind Mishka and hugged him.

"Oh, there, there," Jason teased, as he held Mishka tight.

Jason tightened his grip and started swaying from side to side, to the sound of 'Anything goes' playing in the background. After a few minutes of quiet, tender embrace, Jason broke the silence. "You know I love you," Jason said, softly and factually.

Mishka laughed it off. "Of course you don't. I know you and I know what this is."

Jason shook his head and laughed in self-assured superiority, as he exclaimed, "No, I love you!" Jason confidently argued.

Mishka didn't like it, when Jason made these declarations, he knew they weren't true. Rather than arguing, Mishka just stayed silent, hoping the situation would go away if he ignored it for long enough.

Jason looked intensely at Mishka the whole time, examining his face and trying to guess his thoughts.

"Wow! You're so hard. Why are you so mean?" Jason pressed.

Mishka dramatically turned around, feeling on safe ground and said: "It's men like you who made me the way I am. If you loved me at all, you'd feel sorry for my troubles, instead of holding them against me."

Jason looked confused. He knew Mishka had fled into a quote and he was now part of a scene rehearsal of some sort, but he didn't know which scene it was or what it meant for the evening he had planned.

"That's one of your quotes, isn't it?" Jason asked with a skeptical voice.

"It's Marilyn Monroe, in Gentlemen prefer Blondes, but that doesn't make it any less true. Anyway, our bubbly is getting flat, pussycat," Mishka said cheerfully, as he released himself from Jason's hold.

Mishka fetched Jason's glass and gave him a kiss, as he handed it to him.

Jason was a bit annoyed by Mishka's opaqueness and the pretention of his little sketches, so he turned to the practical task of stocking the fridge.

"What do you want to eat?" Jason asked.

"Oh, I'm not really hungry," Mishka sighed.

Jason started laughing loudly and genuinely.

"Of course, you are! You're so silly, why can you never admit to anything?" Jason roared, laughing and shaking his head in disbelief.

Mishka felt insulted and just wanted the situation to go away, so he stormed angrily up to Jason and forced his right-hand down Jason's pants and grabbed his cock.

Jason was pleasantly surprised and quickly adapted to the changed situation. As Jason stared at Mishka, all Mishka's anger evaporated.

They started kissing hungrily, like they were trying to eat each other. Each kiss getting harder, wetter and more intense, as they ripped the clothes of each other.

They banged into the furnishings, having trouble keeping their balance or spatial awareness, seeing only each other.

Their kisses spread, as their mouths eagerly moved all

over each other's bodies, kissing and tasting each other's most intimate areas.

Suddenly Jason pulled away and they intensely gazed into each other's eyes, before Jason sat up on the kitchen counter and Mishka eagerly inhaled Jason's cock. Their passion for each other was intense and Mishka could feel Jason's blood boiling hot inside his penis.

Sex with Jason was very different, from sex with Mishka's other patrons. He sucked Jason's penis fervently, forcefully and without thought of anything else. Both gave themselves unreservedly and quickly. They came multiple times, only to keep going. Every time Jason came in Mishka's welcoming mouth, they just continued, without stop or hesitation. After three consecutive orgasms, Jason's erection was winding down, so they moved on to other things. While they kissed, in this intermission, Mishka grabbed a spatula. Jason came down from the kitchen counter and they moved on to a nearby chair, where Mishka sat down and Jason laid over Mishka lap.

Mishka plied the spatula to Jason's plump ass, continuously increasing the tempo and force of his lashes. Jason's ass cheeks become redder and redder and his moans become louder and more intense. As their enthusiasm intensified, their cocks became more and more erect and pressed increasingly hard against each other. This shifted their focus and the spatula gradually slowed its pace. As Jason lay across Mishka lap, they started humping up against each other, massaging their penises up against each other's.

Jason suddenly jumped up and grabbed Mishka, led him into the bedroom and carefully situated Mishka on the bed, with his stomach down. Jason kneeled down on the floor, took Mishka by the ankles and drew him closer. Then, Jason buried his face between Mishka sweaty ass cheeks and thrusted his tongue in and out of Mishka's ass. Jason kept going, massaging Mishka ring muscle with his tongue, going round and round in circles, wetting Mishka's ass and opening him up. Mishka started to come in his bed sheets, unable to hold himself back.

Sensing Mishka's climax, Jason got up and moved up on Mishka, laid on top of him, letting his fingers maneuver his cock into Mishka. Mishka let out an instinctive, confirming "yes", as Jason entered him.

Jason fucked Mishka hard and fast, both eager for each other's feel. When Jason came, he thrusted himself as deep inside Mishka as he possibly could, before slowing down. Hungry for Jason's attention, Mishka instructed "more" and Jason started thrusting hard again, until they were both exhausted. There was no more air in the room and there was a stench of man and sperm. The room was in complete dark. Neither of them had noticed the sun go down.

"I really do love you, you know," Jason said quietly.

Mishka turned around and laughed Jason in the face. "Sure you do. I guess you love all your other boyfriends too?"

Jason shook his head. "They're just a bit of fun. Anyway, you're one to talk, whoring around with any silver fox, that comes your way. I hear things about you too, you know."

Jason started tickling Mishka. "Are you my little whore, huh. Are you my little whore?" Jason teased in a baby voice.

Mishka didn't like it, when Jason was so crude and refused to play along. Instead, Mishka looked disapprovingly at Jason.

"It's just a joke, relax. I just think it's hot to say," Jason reassured.

They fell back into silence, as they lay in bed, clutching each other. Despite how in tune they were sexually, their conversation never really flowed. They both felt inadequate, like they just weren't enough for the other emotionally. So instead, they just enjoyed each other's bodies.

When they woke up the next morning, they smiled at each other and shared a sweet kiss. They stared into each other's eyes. They both knew what they wanted and Mishka merely nodded quietly and Jason pulled him close. Mishka wrapped his legs around Jason's body, while Jason hardened and his cock found its way into Mishka's ass. The whole séance was done without words, only muffled moans as they perpetually kissed the whole thing through, occasionally stopping to share a look, in order to take each other in.

Afterwards Jason and Mishka said goodbye to each other with a series of hugs and kisses. Then Mishka went to the bathroom to clean up, while Jason got dressed and left.

When Mishka sat down in front of his bedroom mirror, there was a note, some cash and the usual gift card on the table. The gift card was for 1,500 kroner to the nearest grocery store, there was only little ready cash and the note read: "Buy food too, not just booze. Love Jason."

Mishka looked into the eyes of his own reflection and sighed of disappointment. His reaction had nothing to do with the gift card or the petty cash, this was all standard for Jason and Mishka appreciated it. No, he was sad about Jason's insistence, that he loved him and Mishka feared what consequences it would have.

He'd once believed Jason, when he'd said it the first time, back when Mishka was still in school. Mishka had been forced to leave his sublet and was looking for a new place, when

Jason had suggested, they moved in together. At first Mishka had declined, but as he got more used to the idea, he ended up accepting. Then Jason had panicked and backpaddled, suggesting that he could get another apartment for Mishka. The whole thing got very strange. It turned out, that Jason owned several small apartments across the city, which he at times sublet and other times installed boys in. Jason had several boyfriends at a time, which he would house and lived with some of them. Mishka had been furious, when he had found out and had initially ghosted Jason, changing his number, email and social media accounts, when he moved into a new place. Yet, Jason had found him and they'd started seeing each other again. Mishka's anger went from Jason, to himself. What Mishka had ended up taking from the whole affair, was that he had been wrong to give his trust and invest thoughts of a joint future, with someone who didn't deserve it so readily. It had been the finishing touch to Mishka's transformation to a dandy, since it had taught him not to trust or emotionally invest in anyone, only to look out for himself and to grab any resources he could, out of any relationship.

Feeling inexplicably sad, Mishka put on his makeup, got dressed and prepared for a quiet day at home. He was in no mood to see anyone today, he needed time alone to fix the small cracks in his façade.

Chapter 8

Mr. P was coming in a couple of hours to pick him up, but he didn't know where Mr. P was taking him. All he had to go on was a text message, saying; "Picking you up at eight, don't dress too faggy, but I don't mind if it's tight. I love that ass."

Mishka was struggling to decide, whether he should comply or deny. He was tempted to dress in something loose fitted with sequins, just to be contrary, but if Mr. P was taking him to a very conservative place, he would feel more embarrassed than Mr. P. Besides, he wasn't in the mood to be entertaining tonight, but he could really use the money and Mr. P would be more lenient with him, if he seemed obedient.

So, Mishka put on a simple white shirt, pleated, black trousers, a black, double breasted dinner jacket with satin lapel and black lacquered shoes.

He looked in the mirror and was terribly bored with what he saw. The reflection looking back at him looked dull and uptight, so opened up the first few buttons of his shirt, to show off his out-sticking collarbones and just a hint of his chest, so it looked a little less tense.

Yes, that was it, neutral, not overtly gay, but still with a hint of queerness. Any interesting men he might meet tonight, would still be able to see what he was and guess he was open to being approached.

He fixed his hair, so it looked a bit messy, like he'd just rolled out of bed.

Now he was ready, he went to the door and unlocked the extra lock, so Mr. P could come in.

To kill the time and get himself in the mood, he danced absent mindedly to the endless stream of music, that was always flowing from his Bluetooth speakers. Mishka was still dancing, when Mr. P locked himself in the door.

At first, Mr. P was confused at the scene he was witnessing, that seemed uncharacteristically unstaged for Mishka. It quickly became clear to Mr. P, that Mishka was unaware he was no longer alone and Mr. P relished the unforeseen invasion into Mishka's private sphere. It was a part of Mishka he'd feared he'd never be able to force himself into, but here he was.

Mishka's private life held a lot of fascination for Mr. P, who often wondered how Mishka behaved, when he was alone. He had bought himself access to the bodies of many young boys and knew how they guarded their private lives. He also knew Mishka well enough to know, that he would never willingly let him into his little world and that made it important for Mr. P to gain entrance.

He enjoyed this look into Mishka's private world, so he discretely leaned up against a wall watching Mishka move freely to the music, as he screeched along to the lyrics. Mishka never sang in public, for the very simple reason, that he couldn't carry a tune and he knew patrons treated him better, when he didn't show his weak spots. By the end of Monroe's rendition of 'My heart belongs to daddy', the playlist had finished and everything fell silent. Mishka stood still, gasping for air, when he was startled by several large smacks.

It was Mr. P clapping his hands in applause. Mishka shuddered in shock. Realizing what had happened, he felt a loss of control as he saw Mr. P standing leaned against the wall, smirking.

In a state of confusion and to take back control of his image, he stammered out: "Well, hello daddy", in a bad Marilyn Monroe impression.

"I prefer your performance in bed, but that was really something. I had no idea you were such a showgirl," Mr. P barked out between bursts of laughter.

"Wow!" Mr. P added mockingly.

"Oh, yeah. Well, I can do all sorts of things. Give me a ring and I'll give you a lap dance!" Mishka said, winking, testing the situation.

A change in power had happened and they both knew it. Much of Mishka's power rested on his opaqueness, discretion and his ability to adapt to his patron's fantasies, in other words in being able to be something other than himself. Now, Mr. P had gotten a backstage view of Mishka, when he was out of character.

"Not so fast, lambchop," Mr. P chuckled.

"But, you promised last time!" Mishka said, with a purposefully childish pout, as he stamped a foot in the floor.

"Oh, I know, baby. Come here," said Mr. P and lit a cigarette, while he waited for Mishka to come to him, but Mishka stood completely still.

Then, giving up, Mr. P walked over to Mishka until he stood so close their bodies touched. Mr. P grabbed Mishka's cheeks and continued, "My little baby," while he exhaled cigarette smoke in Mishka's face. Mishka didn't flinch.

"Missed me?" Mishka asked with a sly smile.

"Didn't have time," Mr. P lied, avoiding Mishka's persistent stare.

"Been shopping I hope," said Mishka.

"Shopping?" Mr. P repeated, genuinely confused.

"The ring. Last time you promised me a ring." Mishka calmly clarified.

"Oh! Forget about that for now, let's just go," Mr. P rushed, while he blew cigarette smoke in Mishka face again.

For a couple of minutes, they just stared at each other, both stubbornly waiting for the other to back down into some expression of submission.

"How about this, I'll make you a trade," Mishka said.

"A trade?" Mr. P inquired, smiling a crooked smile and looking Mishka up and down.

"Yes, the ring for a whiskey, that's what you drink right, big boy," Mishka teased.

"Seems a bit steep" Mr. P said, disappointed it wasn't a sexual proposition. He walked over to an ashtray and put out his cigarette, again avoiding Mishka's eyes.

"Well, if Richard III would trade off his kingdom for a horse, I think a stiff drink for a ring is quite modest, in comparison," Mishka said, as he went to the kitchen and came back with two glasses of single malt.

"Modest isn't exactly the word that comes to my mind, when I think of you," Mr. P said.

"I'll cheers to that," said Mishka and handed Mr. P his drink.

"You'll cheers to anything," Mr. P scolded.

"Well, ascribe it to my cheerful disposition. Anyways, I got you. You think of me!" Mishka said, clanking his glass into Mr. P's, then downed his drink and laughed out loud.

Mr. P got nervous, this was getting too emotional for him, so he downed his drink, reached into his pocket and got out a small jewelry box.

"Here," Mr. P said, handing Mishka the box, looking away. "Payment for last time."

Mishka snatched the box and opened it, like a greedy child on Christmas.

Inside the box was a white gold ring, with a big onyx, surrounded by small black diamonds.

"They're black!" Mishka exclaimed in surprise.

"Yeah, to match your low morals," Mr. P joked, then gave Mishka a look up and down, came closer to him and whispered in his ear: "You're my dirty little whore, aren't you," and gently kissed Mishka's neck and tussled his hair.

"Perfect," Mishka said, as he slid the ring onto his bony fingers. This was what it was like with Mr. P. It was always a punch and a kiss. Mishka knew Mr. P feared his own feelings, that's why he always had to cheapen it, when he did something nice for Mishka. It was so Mr. P could convince himself, that he didn't like Mishka, as much as he did. Mishka knew this, he used and abused it for his own gain. But Mishka also gave Mr. P some social allowances because of it. If Mr. P needed to say something nasty, to do something nice, then Mishka would let him without opposition, as long as it was to Mishka's benefit.

"It suits you," Mr. P said. "I can't wait to see it shine, when you give me a hand job. But there's no time for that now, we better be going. The taxi is downstairs," Mr. P said very determined.

"Right, but where are you taking me, you didn't say?" Mishka asked.

"To a restaurant," Mr. P said factually.

"Restaurant? We're going out to dinner? Why?" Mishka

asked perplexed.

"Oh, just some place I had recommended," Mr. P said hurriedly.

Then, after some thought Mr. P defended himself. "Maybe I just want to see something else in your mouth than my cock, that's all. It's not like you have any food here," Mr. P said as he slapped Mishka ass.

Mishka had lost his interest by now and blindly followed Mr. P down to the taxi. Mr. P was silent and stared out the window the whole car ride.

Only after twenty minutes of silence, Mr. P broke the silence.

"Let's get a drink first. At Balthazar."

"Sounds scrumptious," Mishka said detached. He knew the bar, it specialized in champagne and was exactly the place that brought escorts together with rich, randy men, where the former hunted the latter and vice versa.

Balthazar was almost empty and they had the place almost to themselves, except for a few men in suits, that had taken up a corner table and its surrounding lounge chairs, where they were loudly enjoying after work cocktails. A few glamor girls sat at the bar, trying to figure out if the guys in suits were worth pursuing.

Mr. P went straight for the opposite corner of the suits, so they were far away from everyone else and ordered a bottle of Dom Perignon from the overtly conscientious waitress, that had recommended a range of more obscure champagnes. Mishka couldn't help but be reminded of the lectures on conspicuous consumption, he had attended at design school. That was Mr. P to a tee, a conspicuous consumer, who consumed goods, services and people to boost his own ego and demonstrate his power and wealth. It was all playacting.

Mishka drank most of the bottle, while Mr. P sat in his chair and stared at Mishka, with deep eyes and a cagey smile. He only occasionally sipped from his glass, but never took his eyes off Mishka.

Mishka wondered if Mr. P even liked Dom Perignon or if he had truly just ordered it for its brand value.

The restaurant was close by, so they walked from the bar, once Mishka had finished the bottle. Mishka didn't know the restaurant at all, not even by name, which he thought strange, since he usually knew all the fashionable restaurants, bars and night clubs. It had a remarkable décor, dim lights, white lacquered walls, and there were flowers and crystal chandeliers absolutely everywhere.

Mishka became more and more intrigued by the place and curious why Mr. P had taken him there, of all places. What had been said about the place, when Mr. P had gotten the recommendation?

They were shown to their table. Mr. P held out a chair for Mishka, which was uncharacteristically gallant of him and put Mishka on his guard.

Mishka looked around and examined the ambience. The dining room had a lot of pillars, to create intimate corners. All he saw was couples, real couples out on dates. It was altogether too romantic for their 'arrangement'. Patrons didn't take their lovers here; this was a place you brought spouses. Suddenly it dawned on Mishka. Was this Mr. P's attempt to make them into a couple? Had Mr. P suddenly come to terms with his own sexuality and his feelings for Mishka. Did Mr. P. love him or was he just unaware of the kind of place it was...?

"I've never been here before. Lots of couples here,"

Mishka said, baiting Mr. P for some answers.

Mr. P looked around. "Yes, there seems to be. Nice, isn't it. I heard the food is great. What do you want?"

Mishka was frustrated, he didn't know what this situation was. They had never been on a date before, when they went out they had always met up in bars, where Mr. P was sure he wouldn't meet anyone he knew and every time, they had gotten emotionally close, Mr. P had always sexually harassed the nearest woman or suggested they went to a strip club. This was something else, this stunt was uncharted waters in their relationship. He wondered if they could get married, if Mr. P was unexpectedly inclined to it and if his financial assets were worth marrying for.

Mishka browsed the menu.

"Oh, I don't know. Maybe just a salad," Mishka said, distracted.

"A salad! I take you here and you want a salad. Come on, get something real, you barely looked," Mr. P cried.

Just then a waiter appeared and politely asked for their order.

"Yeah," Mr. P said. "We'll start with a bottle of your most expensive champagne and some oysters, then I'll have the ribeye, rare and he'll have some precious fish dish or something. That'll get us started."

The waiter's smile got more and more stiff, as if he too were repressing a sigh to cope with Mr. P's roguish manner and clichéd orders. Then the waiter turned to Mishka, to enquire about which fish he wanted. Before Mishka could answer the waiter's question, Mr. P practically yelled at the waiter. "You know what, just get him the most expensive one, all right."

Mishka just looked down at the tablecloth, as the waiter looked at him, before creeping away to attend to Mr. P's orders.

Mr. P clearly had a specific idea of how this evening should progress, which was very common, not just for Mr. P, but for patrons in general. They paid partly for control of the experience, which they would not have in a more traditional relationship. If there were any disagreement about events, they would negotiate terms and costs until they made a deal. Everything had a price.

The waiter brought the oysters and champagne, which Mr. P kept pushing, so he could feel like a big shot. Mishka guessed that Mr. P's stocks were yielding a nice profit, since he spent so much this evening.

Mishka couldn't put his finger on it, but something about this dinner made him uncomfortable and he wished, that he hadn't drunk so much of the champagne at the bar, it made it hard to concentrate. Normally he didn't have to be on his guard with Mr. P, he could usually handle him, even drunk. Often it helped being tipsy with Mr. P, since it made Mishka less sensitive to Mr. P's pathetic displays of masculinity.

Mr. P kept staring and smiling at Mishka, as he slurped back each oyster and Mishka carefully sipped champagne. It was the same with the main course. Mishka hardly ate anything at all, but Mr. P didn't seem to notice nor care.

"You like the fish?" Mr. P asked.

"Oh yes, it's just what I wanted," Mishka lied docilely.

Mr. P smiled, as to congratulate himself, winked and said, "See, daddy knows what you want."

Mishka smiled back, demonstratively looked down at the ring and said; "You sure do."

"Yeah, I think we have a good thing going here," Mr. P replied, while chewing a massive piece of steak and continued: "That's why I took you out tonight. I just wanted to see, what it would be like. I can be a good guy, I can treat you right," Mr. P explained.

In that moment, Mr. P got distracted, as a well-kept, forty-something blond, in a very tight cocktail dress, walked by their table, probably looking for the bathroom. Mr. P gawked at her demonstratively.

"Hot piece. I'd fuck her. What do you think!" Mishka said mockingly, the alcohol influencing his voice.

Mr. P looked at him in surprise and grinned. "Nah, you wouldn't. You're a total fag. But I could, I would. She's hot," Mr. P challenged him.

"She's certainly mature. Although I don't think she's changed her outfit since her fourteenth birthday. She must be someone's second wife. You'll have an angry husband and a divorce lawyer after you, if you pursue her," Mishka said, eyebrow raised.

"Ah, is my little girl jealous," Mr. P said, pinching Mishka's chin.

"Of the elderly, not really. I enjoy being before my sell-by-date," Mishka said, punctuating his words by emptying his glass.

"Fine, I won't tonight. Tonight, it's just you and me. Let's go," Mr. P said.

Mr. P paid for the check, escorted Mishka out and hailed a cab, to take them back to Mishka's place. This part was well rehearsed on both sides. Most of the patrons acted this way. They paid the bill, led Mishka to another place or into a car, to take them back to his place or to a hotel. None of the times were Mishka asked what he wanted, he was expected to be silent and be directed, in accordance with their wishes. Both their intentions and his consent were forgone conclusions, that was the deal. It was always the same and Mishka liked the routine and often liked, not having to decide anything by himself, other than the odd ultimatum, like whether he should be on his back or on his stomach.

In the cab ride home, Mr. P demonstratively took some cocaine and offered Mishka a little, but Mishka reclined.

"You know coke takes your looks. I heard of a model that lost that thing between your nostrils," Mishka said, suddenly remembering he'd said it before.

While he huffed and snorted, Mr. P indifferently said, "Doesn't matter, I'm not the one who has to stay pretty. I have money."

"Hmm," Mishka answered in recognition. He knew Mr. P was right. The rest of the cab ride was quiet, the only noise was Mr. P's small sniffs and grunts.

They didn't speak until they were back at Mishka's apartment and Mishka handed Mr. P his scotch.

"Didn't even have to ask. See this is what I like about us. You get it. No one else ever gets it. They don't get it," Mr. P said, excited and jumpy from the cocaine.

Mishka didn't answer, he knew Mr. P was talking to hear himself speak, not to engage with him. Instead of answering, Mishka went back to the kitchen and downed a sedative with his scotch, to numb him for the rest of the night.

When Mishka got back to the living room, Mr. P was walking around in a circle, where he had interrupted Mishka's dance at the beginning of the evening. "I like you better, when you don't sing," Mr. P said, without thinking. "I love the way you move. Like you're begging for it," Mr. P added in a husky voice.

Mr. P got up, scotch in hand and rushed over to Mishka, grabbing him hard from behind and biting his neck.

Mishka froze up and let Mr. P do what he wanted. He didn't want to have sex right now, but he couldn't stomach the fight either, not when Mr. P was on coke. It would be easier to just submit and get it over with. Sometimes saying no costs too much.

Mr. P took Mishka's passive resistance as an open invitation, so he unzipped Mishka's pants and pushed him down over the chaise, before thrusting his cock into Mishka.

Without foreplay or lubricant Mr. P's cock felt like a wooden stake, that tore Mishka up, from inside his rectum. Mishka bit down on a cushion, to muffle his cries.

Panting, Mr. P whispered, "Oh yeah, that's a good girl. You're so fucking good, you fucking little whore. You fucking faggot, that's what you get!"

Mishka could feel he started to bleed, which suddenly made him conscious of the fact, that Mr. P wasn't wearing a condom. Now, he'd have to get checked for STDs. He hoped he wouldn't get sick. The blood made the sex a little easier though, working as a sort of lubricant, allowing smoother friction.

Mr. P's tempo increased rapidly, signaling that things were about to end.

As he started to bleed more and more, his thoughts turned to the fabrics on the chaise. He hoped it wouldn't stain.

Finally, Mr. P let out a final roar, pulled himself out and smacked Mishka on the ass.

Mishka was wiping tears off his cheeks, before he got up

and put on his underpants. Instinctively Mishka grabbed the whiskey glasses for a refill.

"Woof, that was good. Wow, is that blood. Is daddy's dick too much for ya," Mr. P said satisfied and proud of himself, as he slowly got dressed.

Unaware of it himself, a sly, psychotic smile crept over Mishka's lips. His hands tightened around the glasses, until he was afraid, he'd break it or throw it at Mr. P. Instead, he filled up both their glasses and said: "Nothing is too big for me, but you do just fine."

Mr. P smiled and took the drink happily. Mishka caressed Mr. P's penis and kissed Mr. P on the neck, whispering, "Thank you, daddy," into Mr. P's ear.

As Mishka went to the bathroom to clean up and assess the damage, Mr. P was smiling from ear to ear.

The damage wasn't too bad externally, Mishka thought as he washed the blood off. When he was done, he meticulously washed his hands, fixed his face and hair and put on a kimono, before joining Mr. P in the living room.

Mr. P was finishing his drink and started to count out bank notes to leave for Mishka.

"I'm leaving a little extra, since you've been such a good sport tonight." Mr. P. explained, without turning to Mishka.

When he was done, he gave Mishka a kiss on the cheek and said, "See, I'm a gentleman, I take care of my baby" and then left Mishka to himself.

Not knowing what to do, Mishka cleaned up, did the dishes and inspected the chaise, which hadn't been stained, as far as he could see. When there was nothing more to do, he took the bank notes and counted them. There was about 5,000 kroner, a tidy sum, but not that impressive.

Suddenly the sedative and all the booze were taking its effect, making Mishka drowsy. He climbed to bed and fell into a deep sleep, clutching the banknotes Mr. P had left him, like a toddler clutching their favorite teddy bear.

Chapter 9

Mishka was sitting in the waiting room of his doctor's office, which was placed in the rich, conservative part of the city. He was waiting to be tested for any sexual transmitted diseases, Mr. P might have given him, when he fucked him raw and drew blood. He always got nervous when he got tested.

Several of the men he'd been with, sporadically forewent protection and it scared Mishka every time. He facetiously got tested each time a patron took him bareback and additionally had a routine checkup every sixth month. Whenever he got tested, he felt like he was gambling with his life and always imagined himself playing chess with death, like in Ingmar Bergman's 'The Seventh Seal'. Mishka didn't feel particularly good at chess and had very negative associations with the game. His father had forced him to play endless games of chess, throughout his childhood and as a result Mishka had developed an intense hatred of the game. In his head, Mishka was in the middle of playing the Winawer Variation of the 'The French Defense', when his name was called up and he was led into his doctor's examination room.

The doctor looked at him, with a disinterested expression, asking what brought him to his office. It was very clearly a matter of routine for the doctor, who probably didn't even recognize Mishka, as a regular client.

When Mishka explained, that he just felt the need for a checkup, the doctor looked at him disapprovingly, from behind his brass half-glasses, as if something in his mind was triggered. The doctor pulled out a file and repeatedly shifted his gaze, between the papers in his hands and Mishka's courteously smiling face.

"Didn't you just have a test a couple of months ago? How much sex are you having?" the doctor cried out in surprise, forgetting himself and the pretense of professional courtesy.

Mishka shrank a little in his chair. Putting on his most charming smile, he tried to defend himself: "Yes, well. You can never be too careful, can you and the board of health is recommending gay men, to get checked frequently."

"M'yes," the doctor said wearily, as he looked through Mishka's chart. "M'yes. I guess I'd better send you in to the nurse for a blood test. I just need a cotton swab, before you go." The doctor put down the chart and started getting ready for the test.

"If you could please stand up and pull down your trousers?" the doctor asked, while he put on his rubber gloves.

As the doctor got to work, Mishka distracted himself by scrutinizing the examination room. It was very white, minimalistic and modern, with bare surfaces, clean lines and designer lamps everywhere. The only smidgen of personality in the room was a staged family photo, placed on the doctor's desk. In the photo the doctor posed on a flawlessly pedicured grass lawn, with his wife and their five blond sons. They were all dressed in matching pastels and all the boys looked exactly alike, right down to their haircuts. Mishka looked down at the doctor and noticed, that underneath his robe, he was wearing khaki chinos, with a brown belt, a peach colored Lacoste polo shirt stuffed into his chinos and brown, suede loafers.

'Ironic,' Mishka thought to himself, as he felt the pain of

the cotton swab inserted into his penis. This doctor was conservative to the extreme, that it almost made him camp and yet, the queer-looking doctor showed no regard for Mishka and seemed very disapproving of his sexuality and libido. He'd previously tried to flirt with the doctor, but the doctor never seemed to notice. While this absolutely proved the doctor's heterosexuality in Mishka's mind, it still annoyed him, that the doctor refused to admire him.

The doctor finished with the cotton swab and without looking at Mishka, he instructed him to get dressed and go to the nurse's office.

The nurse was a kind woman in her late fifties, who had a strong motherly air about her. She always took her time for pleasantries and always treated her patients with empathy and warmth. She carefully took the blood samples she needed, while she assured Mishka, that he had no need to worry and complimented him, for having the good sense to get checked in the first place.

Her caring manner worked its charm and when Mishka left the doctor's office and went home, he felt confident. Unlike the chess games with his father, he'd won this round and had warded off doom once again, like he had many times before.

However, his good mood didn't last. Over the next days, as he waited for his test results, he kept playing out imaginary chess games and toyed with the possibilities of his test results.

There wasn't room for something as ugly as disease in Mishka's carefully constructed world. It was one thing, if you got chlamydia, it would stain your reputation and rob you, some of your gleam. But after a treatment of antibiotics, you were still part of the game. If you got a permanent disease, you were out for good. So many of the boys and girls from the hotel bars ended up with something and they would be left by all their patrons and disappear from their world. Mishka remembered Zola's Nana, where the title character wound up in a hotel room, with horrible boils all over her, all her beauty gone and dependent on the kindness of her former rival.

He tried to distract himself with books and movies, but his mind kept drifting back to the possibility of disease and each time he cursed Mr. P for his possible misfortune. It was all right for men like Mr. P to have a disease, it was somehow part of his worldliness and experience. If boys like Mishka got a disease, they were ruined and would be discarded like an old, battered toy, that no child wanted to play with, now they'd had their fun with it.

Feeling unsure of himself and his future, he even stayed off social media.

When the test results finally came in, they were negative. Mishka had won the game and was completely disease free. In fact, Mishka had never caught any sexual transmitted disease ever, which he prided himself on.

Having dodged any diseases, Mishka felt like Dorian Grey, escaping the consequences of his depravity. He wondered if there was a picture of him somewhere, which paid the price and bore the scars of his sins. Or, did his sins cause a cosmic unbalance, which would spell disaster at a later date?

Mishka didn't have time to finish his thoughts, before he was disturbed by a call from Phillip Jaeger, who invited him to join him for a private poker game that night, hosted in a suite at the hotel, where they'd first met. Mishka readily agreed and asked for any guidelines for the evening. Phillip had merely scoffed and said he'd see him at the hotel.

Chapter 10

Mishka was running frantically around his apartment, as he was trying to get ready for tonight.

In the background, the tones of Shirley Bassey's 'Diamonds are forever' was blasting through the speakers, enhancing Mishka's good mood. As Mishka jumped from room to room, he intermittently mumbled along to the lyrics and occasionally danced along to the music.

He was preparing to go to Phillip Jaegers poker game and he was in youthful high spirits. There was something very Ian Fleming, about attending a poker game as an old man's doll, which excited Mishka. It was great to hear from Phillip again and he hoped it meant, that Phillip would become a regular, if he did Mishka would go from getting by, to thriving economically.

He dressed in a classic black smoking, with a bowtie in a golden leopard print and gold cufflinks. On his feet, he wore patent leather dress slippers, which pinched against his bare toes and heels. Not sure what kind of party he was walking into, he kept his makeup relatively discreet, only using some concealer and a little powder, highlighting his cheeks, eyelids and lips, with some pink crème blush. The blush made him look like a flushed little boy. Before leaving he took a full mirror selfie, where he posed like a pouty gun man, posting it on Instagram with the caption 'P-P-P-P-Pokerface?'

When he arrived at the hotel and was ushered to a suite,

he found the game to be much like he'd hoped. In the middle of the suite a round palisander table, in the style of Louis Philippe, had been converted into a poker table. Around the table sat a bunch of grey-haired men, in simple suits, smoking cigars and drinking hard liquor. Scattered about the suite was a few bored-looking, glamorous girls and one other young man, all around Mishka's age. He knew a couple of them and had seen most of them hanging around the same hotel bars, where he fished for patrons. While the men were drinking greedily and already getting rowdy, the youngsters were carefully sipping their drinks, measuring out their alcohol intake. This was an opportunity for the young companions, so they had to keep their wits about them, if they were to get the commission they wanted from tonight's game.

Phillip, already seated at the table, signaled to Mishka to come over. Continuing his talk with his friends, he grabbed Mishka's ass and then kissed him on his mouth. The age disparity seemed higher as ever, as the odor of Phillip's cigar-breath washed over Mishka. Without a word, Phillip emptied his glass and signaled to Mishka, where he could refill it. Only communicating through a docile smile, Mishka refilled Phillip's glass with a nearly empty bottle of single malt, sitting on a nearby console table. When Mishka placed the drink by Phillip's seat, he noticed the mixed facial expressions on the other men at the table. Most stared with curiosity, some with awkward confusion and fewer still with appreciation.

"That's a good girl. Why don't you join the others," Phillip said, pointing at the youngsters, without taking his attention away from the table.

It was odd. The fight for gay rights and social equality for gay couples, had changed the circumstances for boys like

Mishka. When Mishka first started out, just a few years ago, boys like Mishka were kept in the shadows and patrons only met up with him in the privacy of hotel rooms or his apartment. There was a great deal of sneaking around. But the social movement had brought boys like Mishka somewhat out of the shadows and some men, like Phillip, had no qualms about bringing them to events like this or out for drinks or to parties. In short, the fight for gay equality had made Mishka and boys like him, into 'one of the girls'. However, this brought about new social negotiations, hence the looks of the other men at the poker table. Some were clear set against it, but most of them knew an open discussion would be too disruptive and so they kept their tongue. Also, events like this, where boys like Mishka were brought as companions, was ruled by secrecy. The participants were silent of each other's proclivities, since most of the men were married and worked with companies or institutions, that were in the public's eye. Most people where not directly against the presence of gay boy toys, but merely confused by the change in social customs and were curious about homosexuality, as a social study. These were the men, who would get drunk and ask personal questions about gay sex or suddenly start bragging about their social tolerance for LGBTQ+ people and say something like 'I always wanted to see a gay weeding' or 'My wife and I regularly dine with a gay couple, do you know Frank and Harry?'

Mishka shook off his social observations, poured himself a glass of champagne from an open bottle and joined the other girls. Darting over to one of the girls he knew, he tried to entertain himself with conversation.

"Hey, Genevieve. Nice to see you again. Who are you with?"

"Darling, nice to see you too. I'm with the tall one, there. The one who's dyed his hair way too dark. The one over there. He's a patent lawyer and has made some very clever investments, in something equally boring, but they yield rather well and he's very generous. He's widowed, you see, and his kids are grown, out on their own and financially independent, so he has no one to answer to, about his spending on me. Isn't that nice. And you? You're with Phillip Jaeger. Nice catch. A step up for you, isn't it?" Genevieve chirped away, trying hard to sound passive aggressive.

"Well I haven't landed him yet, this is only the second time I've seen him, but he'll make a welcome addition to the collection," Mishka said haughtily, trying to sound impressive.

"I bet he would," Genevieve responded, with a knowing smile, as if she saw right through him.

Genevieve was dressed as she usually was, in a black, embroidered, silk cocktail dress, worn with a black fox stole and razor-sharp stilettos. As she smoked her black, gold tipped Sobranie cigarette, she looked very much like a movie star, from Hollywood's golden era.

Mishka liked Genevieve, because she was fun and didn't hold a grudge. She simply went about her own affairs and lived her life, following her momentary moods and inclinations. Genevieve was the epitome of a champagne girl. Working as a freelance art consultant, she already earned the money to cover her living expenses. This allowed her to be picky about her patrons, which had helped to drive up her value. Her pursuit of patrons was mostly for sport and her own amusement. She enjoyed toying with dull, powerful men and she enjoyed the freedom and luxuries the extra cash bought her. Using her extra earnings as mad money and to have a financial cushion.

This had bought her a wide-ranging collection of furs and a small collection of rare jewels. Mishka was still playing the field for prêt-à-porter men's wear and mass-produced designer jewelry and he still had to worry about basic living expenses.

The poker game was starting, and the young companions intuitively quieted down, keeping their chitchat to a whisper. As the men played, Mishka and the others were occasionally called to refill their date's drink and the drinks of some of the players, who hadn't brought a companion. When the stakes seemed to be high, some of them would go and stand by their dates chair, striking poses and following the game. This was mainly to keep tabs on how the money was fluctuating, so they knew, if their date was still worth their time tonight. Games like this, where money was at stake, were just as much a gamble for the cocottes. They all knew, that if their date lost too much, it would come out of their gratuity, at least in part. On the other hand, if their date won, especially if they won big, they would share their luck with them and they could expect a much larger reward, than they usually got 'for their time'.

So, the game went on, the older men sitting in their chairs, playing poker, trying to one-up each other, while sharing tales of dirty adventures or bragging about their recent financial successes. Tonight, there were few losers, but also few winners. Despite a few risky bets, the players mostly ended up with approximately the same amount, that they had brought.

Perhaps the game was simply a way to feel risk, without being in it. An occasion for the men to feel like high rollers, while in fact staying in the same bubble of safe conformity and social privilege, that they'd lived in their entire lives, or so Mishka thought to himself. This observation suddenly made him aware of his own privilege, that he was merely playing the harlot. That he had worked very, very hard to be loose and that this life was an option he had chosen. While he'd worked hard for his lifestyle, it was one he could leave immediately and retreat back to his white, middle class background, as soon as he wished. Unlike the street walkers, working just a few blocks from the hotel, he had choices and he would probably always have choices. He looked at his reflection in one of the countless decorative mirrors, in the lavish hotel room and was somehow hurt, by his own pale, rich, whiteness and the privilege it represented. Silent and barely conscious of it, Mishka scanned the room and the lack of equality and diversity dawned on him. It made him feel shy and embarrassed.

The white, older gentleman all looked, talked and behaved like one and other. The young ones had more diversity, both in ethnicity and in social economic background, but it was diversity born out of the older men's fetishes and sexual craving, not out of equality. There was also the disparity between the older men and their dates. Their relationships all had the same power dynamic, where one part had social power and resources and the other had aesthetic power and cultural capital. All these relationships were born out of a quest for power, each part thinking they could gain power from the other, if they wrestled it away from them.

Mishka wasn't able to finish his thoughts, before Phillip beckoned him with the waive of a finger. People were clearing out of the room and the few people left, were hanging out at the console table, getting one last drink.

Mishka emptied his champagne glass, down to the very last drop, and strutted over to Phillip.

"Good night?" Mishka asked, testing Phillip's mood.

"Oh, bit of a boring game, but it's always nice to see the fellas," Phillip said detached and looked at Mishka for the first time that evening. He fixed his eyes on Mishka and examined him, like a microbiologist might look at a virus through a microscope. "But I have great hope, that the evening will increase in excitement," Phillip proposed, as he stretched out his lips in a wide and stiff smile, that made Phillip look like an adaption of Victor Hugo's character Gwynplaine, from 'The Man Who Laughs'.

"Excitement is just what I'm looking for," Mishka sighed disingenuously, as he sat up on the table, across from Phillip's seat.

Mishka felt jealous and inadequate, that he hadn't had Phillip's attention tonight and so he was punishing him and giving Phillip the chance to come to him. But Phillip seemed satisfied to just look at him, without doing anything to boost Mishka's ego.

"Where should we go from here?" Mishka asked, as he looked about the room. The last people were leaving, amongst them was Genevieve, who waived and mouthed goodbye.

"We don't have to go anywhere, we have these digs for the night," Phillip said proudly, as he took a last toke of his cigar and put it out in a crystal ashtray.

Mishka's eyes followed Phillip's movements. He could tell by Phillip's manner, that he was meant to be impressed, but he wasn't in the mood.

"You just want to stay here, alone? Isn't that a bit boring? Anyway, I can see you have won something. Shouldn't we celebrate in some way?" Mishka chirped.

Phillip scoffed in arrogance and amusement. "You can earn your reward right here, don't worry. What do you want?"

"Too much," Mishka said dryly, since he'd learned it was always best not to make an opening bid, because he'd might sell himself cheaply.

"Huh, you don't need to play this game. I'll make your fantasies come true, if you make mine come true. It's that simple," Phillip explained. Then he pulled Mishka closer, by Mishka's neck hairs and sniffed his throat, before biting into it.

Mishka scanned the room to make sure, there was no one else left and was relieved, when he found the room to be empty. While Phillip kissed and groped him, Mishka admired the lavishness of the hotel room.

He treasured all the pomposity of the replica antiques, the pointless, glossy knickknacks and the plush fabrics, all spread about the room. It made him envy Phillip, that he could check in and out of frilly hotel rooms, order whatever he wanted at the bar and had money to spare on anything, that caught his eye. Mishka's envy didn't consider all the work Phillip had done, and still did, to earn and maintain his wealth. Mishka only thought of the fun and freedom of disposable financial capital and the lifestyle it could buy.

As if Phillip had read his mind and tried to correct him, Phillip pulled himself away and said, "Let's put you to work."

Without waiting for a response, Phillip shepherded Mishka to a seating arrangement. Phillip dragged a sofa into the open space and placed Mishka on it. When Mishka was seated, Phillip took a few steps back and stood across from Mishka, looking down on him. A few moments past in absolute silence, before Phillip slowly took off his Hermes belt. Phillip kept staring possessively at Mishka, while Mishka jealously admired the shiny, brass H-shaped buckle. Then, with a swift movement, Phillip raised the belt up above his head and swung it through the air, making a loud, sharp noise, as the long leather strip came swishing down through the air and struck Mishka across the face. Mishka's head was forced to the side, down to his shoulder. It had happened so fast, that Mishka didn't really know what was happening until he could feel his left cheek swell and turn red hot. Mishka didn't know what to do, so he did nothing. He'd never been in this situation before and he'd never researched in preparation for it, so he didn't know the proper etiquette of this particular game or what Phillip might expect from him. It made Mishka feel awkward, since he was usually so sure, what he was supposed to do.

Phillip just stood there, towering over him, grinning like a hyena.

"Yeah, this is going to be fun," Phillip said.

Mishka smiled timidly in response, happy that he was of some use.

Phillip raised his left eyebrow, smiled crookedly and swung the belt again, striking Mishka. This time, Mishka let out a small, involuntary croak. This seemed to spur Phillip on. Phillip's grin widened and he let out a low-pitched grunt, as he nodded his head and raised his arm again and struck Mishka with the belt again, again and again, in an incessant series, until Mishka lost both count and feeling.

With each stroke it hurt a little less and by the third stroke, Mishka had learned to roll his head, when the belt came down, moving with the lashes, instead of against them. He fell into the rhythm of the beating. The whole time, Mishka kept his arms stiff down his sides and folded his hands in his lap, sitting like he was at a tea party. It was a struggle against his baser instincts, not to raise his arms in protection of himself, but he was determined to see the game through and prove to himself, that he could take it, that he could behave himself, in this situation too. But, as the lashes increased in tempo, Mishka got dizzy from the rapid movements and it started to become too much for him.

Tears were pressing in Mishka's eyes and despite trying to hold them back, they started to silently stream down Mishka's red hot cheeks. The tears added a painful friction, when the leather made contact with his skin.

"Please stop, just stop for a moment," Mishka pleaded in a hushed voice, ashamed that he had to draw a line, instead of just going along with Phillip's fantasy.

Phillip dropped the belt to the floor and stood there staring at Mishka, with a wide, creepy smile. As Mishka looked up at him, he noticed that Phillip had a huge erection. The sight of Phillip's penis, bulging out his pants, pleased Mishka. The bulge was evidence of Phillip's attraction to him. That he was something to Phillip, something of value, something desirable.

"What?" Phillip said teasingly, gesturing his arms dramatically. "We're not done, not by half! Or are you afraid I won't hold up my end of the bargain?" Phillip lured.

Mishka was so confused and felt so many conflicting things, that he simply couldn't answer, so he just sat there, silently sobbing. Internally Mishka was reprimanding himself, for behaving in such an undignified manner.

Phillip bowed down and wiped Mishka's tears off with his hands and licked the tears off his own fingers.

"Fine," Phillip said in a soft paternal voice, holding Mishka's face in his hands. "You said you wanted too much, but I'm asking a lot of you, so that's only fair. Besides, I'm a very rich man. I can give you what you want." Phillip boasted, gleaming with pride as he said the last two sentences.

Without knowing why, Mishka thought of Jesus, walking in the desert, being tempted by the devil. Bible stories, as told to him by his mother, sometimes came to his mind, when he was with patrons. Right now, Mishka was tempted to sell himself to the devil, just to see what would happen, to see if he could take it. After all, what else did Mishka have left to offer anyone?

"May I use the restroom, please," Mishka asked carefully.

Phillip stared in surprise and possibly disappointment.

"Of course…" Phillip said, gesturing the way to the bathroom, adding "… I'll fix us some drinks in meantime."

Still dizzy from his trashing, Mishka stumbled out to the bathroom, to check his reflection and gather his thoughts.

The bathroom was just to Mishka's taste. It looked like something out of a French film, with black and white marble tiles, ornamented House of Hackney wallpaper, an old-school freestanding bathtub and a large golden mirror in Louis XVII style.

Mishka examined himself in the mirror. His face had already swelled, there were several marks from the belt and streams of blood were running down his cheeks. There were also blood spatters on his coat, shirt and bowtie. The sight of himself battered and bloody almost made him cry again, instead he took a deep breath and collected himself. Focusing on his breathing, he was able to bring himself back to his usual opportunistic self. What was done, was done. What mattered now, was what he could gain from the situation.

It wasn't that Mishka was lying to himself, about Phillip's sadistic behavior and the way it hurt him, it was just that Mishka preferred to think of things in a constructive way. He'd learned he couldn't avoid trauma or pain, so he saw it as his job, to make the most out of it and make the pain worth bearing. He wetted a towel under the faucet and was just about to clean his face, when Phillip appeared in the doorway.

"Don't wipe it off," Phillip said sternly and clearly annoyed, like Mishka should know better, than to do something as foolish and complacent as clean off the blood.

Mishka's blood turned cold and he tried to figure out, how much he could ask for. What was this pain worth? And, how bad would things get tonight? Would he die? He forcefully threw the wet towel across the bathroom and stormed back out to Phillip, to make him pay.

It was time for Phillip to prove it was all worth it.

Seeing the greed in Mishka's eyes, made Phillip smile.

"Champagne?" Phillip offered cheerfully, as he handed a glass to Mishka.

"I want diamonds!" Mishka clumsily blurted out, as he took the glass from Phillip's wrinkled fingers.

Mishka saw the image of Genevieve in his mind. He thought of her glimmering jewelry, her fur pieces and her overall glamor. Mishka blindly wanted to reach Genevieve's level of luxury and he had decided that Phillip was going to be the one, to give it to him. Why not, if he was going to beat the blood out of him, then he would bleed Phillip dry. It was only fitting, there was even an air of poetic justice to it.

"I want a necklace from Cartier... with diamonds!" Mishka tested, continuing making demands in a disrupted manner. Phillip had boasted that he could give him anything, but what was the real limit?

"I want a white gold timepiece... with diamonds... from Backes and Strauss... their Regent collection!"

"And I want a Chanel bag!"

"I want… I want…"

"I want a fur coat!"

"Yes, that's what I want!" Mishka said angrily in conclusion, as he accidently spilled some champagne, as he gestured his arms.

Phillip, who was obviously amused by Mishka's little list, had used it as a drinking game, inhaling a glass of champagne at every "I want" that Mishka had uttered.

Chuckling, Phillip nodded his head, saying, "Sure, kid."

Getting his way so easily made Mishka laugh and it put him to some ease.

There was something about Phillip, that reminded Mishka of Ballin Mundson, the power hungry and generous sadist from the movie 'Gilda'. It eased him up thinking of the whole situation as a scene study of 'Gilda'.

"That's awfully cute… more champagne, please," Mishka replied.

Phillip tried to pour Mishka a fresh glass, but he'd emptied the bottle during his drinking game and had to pop open a new one, which Phillip did with a flourish.

As Phillip poured Mishka a glass, he asked: "Is that all settled? Are you ready for round two?"

"Oh, Phillip, I need more assurance than an IOU, if you want to continue" Mishka replied, confidently sipping his champagne.

Phillip sighed. "What did you have in mind? We're not going to get the things now! Anyway, the stores are closed," Phillip said, worrying he was losing his grip on Mishka.

Mishka put down his glass and put out his hand. "Hand me your phone."

Phillip looked confused.

"Hand me your phone," Mishka repeated anxiously.

In eager anticipation of being done with the conversation, Phillip complied.

Mishka opened the browser and went to Chanel's website, where he picked out a large zipped Chanel tote bag, which he added to the online basket and typed in his address. When the purchase was almost complete, he handed the phone back to Phillip.

"Your credit card info!" Mishka demanded.

Phillip looked at him and smiled. "You understand that there's no going back, once I buy this for you? No stop!" Phillip asked in all seriousness.

"I am a greedy child, Phillip, and if you feed me, I'll let you do whatever you want. No stopping." Mishka said, kissing Phillip's free hand. "But, you have to buy everything I said before," Mishka answered, without batting an eye.

Phillip looked giddy and Mishka began to suspect, that few had made it this far with Phillip. That Phillip had been aching for this night for a long time, just waiting for someone, who could fulfill this fantasy. Mishka felt a strange sense of pride, at this notion.

"Fine. You're shrewd negotiator, boy," Phillip said happily and shook Mishka's hand, from habit of his other business dealings.

Mishka continued browsing websites, to find the items he had demanded before. Going to a website for luxury watches, to get his Backes & Strauss timepiece, then to Marni's website for a fur coat and finally to Cartier's website, where he picked out a yellow gold Panthère de Cartier necklace, with diamonds and tsavorites.

As Phillip entered his credit card information to purchase the necklace, Mishka felt euphoric. He'd never been worth so much, to anyone, before. Mishka couldn't believe he was getting away with this haul.

When Phillip was done, he put away his phone and turned to Mishka. "Now, where were we? What next?" Phillip asked himself, as he looked Mishka up and down, trying to bring his various desires into focus.

Mishka straightened his back, sucked in his stomach and pouted his lips, trying to be as attractive to Phillip, as possible. Wetting his lips with his tongue, Mishka got a taste of blood in his mouth.

Phillip led Mishka to the bedroom, undressed him and pushed him hard, so Mishka fell flat onto the large, opulent bed.

Looking searchingly around the room, Phillip found some furniture string and used it to tie Mishka's hands together and bound him to the bed. As he was binding Mishka, Phillip tested the string, to make sure, there was enough room for maneuvers. As he undressed himself, Phillip took his underpants, bundled them up and forced them into Mishka's mouth. The whole time, Mishka was carefully monitoring each of Phillip's acts. Mishka couldn't explain why, but despite his horror during his whipping, Mishka was getting a bit excited by the anticipation and speculation of what was to come. His blood was slowly shifting from his brain to his penis.

However, Phillip was no longer paying attention to Mishka, but was busy preparing something. He went out of the bedroom and came back with a bunch of candles, which he lit, then he left again. This time, Phillip reappeared with a small leather trunk in his arms.

He placed the trunk by the bed table and opened it. From the angle it was placed, Mishka couldn't see, what was inside it.

When things seemed to be arranged, Phillip looked at Mishka.

"Brace yourself," Phillip warned. Phillip's penis was already fully erect, while Mishka's penis shifted between semi-hard and flaccid, as Mishka's feelings shifted between anticipation and trepidation.

From his little leather trunk, Phillip took out a rubber fist and hurled it down on Mishka's stomach. The force of the throw and the heaviness of the rubber fist knocked the wind out of Mishka's lungs.

"I know," Phillip comforted in a gleeful tone, as he sat down on the bed next to Mishka and tussled his hair.

Phillip picked up the rubber fist and turned Mishka around, so Mishka was on his stomach. Then Phillip's hands travelled all over Mishka's body, lingering at Mishka's ass, before he started spanking Mishka with the rubber fist. At first, Phillip raised the rubber fist and brought it down on Mishka ass, hitting different areas at random. Mishka rather liked it, feeling his buttocks turn hot and red, as Phillip slapped him. But, as Phillip continued slapping, he started aiming directly for Mishka's sphincter and the mood changed.

Phillip turned the rubber fist, so the fingers were pointing to Mishka and started thrusting, rather than slabbing. With each new thrust, Phillip tried to jam the rubber fist into Mishka, more and more determinedly.

"Take it," Phillip commanded in a husky, assertive voice and thrusted the rubber fist down between Mishka's buttocks once again and Mishka bit down in his cotton gag.

The force caused a jabbing pain, that went all the way through Mishka's system, spreading from his sphincter to his whole body.

With each thrust Phillip increased his force, stabbing the rubber fist manically down towards Mishka's sphincter, trying to gain entry. Phillip didn't use any lubricant to ease the insertion, so with each new thrust, Mishka's sphincter instinctively tightened itself, due to the brutality of the insertion. It was only through determination and brute force, Phillip managed to penetrate Mishka with the rubber fist. Mishka writhed in pain, noiselessly screaming. Mishka feared his sphincter would snap like a rubber band, that's been stretched further than it can bear, but he said nothing. This was Phillip's time.

Phillip slowly pulled the rubber fist out again, much to Mishka's relief, only to suddenly thrust it back into Mishka. Repeatedly, Phillip slowly pulled the fist out of Mishka and quickly jabbed it back into him, like Phillip was a child playing with a new toy.

Finally, Phillip stopped, leaving the fist inside Mishka. He got up, leaving Mishka lying face down on the bed, discreetly sobbing into the pillow, hiding his tears.

Glimpsing up from the pillow, Mishka could see Phillip light a candle and bring it to the bed. Phillip sat on his knees, in the bed and dripped hot wax, up and down Mishka's back and his buttocks. Despite the burns, from the dripping hot wax, Mishka was glad of the interlude, simply because it was more familiar ground. The hot wax was nothing, compared to the brutality of the dry fisting and Mishka was able to get a hold of himself and stop crying.

The wax play didn't entertain Phillip for long, before he

turned Mishka to the side and kissed him on his lower rib, with a long, wet and tender kiss.

Grabbing the candle again, Phillip brought the flame to the same spot he'd kissed and let it heat up the saliva, the kiss had left behind on Mishka's skin. Phillip held Mishka's body still, as he watched the saliva disappear under the heat and the flame started to burn Mishka's skin. Mishka's entire body clenched up and spasmed, enhancing the pain of the rubber fist launched inside him, which suddenly felt bigger and harder, than before.

Just as Mishka started to panic, Phillip moved the candle away and Mishka sighed of relief, breathing heavily into the cotton briefs, that Phillip had gagged him with.

As Phillip's hands inspected Mishka's burn, Mishka slowly retracted deep into himself and became an empty vessel for Phillip's wants and needs. Mishka had already sold himself, now he just needed to get through it. At some point, it would be over, he just had to wait it out.

Phillip's hands moved down Mishka's body, grabbing a leg and leaving a wet kiss on Mishka's upper thigh.

Once again, Phillip brought the flame to the mark of saliva and watched his kiss melt away and Mishka's clear white skin turn dark, in contact with the flame.

Now, Phillip turned Mishka on his back, where the madras pushed the rubber fist further up inside Mishka and enhanced the spots of candle wax on his back. With his free hand, Phillip stroked Mishka's penis, trying to get it hard. Cheering Mishka on, Phillip kept whispering, "Yeah, there now. There we go."

Mishka closed his eyes and tried to give Phillip what he wanted, by fantasizing about Jason to make himself erect.

When Mishka was finally hard, Phillip wrapped his lips

around Mishka's penis and started sucking him off. Mishka kept thinking of Jason and just as Mishka was getting close to an orgasm, Phillip spat out Mishka's cock and wafted the flame, from the candle up and down Mishka's shaft. Mishka let out a muffled scream, as his body once again tensed with extreme pain. It was getting harder to breathe, with Phillip's underwear still stuck in his mouth and he was starting to get dizzy. Right as the flame was on the brink of searing Mishka's skin, Phillip took the candle away and put it back on a nearby table.

Mishka's body was still tensed in pain, when Phillip was pulling something new out of his leather trunk. Mishka feared, what it would be and hoped it would soon be over. Once again, Mishka thought about Jesus, walking in the desert, being tempted by the devil. Unlike Jesus, Mishka had been tempted and he'd agreed to terms and conditions. There was nothing left to do now, other than to submit and go through the motions, letting whatever would happen, happen.

To Mishka's surprise, Phillip didn't pull out some sexual torture devise from his trunk, like a perverted Mary Poppins. Instead, it was a pair of rubber gloves and some disinfectant wipes.

Phillip put on the gloves, pulled out some wipes and gently wiped Mishka's penis and scrotum. The wipes brought a sharp pain to Mishka's penis, especially on the burnt shaft. Mishka hissed silently into the cotton in his mouth and thought how strangely nurturing and caring this scene was. As Phillip disinfected Mishka, Mishka's penis fell limp.

Mishka hoped, with all his might, that this meant the end of the séance. But, as Phillip carefully packed the disinfectant wipes away in his little trunk of sins, he pulled out a little box of piercing needles. Phillip opened the little box and poured the needles out onto a porcelain tray, sitting on the bed side table. As the needles dripped out of their cage and hit the porcelain, they each made a little clink. Together, the needles made a beautifully incoherent melody, with no rhythm or specific pace like an orchestra tuning their instruments, before playing a symphony.

Phillip sat down on the bed next to Mishka, gently grabbed Mishka flaccid penis with his left hand, as he found a piercing needle with his right hand and slowly inserted the needle in Mishka's foreskin, which first seemed gentle, but then Phillip ended the insertion with a fast twist.

Phillip then proceeded to insert several needles to Mishka's shaft, scrotum and glans. Each time he inserted the needle with a fast, painful twist, increasing the force, with each needle.

Mishka was breathing harder and harder. He felt like he was high and wondered if Phillip had slipped something into his champagne earlier. Would that just be kicking in now? They must have been at this for hours, now.

The high clouded Mishka's thoughts and it seemed to blur the lines between pain and pleasure. He was no longer sure what he felt. All he knew was, that he wanted to scream. Suddenly, everything went dark and he fainted.

Mishka was awoken by sharp, multiplicated pains, from his penis and scrotum. He had no idea how long he'd been out. Phillip was slapping his needle-filled cock, with a leather strap, which caused immense pain as the needles moved inside his skin, tearing through him. With each slap of the leather strap, Mishka's body tensed and jumped a little up in the air, as he screamed. Each time his scream was silenced, by

Phillip's briefs.

Not knowing what to do, Mishka looked up on the stucco ceiling and forced his thoughts to the reasons for his submission. His thoughts turned the Cartier necklace, that shiny, golden panther, reflecting any light that hit it. His fingers tightened their grip on the furniture string, he was tied with, as he thought of the softness of the fur, he was going to get. He suddenly heard the tick-tick-tick of the clock in the living room and thought of the elegant, curved lines of the Backes and Strauss watch, he'd made Phillip buy him.

As Phillip swung the leather strap through the air, hitting Mishka's cock again, Mishka arched his back in ecstasy, as he thought of the smooth leather of the Chanel tote bag.

Arching to a nearly sitting position, the furniture string forced Mishka back and he fell back down in the bed. As Mishka lay there, helpless, but not guiltless, he suddenly had the weirdest urge to pray, like he'd done as a small child. Still staring at the ceiling, he silently prayed:

"Our Father in heaven,
hallowed be your name,
your kingdom come,
your will be done,
on earth as in heaven.
Give us today our daily bread.
Forgive us our sins
as we forgive those who sin against us.
Save us from the time of trial
and deliver us from evil.
For the kingdom, the power, and the glory are yours
now and forever. Amen."

But Mishka didn't feel any forgiveness, nor did he feel

like he was delivered from evil. He felt like he was being fucked by evil.

Tears were forming in his eyes, but he refused to let out a sound. Mishka was broken, like a horse. Instead, Mishka stared daringly at Phillip, while he sucked in his stomach and stretched out his entire body, to enhance its long, thin lines. Even now, Mishka couldn't help, but try to be as attractive as possible.

When Phillip saw this contrasted show of forced flirtation and silent tears streaming down Mishka's cheeks, mixing with the blood from his initial belt-lashing, Phillip smiled.

"Oh, yeah. It's time," Phillip said, as he brutally pulled out the needles out of Mishka, causing blood to flow down his testicles. Once, Phillip had removed all the needles, he put on a condom and came into the bed. With one hand, Phillip raised Mishka up, by his ankles, slowly removed the rubber fist and replaced it with his penis. As Mishka's legs were placed on Phillip's shoulders, Phillip had the best view of the damage he'd done to Mishka.

As he thrusted himself, hard and dry into Mishka, Phillip inspected the fresh blood flowing from Mishka's limp penis, as well as the burn marks and dried blood from the belt-lashing. Now and again, Phillip would look Mishka in the eye, to see the sad, deadened look, in his tear- and bloodstained face.

Mishka no longer felt anything. There was no longer anything burrowing into him, other than Phillip and his penis was nowhere near the size of the rubber fist. The only thing Mishka noticed, was the rhythm of Phillip's thrusts, as he moved along with them. Phillip's tempo was increasing, as did Phillip's grunts.

Phillip drooled, as his eyes travelled over Mishka's body, trying to take in all the alterations he'd made and the power he'd established over Mishka.

Suddenly, Phillip pulled out of Mishka and sat up across Mishka's chest, making it hard for him to breathe.

Mishka just lay there, like he was dead, as Phillip was sitting on his chest masturbating, but Phillip either didn't notice or he simply didn't care.

As Phillip's sweat mixed with Mishka's splattered bloodstains, Phillip became more and more exited, until his excitement reached its climax and Phillip ejaculated all over Mishka's face.

Phillip shook his penis over Mishka's face, as if to make quite sure, he had no more semen left to spill. When Phillip was quite sure, he'd cum all he could, he hit Mishka hard in the face with his still erect cock.

At first Mishka tried to hide his face, but this made Phillip slap him hard, so Mishka stopped hiding away and let Phillip slap him continuously with his penis, as it slowly grew limp.

When Phillip was finally flaccid and Mishka thought it was completely over, Phillip stood up in the bed and started to pee in Mishka's face. Mishka tried to close his eyes and bite down, but Phillip's underpants made it impossible for him to close his mouth shut and as the cotton fibers of Phillip's underwear soaked up Phillip's urine, it leaked drops into Mishka's mouth and he felt like he was about to drown.

Phillip took his urine soaked briefs, from Mishka's mouth and let it drop to Mishka's stomach. Ungagged, Mishka gasped for air. As he caught his breath, it was like he was coming out of a trance or feverish nightmare.

"Thank you for that. Now, you can clean yourself," Phillip

said gaily, all smiles, as he untied Mishka.

Mishka looked at him, with an empty stare and rushed to the bathroom, where he quickly cleaned himself off in the shower. At every small noise, Mishka jumped, fearing that Phillip would join him.

When he was cleaned off and smelled like hotel soap, he took stock of himself in the mirror.

Besides some swelling and some red marks, his face didn't look too bad. The burn marks, however, already looked bad and were swelling up with liquid. His testicles and penis were in the worst condition and Mishka wondered, how much time it would take to heal and if it ever would look, like it did before.

It took a lot of courage for Mishka to go out and join Phillip again, but when he did, Phillip was cordial. In fact, he was running around, in a fresh pair of underwear and a robe, humming happily and sipping some sort of coffee drink.

"Oh, there you are," Phillip said, handing him a bundle of cash, as per routine.

Mishka looked perplexed at the cash.

"You were a good sport," Phillip said in explanation, smiling as he gave Mishka a gentle pat on the cheek.

Mishka just smiled in response, then he picked up his blood-spattered clothes, from the bedroom floor, to dress himself.

Seeing Mishka completely naked for a last time that night, Phillip looked him up and down, as if to take it all in.

"… and don't worry, there shouldn't be any permanent damage. You should be fine in about two to three weeks," Phillip added, winking at Mishka.

Mishka smiled. "Good to know. Did you, uhm, did you

have fun?" Mishka asked, as he put on his pants.

Phillip furrowed his brows and walked straight up to Mishka, put his hand around his neck and gave a hard, dry kiss on the lips. "A great time, don't worry about it. You were great." Phillip answered and slapped Mishka's ass. Mishka jumped up, suddenly feeling how sore his entire bottom was.

As Mishka finished getting dressed, he tried to process, what had just happened and figure out, what he was doing.

Mishka was used to his desires and gratification being ignored. He was used to being handled roughly, with no regard for his pleasure. This was something else though, a different level of possession and he wondered if it was a step up or step down. Again, he thought of Genevieve and wondered if she had to undergo séances like this, if this was the way to the life he dreamed of. Despite the extreme physical pain he endured under Phillips ownership, he mentally enjoyed being of use and being able to attract a man like Phillip.

When Mishka was completely dressed and had collected all his things, he nodded to Phillip, held up the cash Phillip had given him and said, "Bye, thanks for tonight," and hurried out the door, without waiting for a response. All Mishka wanted now, was to get away from Phillip.

Out on the street, the morning light was breaking and the streets were busy with people going to work.

He lit a green Sobranie cocktail cigarette and started walking home. All the way, people took the time to look him up and down. Some in surprise at seeing a young man in a tuxedo at seven a.m., others in horror, noticing the blood stains on his face and quite a few looked at him in amused fascination of someone who was still engaged with last night. He was stopped several times, by people who offered their help or to tell him, he had it coming or to threaten him with an extra beating. Comments like 'serves you right pervert', 'fag' and 'fucking homo' was thrown at him from passing people, bikes and cars. Mishka simply walked hurriedly away from everyone, not answering or looking at anyone.

When he finally reached home, he threw off his coat and blazer, dropped his pants and opened his shirt. Then, he stumbled half naked into the bed, threw the cash Phillip had given him up in the air and rolled around in it. Then, he took a selfie, with one hand down his underpants and his face scrunched in an overtly fake orgasmic look, with sores and red marks across his face and down his partially exposed torso. He posted the picture on Snap Chat and Instagram accounts with the caption "Play with me", before he fell into a deep and desperate sleep.

Chapter 11

Mishka woke up from discomfort, as he turned in his sleep.

"Urgh," Mishka grunted to himself. Almost his entire body was sore or in pain. As he yawned, he hid his face in his hands, but as soon as his palm touched his face, it made his entire face feel raw. Mishka hissed in agony, as he slowly remembered last night.

Besides the various physical ailments, he was hurt from a sharp bolt of shame, which he desperately tried to replace with a forced, emotional detachment.

Yet, his curiosity and fear made him run to a mirror, to inspect the damage. He recalled more and more details, from last night, as he rushed to the mirror. His ass felt sore and he remembered the pain from the dry insertion of the rubber fist.

It was all coming back to him, in vivid detail.

The shiny, brass H-shaped belt buckle and how he'd moved with the lashes.

The hot wax.

The burning.

The needles.

How he'd thought of Jason to fain excitement and how his pain had turned Phillip on.

In the mirror he saw himself, like he'd never seen himself before. His facial features were distorted from swelling, his color had gone from pale white and pink, to flushed red, with darker red stripes and occasional black, oblong sores.

Mishka turned his leg, to see the blistering burn on his thigh and then took off his shirt, inspecting the identical blistering burn on his torso.

Dropping his underpants, he saw his penis, transformed from an average, white, straight-lined penis, to something that looked like a failed brisket recipe. His penis was badly burned, red and orange, with blisters all the way up and down the bottom of the shaft, with big, clumpy sores all over his penis and balls. As he touched his penis, it made a horrific sticky and crackling sound, as the juices from his burns shifted and the dried blood cracked and reopened sores.

Mishka felt sick and ran to the bathroom and threw up, reaching the toilet bowl, in the nick of time.

He threw up again and again and again. Vomiting from each flashback from last night, that came to his mind.

When he finally had no more liquid left to purge, he sat down on the cool tiles, next to the toilet and just existed in a welcome vacuum of silent thoughtlessness. But like all silences, it ended and noise came crashing in.

Last night was bad and he bitterly regretted it today, but he could still make something of it. Change the narrative. There was nothing to gain, by remembering it as a mistake or a trauma. He had to figure out a way to spin it, so he could move on, he knew that.

Having confidence in his ability to change the past, by changing the tone of his thoughts, he got up off the floor and gave himself a determined, confident look in the bathroom mirror.

"Right," Mishka said to his reflection. "We will get through this together. We've done it before."

Mishka thought back to other nights, with other men, who

had misused him and how he had recovered.

He thought about the first times he'd been with Mr. P, where he'd slapped Mishka, whenever they'd locked eyes during sex and Mr. P had chanted "I'm straight, I'm straight", as he neared ejaculation. That had been weird and humiliating, but he'd gotten past it and Mr. P had simmered down, about his alleged heterosexuality.

There was also that Russian guy, he'd dated for a year, who kept drugging him and having sex with him, when he was unconscious. "God, he was hot," Mishka thought to himself, sad that he'd never really gotten to experience sex with him.

Oh, and that children's psychologist, Allan something, who had insisted on psychoanalyzing him, while he was anal fucking him. That was weird. He could still clearly remember the first time with Allan, when Mishka was on his back, legs wrapped around Allan, as Allan leaned over him, fucking him nice and hard, while grunting "So! Ugh! T-tell me... Ugh... about your childhood... Ugh!".

Mishka smiled from embarrassment and shook his head, as he cherry-picked memories, bad memories from his mind's 'Pandora's box'.

Last night may have felt different, but it was the same power dynamic, Mishka was used to. It was all about them and their need to exercise power over him or anyone else, they were with. That's why they were willing to pay and were so generous with presents. It was all to gain power, so Mishka owed them and perhaps to ease any moral quandaries, they may have had. It wasn't abuse, if they paid for it, then it was simply an exchange of favors. Their social interactions with him was just a mirage, they used to reflect in and see their own self-concept.

As he analyzed, Mishka felt empowered and more at ease. If he had the ability to describe his experiences, he felt he had some control over them.

Now, he had the mental power to be pleased with the haul he had got from last night and could look forward to receiving them. He went back to the bedroom, to collect the cash, he'd slept on, counting them, as he found each bill. There weren't much, just 1,500 kroner, but with the presents coming, it was a decent tip.

Picking up his phone, Mishka checked the performance of last night's selfie. It had done well, it had a little over 3,400 likes and over 1000 comments, most of them were lurid and suggestive emojis. It pleased him, it meant someone still wanted him and he was on the right track. He still was something, to someone. Catching a glimpse of himself in his vanity mirror, he realized, it would probably be some days, before anyone would want him again, before he could take a decent selfie or see someone. Immediately, he postponed all engagement for the following weeks, sending out the same text to all: "Sorry, darling. Have to cancel our plans. I'll see you some other time. Can't wait (KISS EMOJI)". He thought the mixed message in expressing desire to meet, by canceling for no apparent reason, would be alluring to most of them. They would most likely use the lack of information, to project both their best hopes and worst fears into his message, which would just make him dearer to them. Besides, he didn't owe them an explanation and he didn't want to tell them the truth.

Phillip's rough treatment and his own recent high earnings meant, that he could take this as a sort of holiday, if he would heal in the two to three weeks' time frame, Phillip had estimated.

Mishka sat down and looked about the filthy, messy room, filled with consumer goods. It looked like the wardrobe of a second-rate theater diva. He chuckled at the thought and then tried to find other distractions. The whole time of his convalescence stood before him like a black hole and he didn't know how to handle the silence. He feared the lack of things to do and the lack of parts to play, when he would have no admirers to see him or to play up against.

Just then, his phone pinged in his hand, it was another eggplant emoji sent to him by a follower on his Instagram account. It gave Mishka an idea. He could sell his dirty underwear to his followers. That could earn him some extra cash, while he healed and provide him with some indirect limelight, during his isolation. There would still be an audience to fantasize about him and fetishize him. He knew some of the other boys and girls did it, for easy cash, so why couldn't he?

Jumping up, he ran to the laundry basket and fished out all his dirty underwear. Afterwards he searched the trash for condoms, turning them inside out and rubbing their deposits on the inside of each of the twelve dirty underpants, he'd found. Afterwards he laid them out on the floor and took pictures of them, posting them as stories on his Instagram and his Snap Chat, with the caption "Dirty And For Sale. Gimme a bid, daddy". He had no idea, how these transactions were normally done, but he figured this would work.

As he posted it, he remembered the bloodied ones, he'd worn last night. They could probably go for a lot. He took some pictures of them, making sure, all the stains were captured and posted those pictures too, this time with the caption "For sale: my blood, sweat and tears."

Getting energy from the assurance, that he still had an audience to perform for, even if it was a remote one, Mishka started his day and got in the shower. Today he would treat himself and bathe in warm water, instead of cold.

As the water poured down on him and warmed his body, he felt like all the bad things were washing away. It was his belief, that any shower was like a baptism, that it washed away his sins and distanced him from evil.

The warm water relaxed his thin muscles and got him to relax. Still, he had to be very careful , not to let the water rays hit his blistering burns directly, since it caused too much pain. While the water didn't take away the bad memories, it did wash away some of the scabbing, only leaving small red marks, from Phillip's needles and the steam cleaned his burns.

The actions of last night were over and he could look ahead. Though Phillip had been physically rougher, than he was used to, it was still the same trite power grab, as all the other ones pulled.

Mishka laughed to himself over the irony, that he risked so much in order to procure securities and then continued to explain away Phillip's actions.

Phillip was just another man, he had let himself belong to, in exchange for something he wanted and their night together had added to Mishka's value, increasing his future worth.

Now that he knew what he could get, he wasn't going to take less. That was what he took away from the experience, that he had underestimated his value and he needed to upsell himself in the future. This meant he had to take care of himself now, as he convalesced, to secure his worth.

When he turned the water off, Mishka hid his face in a towel and stood, leaning his head against the wall. He was trying to be nothing, like he usually did after a shower, but in the dark and once safe space of his towel-cave, he was disturbed by glimpses of Phillip's facial expressions, as Phillip had hurt him yesterday. How excited, happy and curious Phillip had looked. No, the towel was a bad place to hide today. Mishka came out of his hiding place and oiled himself up in lavender oil, which he always had lying around for small cuts and bruises. This time, he used it on his entire body, being extra generous and careful to areas with sores that might scar. Being born a country boy, he had great faith in healing herbs, like lavender, and often used them in his daily life.

As he habitually sat down at his makeup table, he realized, that he didn't need to paint himself today, as he knew for sure, that he wasn't going to be seen by anyone, not even in a selfie.

On unfamiliar ground, he simply put on some powder, to soak up the excess oil and put some nurturing serum in his hair. It took all of five minutes. Was that it? He thought to himself. Was he done now? A huge wave of silence came crashing in on him again, leaving room for the little treacherous, nondiegetic voices of his hurt feelings.

In order to drown them out, he put on the soundtrack to Sofia Coppola's film; Marie Antoinette, as he tried to choose a stay-at-home-outfit.

Routines were a great opium to Mishka. His mother had taught him, how keeping up appearances and routines, could numb almost any pain. If you pretended at something long enough, it usually became reality.

Today, he'd pretend to be a golden boy.

He put on a frilly white shirt and tied a purple silk ribbon around his neck in a huge bow, which he paired with a purple velvet smoking jacket, black satin trousers and black and gold velvet slippers. Raiding his jewelry collection, he put on both a yellow gold pinky ring, with a small white diamond and a large amethyst cocktail ring, which he wore on the same hand.

The outfit and the white powder made him look like an extra on the Marie Antoinette film, that had been battered by French revolutionaries.

Walking majestically into his kitchen, he inspected the groceries, that Jason had brought him and decided to make hot chocolate and a fruit plate, which he enjoyed in his bedroom, in front of his makeup mirror, as he listened to the rest of the soundtrack.

When he'd finished eating his fruit and the chocolate pot was completely empty, Mishka once again felt pointless.

He tried focusing his thoughts, by reading books, then watching television, researching makeup tutorials, flipping through magazines and at last, doing the dishes.

Nothing could keep his attention for long and he walked around his apartment, like a caged animal. Occasionally, he'd stand by the windows and watch people on the street, like a caged leopard in the zoo, might look at the passing visitors.

In the end, he sat back down in front of his makeup table and stared into the mirror, examining his own reflection, shifting between disgust and appreciation.

Of course, he hated the marks, Phillip had left, but he also found a million other pre-existing faults, like the tilt of his nose, the unevenness of his brows and etc. But there were good things too. He really was rather thin, with his collar bones sticking out, in from behind his shirt. That made him smile, smug and self-satisfied. His face had a definite jaw line and very clear features, even if it were marred by marks at the moment.

The mirror provided him with company and gave him the benefit of being both performer and viewer. Maybe some time alone wouldn't be so boring, it occurred to Mishka.

He rearranged his makeup table, moving it to a corner, where the mirror could capture most of the room, including the bed.

Then, Mishka changed the music to Madonna's 'Material Girl' on repeat and changed his clothes.

Just because he was alone, didn't mean he couldn't have a party.

Mishka dressed up in white tie, in one of his new suits from Tom Ford, styling it with a golden jacquard vest and black velvet slippers. He even changed his jewelry, putting on the ring, Mr. P had given him, silver cufflinks and a heavy, silver necklace from Tiffany's, which he wore over his white shirt and tie. It amused him, to put such an effort into being alone and he had fun, dressing just for his own eyes. He admired his own reflection and even thought the scars in his face, looked quite distinguished, when in white tie.

After he'd dressed, he fetched a bottle of champagne from the kitchen, popped it open and poured himself a drink.

As he drank, he changed the music and danced in front of his mirror, carefully studying himself, his movements and his poses.

The whole day flew by, like that, where Mishka and his mirror played the game he used to play with his patrons and for his social media followers.

Only, he and the mirror played both parts. The mirror gave Mishka someone to play across, someone to please, but the mirror also substituted Mishka, as an object of admiration and beauty. Just as Mishka substituted his followers and his patrons, by taking their place and admiring and lusting after his own reflection, as they had lusted after him. He and his reflection were both the admired and the admirer.

He continued the rest of his day dancing, drinking and flirting with his reflection. The only time, he turned away from the mirror was to raid his kitchen. Occasionally taking a break to sample some of the snacks Jason had brought him.

As Mishka continued dancing and drinking, he eventually tired himself out and ended his day. He undressed ceremoniously, trying to seduce the mirror, as he carefully removed each article of clothing. Then, he carefully put each item back in their respective places and put on his best pajamas. After he turned off the music, he brushed his teeth, splashed some cold water on his face and went to bed.

In his bed, he could still see himself in the mirror and fell asleep, staring and analyzing himself, trying to flirt himself into liking himself and being enough for himself.

Chapter 12

In the following days, Mishka started dealing with his isolation and bore it better. His reflection had become his steady companion, confidant and even his object of desire.

Before, the mirror had always been a frenemy, which both complimented him and put him down. Their relationship had always been tense, even when he was just a small child. Now, he was doing everything with his reflection. They ate together, exercised together, danced, he talked to it and it kept him informed of his physical development, including his healing.

He'd even begun to feel occasional spouts of sexual attraction to his reflection. Although all such drives quickly dissolved and were replaced by pain, when his blood shifted and his penis erected itself, tearing open sores, cuts and burns. But he secretly looked forward to the day, when his penis had healed and they could be together. Not, that he was fully aware of this himself. It was just, that the mirror was the only one left for him to relate to.

Despite his fears to be stuck alone in his apartment, he'd found productive things to occupy him.

The dirty underwear he'd offered for sale, had received several bids and had all been sold. The bloodied underwear reaching the highest price, which didn't surprise Mishka, it only confirmed what he already knew; people were twisted and out for blood.

Mishka had packed up each item as soon as he'd received

mobile payment from the buyer. Because it had worked so well, Mishka had begun selling each pair of underwear he wore for a fixed price of 1000 kroner each, soiled with the fluid and blood of his burns and cuts. Each week he'd bought new underwear online and ordered a messenger to pick up the previous week's dirtied ones.

Yes, Mishka had certainly stepped into a rhythm. Each day was pretty much the same.

He'd get up late, make a pot of coffee, which he drank in bed, as he watched old movies, to find lines and social tools he could use later on. Then he'd take off his dirty underwear, post pictures of it and put up for sale online, before taking a shower. Afterwards he'd dress up extravagantly, but he kept his skincare routine fixed on healing, rather than looks. He'd almost given up makeup, except for white powder.

Then he'd have lunch, which he usually only chewed and spat out, without swallowing. In the afternoon he'd read, usually French or Russian novels, like 'Bel Ami' or 'The Idiot', looking for social cues, scheming maneuvers and personality traits to adapt.

In the late afternoon till the early evening, he'd watch different types of gay porn, so he could learn to adapt to the fantasy and fetishes of others. He watched the men on the screen perform various acts on themselves and each other, with a detached, academic interest. This wasn't about his pleasure, there was no pleasure in it for him, it was about learning to give pleasure and he tried to attain as much knowledge as he could, so he too could become an object of carnal pleasure, a flickering fantasy like the men on the screen. This was just research for him. He thought of the porn stars as both his betters and his competitors, so he looked for things to adapt from them, but also how he could be better than them. In Mishka's mind, there were two types of men, ethereal beings who gave pleasure and base Neanderthals who took pleasure and he desperately wanted to belong to the first category. Giving pleasure, gave him value and it could give him power.

After a couple of hours, this journey into men's sordid fantasies would tire him out and he'd move on to his evening. He'd fix himself a cocktail and arrange some snacks, which he'd slowly devour, as he changed to an elaborate evening costume. Every evening, Mishka went to great effort to look lavish and make every evening an event. He filled the apartment with music and dancing, while he processed everything he'd learned during the day. As he dressed, Mishka flirted with his reflection, tried to catch his best angles and practiced his delivery of the moves and lines, he'd picked up that day, imagining up future scenarios where he might use it.

His convalescence had become a cocoon, where he built himself up by altering everything, that was natural and instinctive about him. He got thinner and thinner and his own thoughts were replaced by lines from movies and books. As the days' past, fiction gradually changed from being his source of inspiration, to being his reality.

In short, having the time alone gave him the focus to deny himself and replace himself with something better and he joyfully watched the transformation in his reflection. In his mirror, he created the perfect man, much like Dr. Frankenstein had created his creature, out of bits and pieces of other people. It was with joy, he watched his cheeks sink in, making his cheekbones and jawline more and more prominent, as he starved himself, surviving on booze, nuts and cocktail olives. Each day, he felt stronger, as he learned more and more and his scars, burns and sores slowly healed and disappeared.

In his own way, Mishka was using his time very productively.

In the meantime, Phillip's gifts had been delivered to Mishka's apartment.

As the gifts arrived, Mishka felt he gained worth and it boosted his confidence. At the arrival of each item, he'd test it, by wearing it with a large variety of outfits, admiring it in the mirror, deciding what looks the item was best paired with.

When the final gift arrived, after a couple of weeks, he tried all the items on at once and posed for his reflection.

He draped the fur coat over his naked frail body, making sure it exposed the shiny gold Cartier necklace and the sparkling Backes and Strauss diamond watch. He held the Chanel bag up, covering his torso, feeling the subtle leather against his body.

Mishka had healed very well and there were only few marks, that needed to heal completely, the burns being the worst.

The mix in sensations were intoxicating, the smell of the leather, the warm and fuzzy fur, the slinky silk lining of the coat and the cool, heavy touch of the metal, from the necklace and watch. It was like he was being caressed by infinite lovers, each with their own particular touch.

He missed being felt up, having hungry hands, greedily exploring his body and taking possession of him. As he recalled previous orgasms, he reflexively started pushing his crotch up against the Chanel bag. To his surprise, he was healed enough, that he felt no pain, when his penis stretched itself out, as his excitement gradually grew and he held the bag tighter. While he repeatedly pressed himself up against the back of his new bag, he locked eyes with his reflection, making love to his image, rather than himself or the bag.

His breath shortened and he was filled with enthusiasm, causing him to suddenly drop the bag to the floor and rush to the mirror. He kept posing for his reflection, carefully enhancing his best angles and showing off his new jewelry and the new fur, while he eagerly explored his body with his hands.

Before he knew it, he was pressing himself up against his reflection, the jewels clacking against the glass and his open fur coat flowing behind him. Mishka pushed his body up and down the hard and cold surface of his reflection.

In his excitement, pre-sperm transformed his pushes into sliding movements and his erect penis glided up and down its own reflection, enabling some sort of narcissistic copulation. Mishka moaned enthusiastically, as he watched his body merge with his reflection and he felt a new sense of freedom. With each glide up and down the mirror, both his tempo and his volume increased. Losing all sense of time and space, he suddenly felt a vibrating jolt deep inside himself. To his surprise, Mishka suddenly exploded with a bursting sense of pleasure and he ejaculated an abundance of sperm, greasing both himself and his reflection.

For several moments Mishka just stood still, leaning up against the mirror, as he tried to catch his breath.

He had no idea, what had just happened, but he felt it was significant and he needed a few moments, taking in the importance.

Despite the quantity of lovers and the variety of Mishka's sexual experiences, he felt something he'd never felt before. This orgasm, from this encounter with his reflection, had changed him. It was like he was recharged. His pallor had changed, with an attractive flush in his hollowed-out cheeks. His blood even felt different, like it flowed more freely through his body. His whole being was refreshed; renewed.

Out of an odd sense of possessiveness and to prolong the moment, Mishka greedily licked the sperm from his reflection and tasted it, like you'd taste a lover you truly lust after.

Mishka finally stepped away from the mirror and dropped the fur coat to the floor, careful not to sully it with his fluids. Still panting, Mishka didn't know what to do now. He felt like he should be ashamed, but he just felt free and empowered.

Mishka took off his new watch and the necklace and drew himself a warm bath.

Lying in the warm water, Mishka couldn't help laughing to himself. He let his hands wander all over his body, rubbing it with lavender oil. For the first time, he felt glad of his body and he proudly examined every bit of it, as he caressed it with oil. Mishka looked at his body, like his reflection had looked at it and he understood, that he was now seeing his body from the perspective of his patrons, something he hadn't been able to do before.

Now, he understood their desire for him and their inclination to try and assert possession over him, both socially and physically. But the reflection had no mind to control, it only showed him how to look his best. His reflection scolded him, when he was unattractive and rewarded him, when he pleased it. It didn't have the violent controlling grasp of his patrons.

The water was getting cold and Mishka got out of the bath, dried himself and walked naked to his bedroom. He carefully cleaned the mirror, not to erase the traces of his encounter with his reflection, but so he could once again see his reflection clearly.

Mishka spent the rest of the night in silence, drinking scotch and telepathically conversing with his reflection. He had a new goal, to get the means to live alone, just him and his reflection, without any controlling patrons. Before they reached a natural conclusion to their conversation, Mishka fell asleep at his makeup table, stretched out among his makeup, books and recently used jewelry.

Chapter 13

After the course of three weeks, Mishka's wounds had completely healed and he was setting up appointments to see people again, but something in him had changed, since his evening of passion with his reflection. He no longer went aimlessly after more money and more expensive gifts to prove himself. Money had taken on a different meaning for him, it was not so much about worth anymore, but about independence and freedom. This new interpretation of money affected his relationship with his patrons, he cared a little less about their approval. Not that he was indifferent to it, their opinion of him and desire for him was still flattering to him and meant a great deal to him. But autonomy had started to matter more to him, than flattery. He was no longer satisfied being a fantasy for others, he wanted to live out the fantasy for himself and for his eyes only, but that required financial independence and that meant work.

Luckily, Mishka's cold and abrupt cancellation of his patron's appointments, during his convalescence, seemed to have spurred them on. They were all anxious to see him again and had texted several times, which he had simply ignored until he was healed. Now, when he looked good again, he texted them individually and asked if they wanted to meet soon, which they'd all eagerly agreed to.

After a few weeks, everything was back to normal and over the following months, life went by peacefully and prosperously. Phillip had become a generous regular and Mishka still saw Mervin, Jason and Mr. P.

Phillip and Mishka had negotiated terms, that let Phillip live out his violent fantasies, but without causing lasting marks, that left Mishka forced to isolate himself again. So, while Phillip's desire for Mishka was still of a very violent nature, it was now understated enough, that their encounters only left bruises.

All in all, things were going well. Between Mr. P, Mervin, Jason and Philip, occasional one-nighters Mishka picked up in hotel bars and the continuous sale of his dirty underwear, Mishka earned a good, steady living, which allowed him to live expensively and still have a little to spare. Mishka was always busy and had very little time to himself, but he enjoyed seeing his small savings grow.

However, all his patrons had noticed a change within Mishka, a slight abstraction which they reacted to in different ways.

Phillip was beginning to suspect, that he was pushing Mishka near a mental breaking point, which gave Phillip immense pleasure, since it fed his power-hungry id. Phillip's suspicions even made him go easier on Mishka, because he thought he had the upper hand and therefore had no more power left to take from Mishka. Their games now mostly consisted of mild BDSM, like bondage, whipping and spanking. This wasn't to Mishka's tastes at all, but at least it wasn't too damaging to his looks.

Jason and Mr. P both worried, that Mishka was drifting away, wondering if Mishka had met someone else and was falling in love. Even though Jason and Mr. P had the same theory, they reacted in very different ways.

Jason become more caring, in an anxious way, acting almost like a guardian for Mishka, trying to provide for him, as best he could, economically and emotionally.

Mr. P reacted almost manically, shifting between excessive tenderness and sudden outbursts of physical brutality and streams of verbal accusations.

Mishka bore it all nonchalant, seeing it as an unfortunate part of the job, while he longed for his retirement. In their increasing desperation, Mishka saw the opportunity to squeeze generosity out of all their insecurities and conspiracy theories, to grow the stash of cash he called his 'retirement fund'.

The change they sensed in Mishka, was simply his new direction away from them and Mishka's new self-sufficiency. Mishka had become obsessed with pleasing his own gaze and had become possessive of his body, unwilling to share it freely with anyone else. Before, Mishka took emotional nourishment from his sexual encounters, gaining confidence and self-worth from it. Now, sex had simply become work. It was work he did exclusively for the purpose of earning a fortune, so he could buy his freedom.

The only one, who didn't really seem to notice Mishka's detachment, was Mervin. Mervin had gone back to his old self and showed up for planned appointments, played with Mishka and left his usual amount on the nightstand, in keeping with Mervin's old-world-manners. Yet, something seemed to gnaw at Mervin's mind, it was as if he was distracted too, but wouldn't or daren't say what was weighing on his mind.

Mervin's brows were now knitted in a permanent sulk, which were only ever relieved, when he was in bed with Mishka. Mishka didn't know what was wrong, but he knew something was and out of sympathy for his old and generous patron, he was extra attentive to Mervin's needs. Despite Mishka's new resolve, it hurt his pride, that he no longer had Mervin's full attention and Mishka worked harder as a result. In fact, they had never had so frequent or so lasting sex, as they did now. Mervin had become frustratingly slow to reach the critical juncture. It seemed to take him a long time to forget his troubles, which delayed his focus on pleasure. But like all pressing things, it inevitably came to its culmination.

One night, Mervin came unannounced to Mishka's apartment. Luckily, Mishka was alone, having just said goodbye to Jason, before Mervin came by.

Mishka froze up, when he saw Mervin.

It was such a grotesque scene. Mervin came looking like the ghost of the late king Hamlet. Mishka was just enjoying a post coital, lilac Sobranie cocktail cigarette and was wearing nothing but Versace briefs and an open silk robe.

Mishka was startled at the sight of Mervin creeping quietly into the living room.

Mervin looked terribly disheveled, his bowtie was crooked, his shirt was partially untucked and his hair was all mussed. Even his face was different. Mervin's once plump and jolly face was sunken in and completely white. There was little left of the stately gentleman, Mervin usually was.

Mishka had only seen Mervin step out of character like that once before, the only other time Mervin had shown up without an appointment.

It was strange, as Mervin moved further into the apartment, it was as if he had no noises left in him at all and therefore moved noiselessly. Mishka hadn't even heard Mervin lock himself in.

This must be what Mervin will look like, when he's dead,

Mishka thought to himself and took a long slow drag from his cigarette and assessed the situation. Not finding any words, that seemed appropriate, Mishka simply gestured to a chair, indicating Mervin should have a seat.

Mervin mechanically submitted to the gesture and sat down without a word.

Out of habit, Mishka fixed him a glass of scotch and handed it to him.

"Thank you, my dear boy," Mervin croaked, like he hadn't used his voice for years.

Mervin looked solemnly into the air, as Mishka hanged over Mervin and carefully attempted polite conversation, but Mervin stayed silent and just stared at nothing.

Just as Mishka had given up on conversation, Mervin firmly let out: 'We must face facts!'

At the word 'facts' Mishka instinctively withdrew from Mervin, as if the word was poisonous.

"But they're so dull," Mishka said reservedly.

"Such an innocent you are," Mervin responded emphatically.

Mishka didn't associate with the word; 'innocent', but he was touched, that Mervin thought of him like that.

Mishka got down on his knees and sat before Mervin's feet and took Mervin's hands.

"Mervin, what is it? Please, just tell me."

"My dear, dear boy," Mervin said in a desperate tone of voice.

A few more moments passed in silence, before Mervin continued; "It's all coming tumbling down and… I'm ruined… or I'm going to be."

Mishka's first thoughts were of himself. It had been such

a lucrative few months and he was just starting to get a taste for spare cash. Now he saw Mervin's contributions disappear. Mishka made no answer other than to shake his head in refusal.

Seeing Mishka's unwillingness to believe, Mervin went on to a very long and very technical explanation about his finances and investments, which Mishka couldn't make heads or tails of. The whole time, Mishka sat by Mervin's feet, with big, wondrous eyes, shaking his head.

"The point is," Mervin said pointedly, "that I'm found out. What I did wasn't exactly above board and the press has gotten hold of it and they've made it clear, that they intend to publish... They've asked for quote," Mervin sighed, "then there will surely be an investigation of some sort. Even if there isn't, by some miracle, the press alone will finish me."

"I don't understand," Mishka admitted freely.

Mervin noticed the glass in his hands and swallowed his scotch in one giant gulp.

"You don't have to," Mervin said factually. "I've tried to keep it all under wraps, but the truth will out, as they say. I refused to comment. They said the story breaks tomorrow either way."

Mervin tried taking another big gulp from his glass, forgetting he'd already emptied it.

"Who, who wanted a quote?" Mishka asked, mostly to have something to say.

"Just some tabloid trash, it's not important who," Mervin scoffed, as Mishka refilled Mervin's glass.

Mervin continued, "Oh, my dear boy, you've always been kind to me," Mervin said as he tussled Mishka's hair.

Kind? It was such an odd descriptor for his behavior and it dawned on Mishka, why Mervin had come to him and kept him. What a cold life Mervin must have had outside of their relationship, for Mervin to equate his paid subservience with kindness.

"I'll try to keep you out of it and you will keep, what I've promised you, before it all comes down." As Mervin said this, he pulled out some papers and a fountain pen from his inner jacket pocket and continued. "When there's an investigation, they will seize whatever they can get their grubby hands on. After all, I promised you, you could stay here as long as you wanted to, when I put you up. That was the deal and a deal is a deal, however you look at it. Besides, I'd rather just give it to you, than let the tax office have it." Mervin said begrudgingly, adding: "If you sign this, you'll still be able to keep the apartment, just like I promised you."

Mishka was impressed by Mervin and not for the first time. He'd always admired Mervin's old-world charm, it seemed to be the echo of a lost world of elegance, like something out of Edith Wharton or Leo Tolstoy. Mishka took the papers and glanced at them. It was a duplicated set of a 'deed of gift'. He looked up at Mervin, with dotting eyes, but he wondered if it wasn't some trick. It was hard for Mishka to trust kindness.

"What do you want your lawyer to go over it." Mervin mocked, then turning serious. "Now it still needs to be signed and witnessed. I instructed one of the legal fellows to come here, so we can get it over and done with. He should be here any minute."

"What will you do?" Mishka anxiously asked.

Mervin answered coolly, like he has at work. "Oh, don't worry, I'm always prepared. I already have something squirreled away in Tortola and I've talked to the lawyers, who are fast at work transferring as much as they can before tomorrow."

Mishka thought of how Mervin was always prepared when he came, always freshly showered, a new shirt, condoms and lubricant. Maybe the two were related, financial security and sexual caution. Mervin had given him a start and set him up when he was still at school. In many ways, Mervin had made Mishka what he was today and Mishka felt grateful, but also a little resentful. He sat down on the floor, next to Mervin and they held hands, sharing the awkward situation in silence.

Startled by a series of pointed knocks on the door, Mishka rushed up from the floor and looked at Mervin, before going to open the door.

In his doorway was a pompous and arrogant looking man around thirty years, dressed in the same way his kind always dress, in an expensive, tightly fitted, but boring suit.

The man let out a scoff as he looked Mishka up and down, which reminded Mishka, that he was barely dressed.

"Aha, I'uh. Wow! Is Mr. Irvine here by any chance?" the lawyer fellow asked, trying to process the sight of Mishka.

To compensate for his state of undress and to oppose the 'lawyer fellows' waspy judgment, Mishka looked back at him critically, as he pushed his robe back and tried to look provocative.

"You mean Mervin?" Mishka asked in overtly insincere naiveté.

"Oh, no. I believe Mr. Irvine's first name is Eugene," the lawyer fellow said, taking out forms from his Hugo Boss computer bag and looked through papers.

Mervin was getting impatient and let out a loud gasp, that could be heard at the door, before he came rushing to the door.

"Oh, there you are. You're from the firm, aren't you? Please come in." Mervin said, shaking the lawyer's hand and guiding him into the living room.

"Yes, pleased to see you again sir. My name is Oliver. You probably haven't noticed me, I…" the lawyer meekly said, but was interrupted by Mervin, who was eager to get everything sorted.

"I apologize for the confusion. I know this is a bit unorthodox. Did anyone from the firm tell you, what you're doing here?" Mervin asked, looking impatiently at Oliver.

"Uhm, y-yes. I believe I'm here to witness a contract. A deed of gift. I brought all the papers with me…" Oliver mumbled, once again going through papers in his bag.

"No need, I have the papers right here," Mervin said, as he gestured to them on a side table.

Mervin quickly organized the papers and their duplicates and shepherded both Oliver and Mishka through the process, until everything was signed.

No sooner had he squiggled his legal name, then Mervin downed his scotch and got abruptly up from his seat.

"We must go now, lots to do. The lawyers are waiting for me. Don't worry, my boy, we'll get these sealed and finalized and then, uh, Oliver was it, can bring them by later tonight." Mervin said nervously as he grabbed the papers and rushed out the door with Oliver, leaving Mishka standing in the middle of the room in a deafening silence.

Mishka looked at the empty seat, that Mervin had sat in tonight, then he sat down on the floor beside it and lay his head on the empty seat.

He was going to miss Mervin when whatever would happen, happened.

Chapter 14

Mishka didn't sleep all that night, instead he anxiously paced about the apartment, uncertain of his future, now Mervin was leaving him behind. Questions raced through his mind, as he tried to map out the possibilities.

What story would break in the morning?
Would he really get to keep the apartment?
What was the expenditure on utilities and etc. each month?
What would he do without his allowance from Mervin? He'd be right back to where he was, before he met Phillip, unless he thought of a new source of income.

He would have to make a new budget. How much less would he have to spend on shoes each month? Would he have to sell some of his jewelry?

Mishka went to his closet and checked on the jewelry, like a concerned parent checks on their sleeping baby. They were all there, safely tucked away.

A loud, insisting knock came from the door. For a moment, Mishka thought it was debt collectors, like in Thackeray's 'Vanity Fair', until he remembered he didn't live in a novel from the 1800s.

He collected himself and answered the door.

"Oh, you." Mishka sneered as he saw it was Oliver. It was an entirely different knock, than when Oliver had come by previously.

"What, not happy to see me?" Oliver said with a hostile smile on his face.

Mishka saw the change in behavior in Oliver and his entire attitude. As a response, Mishka walked wordlessly back into the apartment, leaving the open door as a passive invitation for Oliver to follow him.

"You know, when I was sent here tonight, I wasn't prepared for you." Oliver laughed, as he followed Mishka into the small living room. "No, I wasn't expecting that. I-I never thought Mr. Irvine was... well you know. Into this!" Oliver said gesturing to Mishka.

Mishka poured himself a drink, trying to numb himself from Oliver's judgmental monologue. It was the same accusatory judgment, that he had been confronted with all his life, that he did not fit into the boring, mediocre confinement of normality. Normativity was something he had opposed since childhood, refusing to submit to the average. His mother had often told him, that normality was a matter of statistics, something that indicated mediocrity and described superfluous people, that didn't matter. Mishka had internalized his mother's words and twisted them into a maxime. If he stood out, if he was different, he mattered.

Mishka knew, that Oliver set himself apart from boys like Mishka, but Oliver was just the same, only he was too blind to see it. Oliver also prostituted himself, to his bosses at the law firm and he also did it to climb a social ladder. But Oliver was also like Mishka's patrons, filled with the same insecurities, the same desperate need to feel powerful and take possession of anyone and anything in his eyeline and full of the same toxic macho pretentions. Oliver was common and just like everyone else, but he'd never be able to see it himself, he refused to and that was Oliver's weakness.

"You'll probably have trouble grasping this concept, but I don't really speculate or care about what you think." Mishka said casually, taking place in the chair Mervin had sat in and drinking from Mervin's whiskey glass.

Oliver went close to his chair, hovering over Mishka and looking down at him.

"Oh, please. You love me don't you. It's okay, there's no shame in admitting it. I love me too." Oliver antagonized.

Mishka recognized Oliver's body language as the same pathetic power grab, he'd encountered a million times before, from a million different men and he wasn't fazed by it. He took a sip of his whiskey and answered detached: "I think you just summarized the foundation of straight, white male privilege. Did you bring the papers?"

Oliver bent down, closer to Mishka and handed Mishka his business card.

"There's this paper, isn't it cute?" Oliver said, smilingly.

"Absolute adorable," Mishka said pointedly and flung the card across the room.

Oliver started massaging Mishka shoulders, not in a caring way, but with a hard, tense grasp, that forced him down.

"You don't deserve it!" Oliver whispered gently into the air.

Mishka sighed and rolled his eyes, wrestling himself out of Oliver's hands so he could get up and create some distance between them.

Oliver looked at Mishka, smiling as he spoke in a hushed, controlled tone. "You disgust me, you know. You really do."

"Is this a peer review? Do you have the papers? You know, the ones Mervin asked you to deliver." Mishka asked firmly.

Oliver looked Mishka up and down, sizing him up. "You're not my peer," Oliver said, spitting out each word.

"We work for the same man. Doesn't that make us colleagues?" Mishka said, baiting Oliver.

Oliver shook his head. "Mr. Irvine is the firm's client."

"Yeah, Mervin is my client too, only I work directly under him. No managers, no bosses." Mishka shrugged as he took a large sip of whiskey.

"Enough of this bullshit," Oliver blurted out, as he took the deed out of his bag and defiantly dropped it on the floor.

Mishka rushed over and picked up the deed, carefully going through the papers, despite not knowing how a deed of gift should look like.

"Don't worry, it's all in order. I know how to do my job," Oliver said calmly, before loudly adding: "I guess all the dick sucking paid off. More, than my ass kissing ever did."

"Thank you." Mishka said meekly. Now, that he'd gotten what he wanted, Mishka felt no need to provoke Oliver any further.

Oliver smiled at him and cheerfully said: "You're a whore and a faggot!" before he picked up his things and left the apartment.

Mishka was relieved, when the door shut behind Oliver and Mishka locked it tightly, to make sure, he wouldn't come back.

But as soon as he was alone, his worries returned.

Even with the deed of gift and Oliver's reassurance of its validity, Mishka was fidgety and couldn't find any calm or stillness, but kept running around his apartment, keeping watch over all his things, which he had worked so hard to procure.

All through the night Mishka was concerned, wondering what kind of scandal that would break and how it could derail his ambitions.

When the sunrise finally came, Mishka took a long shower. He washed his body, hair and face meticulously, already feeling dirtied by his association to Mervin. Sitting naked at his vanity mirror, he carefully tried to hide his lack of sleep, painting on a pale, innocent face, careful not to make himself look too made-up. The silence in the apartment felt like the early stages of a hangover, playing to Mishka's fear, that Mervin's scandal was the end of the party. It made Mishka feel a kinship with Marie Antoinette, since she must have had a similar feeling, as the Bastille was stormed.

Perusing his closet, he selected a blue and white striped shirt, a grey flannel suit, fuchsia socks and blue leather brogues.

He combed his hair away from his face and decided against his usual sunglasses. In a time of crisis, it was important to show one's face publicly, or so went one of his mother's many rules for social survival and Mishka was a good boy, who followed his mother's rules.

After carefully reviewing his appearance and making minor alterations, Mishka was finally satisfied and gave his reflection an approving smile and a nod.

"Wish me luck," Mishka said, kissing the reflection goodbye, before he went out the door.

Out he went, to search for a bomb hidden in the magazine rack at his local kiosk.

As he stood at the newsstand, confronted by the absurd amount of colorful rectangles and their sensational, splashy headlines, Mishka wasn't exactly sure, what he was looking for. Suddenly Mervin's image jumped up at him, from the front page of one of the more serious magazines. It was a small section, with a picture of Mervin and the headline: 'Philanthropist caught in embezzlement, misappropriation and tax fraud'.

Mishka took the magazine and opened it, to read an article juxtaposing 'the well-known Eugene Irvine' as a philanthropic entrepreneur and a fraudulent, financial criminal. It recounted how Mervin had donated millions over the years to fight diseases and human rights campaigns, with money he'd earned from his publishing house, which he had started himself as a small printing press and built it into a huge publishing house. The article then went on to tear Mervin down, saying the big-hearted entrepreneur also cheated taxpayers, frauded investors and then listed a lot of other offenses. The reporter claimed to have proof of huge discrepancies in the publishing houses financial records, which had been leaked to the reporter. Mishka didn't understand half the accusations against Mervin, but he understood the narrative. In short, the article presented Mervin as a wolf in sheep's clothing, whose respectability and many good deeds over the years were now nullified by violations of financial law. This was bad, really bad, but not surprising. Mervin had always been reluctant to relay any information about his finances or his own investments or where the money for Mishka came from. Mishka had always suspected something was fishy about Mervin's wealth, but he had never really cared.

What surprised Mishka was the many facts and facets of Mervin, that Mishka had never heard of before. The man in the article was a completely different man, than the man he had been attached to. Mishka's thoughts turned to Mervin's wife and he pitied her. What would her life be now?

Mishka bought the magazine, along with all the dailies.

Once at home, Mishka situated himself casually on the chaise, with a pot of green tea and his pastel colored cigarettes, puffing smoke and sipping tea, as he read. He carefully went through each single paper and magazine he'd bought, in search of news of Mervin. Luckily, there was only the one article, which he'd seen in the store. But online was a different matter. The article was already spreading fast on social media, mostly by people with attachment to Mervin or his publishing house and those who had received financial contributions from Mervin. Most of them were already distancing themselves, claiming outrage and ignorance, only few spoke out in sympathetic disbelief.

The story had also spread wide among the online press, where all the major newspapers published their own theory of the 'truth'. Mishka scoffed each time he saw the imposturous word 'truth' in a headline or paratext. The press didn't know the truth and they certainly didn't care for the truth and all its complexities and spectrums. This was all easy click bait, to entertain the masses.

What really worried Mishka was, that the story was gaining interest and that meant the reporters would be digging for any information they could sensationalize and as Mervin's gay lover, he would certainly make for a splashy headline, which he imagined could get the authorities digging into his finances and the legality of the deed transfer.

Mishka lit his ninth cigarette of the day and decided to call up a former friend; Ethan Ludgate, an American lawyer living and working in Copenhagen, he'd been in a relationship with a couple of years earlier. It had ended right before Ethan's fiftieth birthday, when it had suddenly started to annoy Ethan, that Mishka was thirty-one years younger and Ethan had broken up with him. It had ended abruptly, but without drama. Hopefully, it was amicably enough, that Ethan would help him now.

Mishka found Ethan's number in his phone – he always kept all numbers and information on his patrons, just in case he would need it someday – and phoned Ethan.

"He-e-ey, you." Ethan's voice sounded both cheerful and nervous.

Mishka realized that Ethan's uneasiness meant, that Ethan knew who was calling, so he was apparently still in Ethan's contacts, which seemed like a good sign.

"Hi sweety. I know it's been a while. I'm afraid I might be in trouble and I hoped you could help me," Mishka pleaded timidly, hoping to gain Ethan's sympathy. Ethan had always loved to step in and save Mishka, whenever he could and Mishka was hoping it was still the case.

"Okay, what kind of trouble?" Ethan enquired, in a solemn tone.

Mishka started to explain, "It's about property. You see, I've been gifted…"

"Oh, Mishka honey. I'm not that kind of lawyer." Ethan cut him off.

"I know," Mishka lied, trying to sound as sad as he could. "It's just, that I don't know anyone else, who could help me. I just need someone to help a bit," Mishka pleaded.

Ethan sighed in the other end. "All right, shoot."

Mishka went right to the point. "I've been gifted an apartment, through a deed of gift and I just want to know the validity of it and if it can be reversed or taken from me, for some reason?"

"Don't you want it?" Ethan asked perplexed, full well knowing Mishka's greedy and consumerist mindset.

"Oh, no I want it. I'm just worried if I can get to keep it?" Mishka scoffed.

"Is it a gift from your parents?" Ethan asked teasingly.

Mishka rolled his eyes and neglected to answer.

"Another family member?" Ethan asked again.

"A friend," Mishka answered, irritated.

"Oh," Ethan laughed on the other end, "I see, you better take me through the contract. Read to me," Ethan instructed, like he was talking to an assistant.

Mishka found the contract and together, they went through it, point by point, as Ethan tried to identify and explain possible problems and asking Mishka to reread certain paragraphs, to ascertain the terms for payment of duties and taxes etc.

In the end, Ethan assured him, that it looked like Mervin had been telling the truth and Mishka would probably get to keep the apartment, as Mervin wasn't under investigation, when the contract was signed and notarized.

"Okay, thank you so much, darling. I really appreciate it. You were always sweet," Mishka said ingratiatingly.

"Yeah, I'm actually seeing someone, so it would probably be better, if you didn't call me again. It's just, I don't want him to worry. Take care," Ethan said, clearly embarrassed, as he hung up the phone.

Mishka was embarrassed too, by the sudden silence on the phone. He hated himself for not having been able to seduce Ethan back to him and he hated Ethan too for not having been tempted, but a small, hidden part of him genuinely appreciated

Ethan's assistance.

Setting aside his vain ego and his feelings for Ethan he concentrated on the matter at hand. The apartment seemed to be his now and he mentally added it to his list of trophies.

All there was left to do now, was to wait and see if anything would change in his life, if Mervin's scandal would rub off on him and taint him.

Chapter 15

It had been a couple of days since the news about Mervin and his financial crimes had broken. Since then, the story had dominated the national media and turned into a social media shit storm. The story was causing public outrage and had instigated a police investigation of the allegations. Mervin was nowhere to be found and so the media speculated wildly about him and his whereabouts, they hounded his stoic wife, who Mervin had left behind, they examined every single aspect of Mervin's work, life and they analyzed anyone, who had ever had any connection to Mervin.

This also included Mishka.

As the police had investigated Mervin, they had found out about Mishka, from Mervin's driver and the police's attention to Mishka had also attracted the media. While the police had been courteous and professional in their dealings with Mishka, the press had been merciless.

The police didn't even seem to care, about the apartment or the deed of gift. All the police wanted from Mishka, was knowledge of Mervin, Mishka's knowledge of Mervin's work and of course Mervin's whereabouts. Mishka had shared the little he knew, which was the times he had seen Mervin, that Mervin had always been vague about his business dealings and that Mervin was most likely somewhere abroad, since he knew he'd been transferring money out of the country, to some tax shelter.

The press however, had been busy taking and publishing as many pictures as they could of Mishka. Pictures from his social media account had already been repurposed for story after story, about 'Eugene Irvine's boy toy' or 'Eugene Irvine's expansive habit' or 'Eugene Irvine; sugar daddy - see his expensive sugar baby'. What annoyed Mishka was that he wasn't actually getting any attention, he was just used as a storytelling device, to demonstrate Mervin's vast expenditure and to scandalize Mervin even further, by using his sexuality against him. Mishka was just another 'bad thing' that Mervin had done. The press didn't care about Mishka.

In fact, for Mishka, the scandal was that no one cared about him anymore. The media coverage had made him entirely Mervin's property and there wasn't any room left, for anyone else.

Phillip and Mr. P had dropped him after the first story, that mentioned Mishka, too scared to risk any coverage of their own affairs. Jason had tried to continue their relationship, but had quickly realized he couldn't go to Mishka's apartment, without being seen by reporters and then Jason had decided 'they needed a break, until things were figured out'.

Suddenly Mishka was all alone, with no patron to support him. It suddenly made more sense, that Mervin had felt he owed him the apartment, because Mishka would have had a difficult time, without his own home.

Yet, Mishka was not without income. Luckily, the scandal had created a huge demand for the sullied cum-stained underwear of Eugene Irvine's boy-whore and Mishka could now sell his dirty underwear for 2000 kroner a pair. This earned him a profit of about 1000 a day, after he'd paid for transportation, the cost of the underwear and tax. Because of the police investigation, he was now forced to pay tax on any money transfer he got. Mishka had even had to register for a business license, so he could continue selling his underwear.

While Mishka wasn't in financial trouble, his lifestyle was no longer luxurious. Mishka desperately wanted a patron, to boost his earnings and to get some positive attention again. The media's treatment of him had badly hurt his confidence and he frantically exercised at home, spent hours grooming himself and had stopped eating altogether. Now he lived on coffee and tea with milk and sugar, Sobranie cocktail cigarettes and booze. This was just as well, since Jason was no longer there, to stock his fridge.

Mishka had lost a lot in the scandal. He had lost security, companionship, faith in himself and the freedom to walk out in public, without being stormed by the press. As a reaction, Mishka had isolated himself, only ever interacting with pushy journalists, couriers and delivery boys, keeping the curtains shut, so no one could spy on him or sneak a picture.

Everything in Mishka's life had changed, except one aspect. Mishka was still an object of fantasy and entertainment, only instead of playing to companions and social media followers, he was now under the vast power of the media, playing for the grubby masses.

Being handled by the media, Mishka felt more like a prostitute than he had ever felt with any of his patrons or even seedy one night stands.

The following weeks, Mishka didn't go out, he didn't look at his feed or notifications. Mishka couldn't even stand to look at his own reflection anymore. All Mishka did was to obsess over, what other people might think of him. He was setting himself apart from the world and sought refuge inside himself, escaping to his inner life, to the wild woods of his own thoughts.

After three weeks of isolation, Mishka had had enough and decided to venture outside, in an attempt to reclaim his old life.

To work up the nerve, Mishka had spent two hours doing crunches, squats and pushups, before he took a long, ice cold milk bath. Mishka had also spent a long time at his vanity mirror, building up armor by plucking, brushing and painting himself to hide his imperfections. He carefully went through his overfilled closet, estimating each item, in every category, before he settled on an outfit. Mishka dressed ceremoniously in a black chiffon shirt, with a pussy bow, which he wore under his Cartier necklace and a black velvet smoking jacket, which he paired with gold trousers and patent leather boots with a Cuban heel. He thought, if he was labeled a gold digger, he might as well dress like one – an expensive one.

When he was finally finished with creating a persona, he thought could face the world, he hurried out of his apartment building and into the car he'd ordered to take him away. They drove in silence to Balthazar Champagne Bar, where he'd already reserved a table. Mishka was mentally preparing himself for the bar, thinking up behaviors, attitudes and lines he could use in every conceivable situation that might arise at Balthazar.

When he got there, he stormed in, clacking his heels against the floor, trying hard to exude confidence. The harsh clack-clacking of his heels alerted the other guest and caused everyone to look up and inspect him, as he was shown to his table and ordered a bottle of champagne from the waitress. Several of the guests clearly recognized him from the tabloid, while others looked confused, as they wondered if they were supposed to know, who he was. But being an upscale place, that puts everyone on their guard, no one uttered a word to display their feelings. In such a place it's only vague gestures, that showcase people's attitudes, like the persistent and repetitive glances of those ready to snub him or the over courteousness of the sympathetic waitress.

Yes, Mervin's scandal had indeed made a spectacle out of Mishka, *the* cardinal sin all bourgeoisie children are brought up to avoid, at any cost. Mishka felt horribly guilty about his current infamy, but there was also a deep-rooted defiance in Mishka, that made him numb to the judgmental stares. He had lived his whole childhood in opposition, in the all-white, heteronormative village, where being different in any way, bore its own punishment. Back then he was constantly talked about, not openly, but in codes. He was labeled as 'creative', 'original', and as 'such a sensitive boy'. This constant social ousting and prodding had prepared him for his current situation and like then, he would not bow down or 'learn his place', no matter how ugly it got.

As he sipped his champagne, Mishka looked indifferently about the room, trying to gain territory by filling the atmosphere with his presence and his gaze. This behavior was apparently too much for some guests. After a few moments, a small party left, sending Mishka dirty looks, as an obliging staff member handed them their coats and escorted them out. Mishka demonstratively rolled his eyes and slinked down in his lounge chair, to mark his reluctance to surrender territory. Places like this were still his domain, he felt.

Of course, Mishka wasn't indifferent. On the inside he was screaming, stung by their refusal to even stay in the same room as him. Outwardly he showed no distress, as he took dignity for a matter of appearance. And in some perverse way, he did enjoy the attention of being the focal point of everyone's interest. Still, he missed being engaged in a positive way, so he scanned the room, desperately looking for a face, that wanted him, someone he could reflect himself in.

Not finding any admirers, Mishka turned his attention to the bottle of champagne he'd ordered, getting more and more restless with each pour. Around his fourth glass, Mishka started weighing his options for the night and planned his exit.

What was the point after all? This little outing wasn't taking his mind off things, if anything, it cemented the fearsome reality of his current situation.

Everyone seemed eager to talk about him, but no one seemed to dare talk to him. Apparently conversing with him had become one of those things you simply don't do, like inquiring about someone's weight or talk about religion at a cocktail party.

Just as he emotionally prepared himself to leave, he became aware of a handsome middle-aged man at the bar, who was glancing at him and smiling. The man didn't look like the typical clientele at Balthazar's. He didn't have the pompous attitude of the other guests. He wasn't aiming to impress or impose himself. He was dressed plainly, with a white shirt, grey trousers, a tan leather belt and sneakers. Mishka tried to smile back, but the man never held eye contact long enough, but he wasn't alarmed by Mishka's looks either.

It annoyed Mishka, that he couldn't get the man's full attention. In his drunkenness, Mishka decided to seek the man's attention more aggressively, determined to have his way. In a single movement, Mishka rose from his seat, grabbed the nearly empty champagne bottle from its cooler and moved in on the man. The wet bottle dripped, as he slowly sauntered to the bar and seated himself next to the man.

"Hope you don't mind?" Mishka said, smilingly.

"Uhm, hello. Yes. No, no, that's fine." The man said a bit befuddled, but courteously.

Mishka kept smiling serenely, as he stared the man down, trying to goat a reaction. The man became increasingly uncomfortable and ended up chuckling nervously, as he squirmed under Mishka's continuous glare. The tension caught the attention of everyone in the bar, who paid a varied amount of attention to the scene.

"What now?" Mishka laughed back and took a long swig of his bottle.

"Wow! Eh, you're really something. You just walk up to a guy and act like that?" The man chuckled uneasily.

"Well, I saw you sneaking peaks at me, sooo, uhm, I thought I'd come over, so you could get a better look at me," Mishka teased.

The man scratched his neck awkwardly and moaned, "Yeah, I'm sorry about that."

Mishka widened his large, round eyes in sympathy and said "Oh, it's okay". Then he swung his bottle around the room and boisterously added "Everyone seems to be in a gawking-mood today".

Nodding, the man expressed his sympathy. "Yeah, I can imagine. It must be hard, everyone looking at you all the time."

Mishka got embarrassed. So, he knew about him and about Mervin.

He took a big swig of his champagne, some of it dripping down on his chin, as he wondered if the man was truly sympathetic.

"Well, it is what it is... I didn't mind it when you looked at me, though. I quite liked it. In fact, it bothered me, that you looked away, when I looked back at you," Mishka explained.

The man looked at him and measured him up.

"You like attention? I'm sorry, I don't mean to... uhm. It's just, you haven't said anything publicly. You never even given anyone a quote or anything. You haven't even said anything on any of your social media accounts. There's been no response from you at all. Why is that?" the man said luringly.

Mishka stirred his head and answered honestly, "I didn't know anyone wanted a quote, no one ever asked for one."

The man looked serious now, which startled Mishka a bit.

"I do," the man said, as he gathered his things and handed Mishka a card.

"We'll pay for an exclusive and I promise you, it will get you attention. A lot of it. You can share your story. Gain some power over the narrative, you know. Call me and we'll work something out. I'm Nickolaj by the way. Nice to meet you." The man said, shaking Mishka's hand, before he rushed out.

Mishka looked at the card. Nickolaj was a digital editor at the high-end lifestyle magazine, The Society Chronicler. He wondered what Nickolaj could do for him and carefully saved the card in his breast pocket.

To escape the gawking people around him, Mishka paid his bill and left Balthazar.

Afterwards, Mishka walked aimlessly around the city, determined to continue the night and find a good time. To do that, he needed to find new hunting grounds, where he was less familiar and he could step out of his current role.

As he walked, Mishka felt a sinking feeling, like when

you've said something wrong or indiscreet. He had felt a loss of control during Mervin's scandal. He'd learned he wasn't as smart or strategic, as he had thought himself to be. All this time, he thought he'd been in control, that he was the one who had taken advantage of his patrons, but as they'd left and he'd been thrown to the media, he'd begun to see how vulnerable and dependent he was. His beliefs had suffered the most during the scandal. The world had proven to be bigger, scarier and more complicated, than he'd imagined.

The outline of his character, which he had so carefully designed, was being erased and his figure was seeping out into the open space.

Now, he was stuck in the role the press had given him, as Mervin's creature, a role he didn't know how to act. The press had given him no lines, no queues nor stage directions.

His new social insecurity had lost him value and power.

His character was no longer exclusive, it was no longer a favor he had the sole rights to bestow on those who were worthy of it. The story of Mervin had made him common property. Anyone who felt for it, could just grab a piece of him, out of the open air and call it what they wanted to.

The bright neon sign of a gay bar pulled him out of his gloomy thoughts. There was no line outside the door and Mishka let the obviously bored doorman usher him in.

The large night club only housed around seven people, who sat scattered at the very long bar counter, two bartenders, taking it easy and an overly dedicated DJ, who looked as if he were performing before a crowd of a million people.

Mishka took a seat at the bar counter, sitting apart from everyone else.

One of the bartenders jumped over to Mishka, glad to

have something to do. He had the look of a fifty-year-old accountant, with glasses to match, but was dressed in a rainbow-sequin-tank top and very short denim shorts.

"What'll ya have?" the bartender asked.

"A gin and tonic, please," Mishka asked politely and smilingly, as he lit a pink Sobranie cigarette.

Everyone was staring at him, except for the DJ, who was too enthralled with his own set. Mishka wondered, if they were staring at him in recognition or because he was very overdressed for the venue or simply because he was fresh meat.

Because Mishka didn't know why people were staring, he didn't know how to react, so he simply ignored their curious glances.

The bartender brought him his drink.

"Thank you so much," Mishka said routinely and overly courteous, as he handed cash to the bartender.

Dedicating himself to his drink and his cigarette, people seemed to lose their curiosity in him. Only one guy still looked in Mishka's direction. The man looked familiar, but he couldn't quite place him... where had he seen him before? Oh, yes! He had met him through the lawyer, Ethan, when they'd dated. The man was one of Ethan's close friends. Mishka remembered how he'd been a little taken with him, when Ethan had introduced them.

He was still hot, with a strong and stout frame, a chiseled face, strong eyebrows and just the right kind of grey hair. However, he looked drunk tonight, in an unattractive way.

What was the guy's name, it was something very ordinary and boring?

As Mishka tried to remember the name, the guy was

making his way over to Mishka.

"Heeeyyyy, hey, you," he said, swerving his entire body as he talked and smiling slyly.

"Hello," Mishka said, with an expressionless smile, not quite sure what this was.

The man just stared at Mishka, occasionally breaking out in giggles.

To break the tension Mishka asked: "Didn't I meet you once? With your husband? And Ethan, Ethan Ludgate?"

"Yeah! Oh, yeaaah. You're the young guy. Ethan's guy," he answered enthusiastically.

Mishka felt flattered and also stupid for being flattered by such a vague compliment, as 'young'. It was hard for Mishka not to be flattered when he'd gone such a long time without validation. The only gaze he'd been objected to, was the mediated gaze of his social media followers and his own reflection. Also, Mishka felt drawn to his broad shoulders and strong and definite muscles, which seemed to scream 'I can take care of you'.

In lieu of an answer Mishka held his head up, took a long drag of his cigarette and slowly blew out the smoke, while keeping intense eye contact with the man. It was a mannerism he'd purposefully picked up from watching old Hollywood movies about femme fatales. He'd rehearsed it like mad, until it had become second nature to him. Since then, he'd instinctively used it to distract, deflect or simply to give himself time to think. Now, he remembered the name!

"Yes, and you're Michael, aren't you? So... Where's your husband tonight?" Mishka enquired to gauge the situation.

"Home. With our son. Asleep. Sooo, it's just me here," Michael said, smiling and moving closer to Mishka.

Mishka avoided Michaels eyes and put out his cigarette in an ashtray. "Sounds like trouble." Mishka flirted insincerely.

"Well, what they don't know can't hurt them," Michael said, moving close enough to put his arm around Mishka.

"Not sure that's true," Mishka said, looking disapprovingly at Michael's hand, on his waist. He was a little wary of being with men with small children. Most of his relationships were so dramatic, he didn't want innocent children to be caught in the expected crossfire.

Michael put his nose to Mishka's neck, took a big, long sniff and said, "Orgh, you're so hot."

"You're sweet," Mishka said with a smile, as he swatted away Michael's hand.

"Orh, you're so sweet," Michael said in a baby voice, as he pressed his whole body against Mishka's.

It was getting a bit too much for Mishka. Michael's advances didn't seem like a compliment, it was too clumsy and too forward. Mishka struggled free from Michael and headed towards the bathroom, to avoid him.

As Mishka walked away, Michael followed him. Confused, Mishka increased his pace to slip away from Michael, but Michael was right behind him. The situation was getting odd, it was like a war of wills. Mishka practically sieged a bathroom stall and was on his way to close the door, when Michael started pushing back, from the other side, trying to force himself in.

They both pushed on either side of the door, but Michael was big and strong, so he quickly forced his way into the stall.

"Please leave," Mishka sneered in annoyance, but Michael just stood there, looking at him, blocking the doorway of the small bathroom stall.

"GO AWAY," Mishka yelled, but Michael moved closer and pressed his entire body up against him and started kissing his neck.

"No, no," Mishka said, as he tried to push Michael away, but Michael grabbed both of Mishka's wrists and held them tight up over his head.

"No!" Mishka repeated in frustration, but Michael still didn't answer and Mishka started to realize the severity of the situation.

This was something new.

"Stop, please stop." Mishka pleaded desperately, as he felt Michael's erection against his thigh, but again, Michael didn't seem to hear him at all.

Mishka's mind raced. What could he do? What were his options here? Obviously, struggling was useless. Michael was strong and he was weak. But there had to be something he could do? Mishka had a hard time processing his powerlessness in the situation. In his experience, there was always something to do!

While Mishka was trying to assess the situation and weigh his options, Michael had started to undress him.

Michael stopped kissing Mishka's neck and pulled a bit away. Alarmed by the shift, Mishka snapped out of his thoughts and paid careful attention to what Michael was doing.

Michael shifted Mishka, so he only needed one hand to hold Mishka's wrists tight, using the other hand to unzip his own pants and take out his cock. Mishka noticed an unabashed look of pride in Michael's face, as he unveiled his manhood, which seemed strange for the situation. Then, in a quick series of movements, Michael let go of Mishka's wrists momentarily and just for a second, Mishka thought he was safe, but Michael roughly turned Mishka around and slammed him up against the stall wall.

This was it; it was going to happen.

The severity of the situation hit Mishka all over again, as Michael leaned up against his back, so Mishka couldn't move. Mishka panicked and quietly stammered out; "No, no. I-I don't want to."

"Sure you do," Michael rebuffed, as he penetrated Mishka with a hard, sudden thrust. Mishka let out a shriek, as Michael continuously thrusted himself deeper into Mishka, in a sporadic rhythm. Michael didn't even hear Mishka, so Mishka screamed louder and more deliberately.

"Hey, none of that. Schh, schh, schh. It's okay. It's okay," Michael said in a soothing tone, like he was comforting a child and covered Mishka's mouth.

There came a mechanical rhythm into Michael's thrusting movements, as he steered Mishka, with one hand over Mishka's mouth and his other hand around Mishka's stomach.

It was characteristic, that even in this moment, Mishka couldn't help sucking in his stomach, so it seemed as flat and thin as possible. Even now, Mishka wanted to be attractive.

With each dry thrust, Mishka let out a muffled scream, from behind Michael's hand and each time Michael answered it with the same sentence; "Sch, sch. It's okay, all okay."

Mishka gradually stopped struggling, physically or verbally and tried to escape the situation in other ways. To distract himself, he looked around the stall. The stall was cold and filthy, it needed to be cleaned. There was a spider web, with a spider at the ceiling. Mishka wondered what the spider made of this scene, if it was even aware of what was happening? He focused on the feel and weight of his necklace, as it bounced on his neck or the strong, pungent smell of the room or wondered how many bruises he'd get from tonight and how long they'd last. With each observation, the world got a little bit bigger and the situation became a little less imposing and a little less critical. It made it easier for Mishka to simply wait for the thing to end.

After what seemed like an eternity, Michael's thrusts got deeper, more painful and with less intervals between the thrusts. At the same time, Michael's grip on Mishka's mouth and stomach became tighter and crampier.

Michael let out a hushed moan; "Yes. Yeah, that's it. Orgh, orghhhh," before his thrusts faded into small pushes and eventually stopped altogether. While Michael was still inside Mishka, he hugged him from behind, kissed his neck and whispered, "Mmmm, that was nice." This small act of tenderness was somehow harder to bear, than the rape preceding it and it broke something in Mishka. He became aware of the disparity between their joint experience and froze up. To Michael, this had been nice. It had been nice to force him up against the wall and nice for Michael to force his cock into Mishka's unwelcoming orifice. Mishka had never been aware of it before, but he had had an innocent trust in the world that Michael had now broken. It was a strange sensation, to feel the shambles of a thing you hadn't believed existed.

Mishka just kept clinging to the stall wall, as Michael cleaned himself off and put on his pants. On his way out of the stall, Michael nuzzled Mishka's hair and said, "Thank you for that. See you around, champ."

It wasn't until several minutes after Michael had left the bathroom, that Mishka could let go of the stall wall and put his pants back on. He left the stall and went over to sinks to inspect himself and freshen up. In the mirror, he could see two clear streams from his eyes.

He'd been crying! He hadn't even noticed and it surprised him. It was unlike him to cry. He splashed cold water on his face, checked his clothes for spots of dirt or Michael, but found none.

Thank you! Had Michael really said thank you?

He looked into the eyes of his reflection and remembered that scene in Breakfast at Tiffany's, where Audrey Hepburn talked about how she could tell a lot about a man, based on the earrings he'd given her: "I must say, the mind reels" Mishka said out loud, as he stared at himself and fixed his hair.

Despite the physical pain from the 'scene' with Michael, he didn't know what to feel. At least there were no visible signs of anything bad, he thought, as he looked himself over.

Mishka stomped confidently out of the bathroom and back out to the club, but his knees were still weak. He could feel the few guests in the club staring at him, including the bartenders. Some of the guests were even smiling. Michael was sitting at the bar, drinking a beer and followed Mishka with his eyes. Michael had a strange, perplexed expression on his face, like he didn't know what had happened either.

Mishka was so confused, he desperately wanted to be home, so he went straight for the door.

As Mishka reached for the door handle, one of the bartenders mirthfully jeered; "Bye, hope you had a good night!". Without turning around, but staring at the floor, Mishka took a deep breath and contemplated whether or not the bartender knew what had taken place in the bathroom stall. Did they all know? He didn't know what to do, so he just answered routinely and politely; "Delightful, hope you will too," and left the bar.

Out on the street it was approaching dusk. There was a cab just ten steps away from the club and Mishka jumped in. The cabdriver kept looking at Mishka all the way home, not a lustful or disapproving look, but a pitying look. Mishka was sweating cold and panting, he was so weakened from the shock of the whole experience. It was like the cab driver could guess what had happened and felt sorry for Mishka. It made Mishka paranoid. Could the 'scene' be smelt on him, could the driver smell Michael and everything he had done? Oh, what did it matter, he didn't have to impress the driver.

When they arrived at Mishka's apartment building, Mishka handed the driver a wad of cash, without looking at neither the driver nor the money. The driver quietly took a few notes and handed the wad back to Mishka, then opened the door for him. Mishka's knees buckled as he got out of the car and the driver had to help him up. The driver even kept looking after Mishka, until Mishka had made it inside the building.

It was surreal for Mishka, to experience kindness from a strange driver, just moments after experiencing Michael's brutality. It wasn't that the driver did or said anything special, he was just polite and helpful and unimposing.

Mishka struggled up the stairs in a haze and locked himself into his apartment. He headed straight for his bed and crawled in, without changing his clothes or even taking off his shoes. It didn't matter what he looked like right now. For the first time, his looks didn't enter his mind.

He just laid in his bed, in the fetal position, without thinking, without feeling, just clutching his knees and listening to his own panicked breathing.

Chapter 16

Mishka woke up in his bed. His mind was still in the bathroom stall, hearing Michael say 'thank you'. The words echoed in Mishka's mind, because they seemed so out of place and unsuited for the situation.

Instantly, his mind was racing, going through the events of last night.

What had factually happened?
Which words could capture the situation?
What had *he* done?
How much of the responsibility did *he* bear for it all?
What could he have done differently, to prevent what had happened?
And what about Michael?
What had Michael actually done last night?
How did Michael feel today?
How did he feel about last night?
To which degree was Michael really at fault?
Would Michael ever do it again if he met him?

Mishka curled himself into a ball under his covers, trying to minimize himself as much as he could. It felt like a dark wormhole had opened in his stomach and would swallow him whole and a part of Mishka wanted to disappear into it and dissolve into nothing.

So Mishka waited for the nothingness, but unsurprisingly he did not dissolve into nothing. He was trapped in his mind, which kept obsessing about the past and the possibilities of the future. His thoughts turned over it all, again and again, like a stone milling wheat.

Would Michael tell Ethan about it? They were friends!

And what would Ethan say to it?

He'd probably hate Mishka for it! And after Ethan had been so nice, to help him with the legal thing about the apartment.

Mishka felt awful, embarrassed, and guilty. What would Ethan think of him now – he would never be attracted to him again.

The phrase 'spoiled goods' made a surprise appearance in Mishka's consciousness. It was a phrase from his childhood, that he had packed away and forgotten, but now it leaped back into awareness.

He was spoiled goods to Ethan now, because of Michael. But he was spoiled goods before too, because of Mervin.

Maybe, all he was now, was whatever he had been to Michael yesterday? Something to be taken, without regard or consideration.

Slowly, Mishka's thoughts slowed down and he became present in his body and in his bed. He looked around his bedroom and stretched out his body.

What should he do today? What did one do, after something like that?

He could report it! But what would he gain from that?

Would anyone believe him? Probably not!

He was a man, so the police would be skeptical of rape. He was also gay, which would make them even more skeptical and thanks to Mervin's scandal, the media had branded him as an over glorified prostitute, which wouldn't be helpful either.

That was three strikes against him, three stereotypes, that were incompatible with a rape allegation.

Yes, a rape allegation would probably be hard for the police to take seriously.

Besides, what would a rape allegation do to Michael's family?

Oh, and Ethan would surely never speak to Mishka again, if he reported one of his best friends for rape.

No, there was nothing to be done, other than to move on and be more careful in the future.

It was the only real option for him.

In the eyes of the world, he was beyond giving or declining sexual consent. Wasn't that what had happened with Michael? Michael simply hadn't cared about his consent. No one cared or thought he would object.

Mishka got up and rushed to the kitchen, angrier with the world, than with Michael.

This was no ordinary day; this was the first day he realized how little power he actually had and how low people really are. He knew it of course, he had been told so over tea with his mother, a long time ago. But there's a big difference between theory and praxis. This was the first time, he'd really felt his own helplessness. It was the first time, he'd been ignored and overpowered, like Michael had ignored and overpowered him. With his patrons and everyone else he'd been with, he was a focal point and he was treated as such, with attention to everything he did and said. All the other sex he'd had, had been dialogical, with Michael it had been a monologue. The patrons all paid tribute to him and their relationship was based on interaction. Michael had simply used Mishka, pleasured himself in him and disposed of him, like a used-out flesh light.

In the kitchen he drank glass after glass of water and downed some painkillers, as he meditated on his options, but he didn't see any. What could possibly be gained from his current situation?

Not being able to discern a clear path ahead, he decided to act, like there wasn't one and had a cigarette for breakfast.

Smoking was a way for him to destroy himself in a small, but concrete act. To him, smoking in the morning was a passive aggressive suicide, which always made him smile.

When he was angry with the world he could always smoke.

Smoking was something to do, something actively self-destructive, but socially acceptable and without the finality of an actual suicide. The world always seemed to be raging against him and he needed a way to win back some autonomy. While he could never win in a fight against the world, he could help his destruction along and there was something empowering in that.

A little calmed by pills and his cigarette, he poured himself a large glass of gin and went into the living room. Sitting on the living room floor, sipping his gin, he noticed he was still wearing last night's clothes. He carefully took off the Cartier necklace, admiring it in the process and carefully put it on display on the coffee table. Then he took off his clothes, without getting up, pausing when he got to his underpants. If the world were as depraved and low, as he thought it was, he could probably get a record high price for underwear he'd been raped in. It was a perverse notion to Mishka, that people would pay for something like that and it was also perverse to him, that he was opportunistic enough to profit from it.

Mishka started laughing to himself. There was something

so absurd, about profiting from being raped. Still, it was nice to have been wanted and to have been useful again, after so long in his own lazy company.

Mishka took a big slurp of his gin and took a selfie, looking sad, posing on the floor in his underpants. He posted the selfie in his stories and asked for bids, with the caption 'Got raped wearing these. Give me a bid.'

He laughed again. Was this really his life, was this really all he was worth now? Was he just something to soil underpants for dirty men? A human-formed sleeve that men like Michael could masturbate into. A series of dirty social media stories to entertain horny toads?

Not wanting to deal with his depressing line of thinking, he put on music and let the aggressive tones of Stravinsky and streams of gin drown out his anxiety.

He took off his underwear and packed them up, ready to be shipped away to the highest bidder. The underwear was a reminder of last night and he wanted it gone.

Strolling around naked, he looked for something to pamper himself with. In the end he found a bottle of champagne and opened it en route to the bathroom. Not bothering with a glass, he drank straight from the bottle. He didn't see a need for formality or ceremony today.

Standing before the big mirror over the bathroom sink, inspecting his reflection, he wondered if the experience had changed him. Was he different now? Had Michael turned him into someone else, like a frog transformed into a prince with a kiss?

Mishka wondered, what rape victims did, how they were supposed to behave after their rape? In the movies they always sat in a bathtub, clutching their knees.

But he couldn't stand to view himself in this way, so he covered up his face with a healing face mask, eagerly observing his reflection's face slowly disappear.

Afterwards he drew himself a bath and let his body fade into the water. All his senses were occupied now and the inner image of Mishka-the-victim was gone.

His ears were focusing on Stravinsky.

His eyes were wandering all over the bathroom tiles and occasionally created fantasies to fit the music.

His hands were busy washing his limbs and examining his body.

His tongue was indulging in champagne.

And his nose was soothed by the many different aromas of his bathwater and facial mask.

This was the way Mishka dealt with things, by tearing himself away and shifting his focus to new perspectives. He'd always done things this way. It was the same way he'd dealt with the strict guidelines of social identity in his childhood; he had moved away and invented a new identity as Dmitri 'Mishka' Balzac.

It wasn't that he was cowardly, he just didn't like to feel broken. When things seemed like they'd fall apart, he'd built something new and inhabit it. He was usually very honest about the lies he told himself, because he didn't tell them to fool himself, but simply to live in another reality. In a way, he saw the constructed narratives and characters he inhabited to be more real, than fact, because he invented it himself and it came out of true feelings, unlike hard unsympathetic facts.

Now he was creating a new narrative, one that was constructive to him and empowering. Mishka wasn't a victim, he didn't do victimization. So, he had to do something else.

When he was with his patrons, no matter how demeaning their handling of him had been, he'd always been given something in return; cash and trinkets to distract him. They'd given him something else to focus on, bricks to help him build himself up.

Michael had broken that precedent and that was what was upsetting for Mishka. Michael had taken, without giving anything in return and now Mishka felt like bricks were missing from his foundation.

That's why he needed to be a little extra today, so he could be something else than a victim and to find a way for Michael's actions to be constructive. He needed to rebuild.

Mishka removed the face mask in the bathwater, by dunking himself repeatedly in the tub, before he stepped out of the water and dried himself off.

As he stood, hiding his head in his towel, per usual, he had a hard time freeing himself from his hiding place today. It was so comforting and safe, to hide in the silence and darkness of the towel, where he could be nothing. It took courage for him to unwrap the towel from his head, but he knew he had to eventually.

There was no other way but forward, so he focused on the music again and got on with it. He moved arrhythmically to 'The rite of spring', as he moisturized, fixed his hair and painted on a brave face.

He tried to find something to wear, but couldn't settle on anything. Irritated, he went through the racks and piles of clothes, without finding anything that spoke to him. No, no, no, he said to himself, as he went through his closet a fifth time. He was getting increasingly agitated and, influenced by alcohol, he decided to drop the whole thing. Not knowing what to do, he walked around his apartment naked, with the bottle of champagne in hand and tried to find something to do.

When the bottle was empty, he ransacked the kitchen, where he found another bottle of champagne, hidden in the back of the vegetable draw. In the back of a cupboard, he found some old filled chocolates, that Mervin had once brought. He took the goodies back to the bedroom, found his computer and switched out Stravinsky for a movie. As the pre-movie credits of Hitchcock's Marnie rolled over his computer screen, he popped open the second bottle and situated himself across the bed, with his chocolates, his bottle and his computer.

That's how he spent the entire day, eating chocolate, drinking champagne and watching one classic Hollywood movie after another. Distracting himself from the seriousness of what Michael did to him and ignoring the pain Michael had caused him.

After his fourth movie from Hollywood's golden age, the bottle of champagne was empty and he'd eaten the last piece of chocolate from the box. With no distractions left, he grew serious and sad.

Feeling a loss of control over his emotions, he went to the mirror. Had he gained weight? He'd eaten a lot of fat today. How many calories were in the chocolates? Snatching the box, he looked for the calorie content. 568 calories per 100 grams. How many grams were in the box? 360!

A sense of doom came over him. He could feel a loss of control over his body, imagining his beauty and thin body was slipping through his fingers. It was like his reflection was reprimanding him, for his lack of restraint and lack of power over his situation.

Wanting to see just how deep he was in, he did the math.

So it was 568 per 100 grams and he'd had 360 grams, so that would be a total amount of... 568 x 3,6 = 500 x 3 = 1500... 60 x 3 = 180... 8 x 3 = 24... hm, that would be 1500 + 180 + 24 = 1704 and then add 568 x 0,6, so 1/10 of 568 was 56,8. 56,8 x 6 was... 113,6... 160,4. 170,4 x 2 = 340,8. 340,8 + 1704 = 2044,8 calories. He was stunned. 2044.8 calories worth of chocolate, plus the roughly 570 calories per bottle of champagne, so 3184.8 calories in all. No, there was also the gin. Gin had roughly around 217 calories per 100 ml and the glass he'd drunk it from could hold about 30 cl, so with 100 ml equal to 10 cl, he'd drunk about 600 + (17 x 3)... 17 + 17 = 32. 32 + 17 49, so 649 calories for the gin, totaling a calorie consummation of 3833.8 calories and he hadn't actually had a single meal.

A man of his age and size only burned about 2400 calories a day, excluding exercise and he'd consumed 3833.8 calories. That meant he was now officially gaining weight, with a surplus of 1433.8 calories. He'd read somewhere, that it took 7000 calories to gain or lose a kilo of fat. If that was true, then he'd be gaining roughly a quarter kilo of fat or 250 grams.

Looking in the mirror again, he thought about the beautiful men and women he'd just seen in his movies and by comparison, he felt worthless.

Mishka rushed to the bathroom, got to his knees and shoved his index and middle finger as far down his throat as they could reach.

It didn't take. Due to his years of forced vomiting and sucking off his patrons, he had almost no gag reflex left at this point. He was too used to ignoring his body for it to behave normally now.

Determined, he repeatedly forced his fingers down his

throat, harder and harder. He felt like he was choking, but nothing was happening. His face was all red, tears were streaming down his cheeks and he could feel scratches from his nails, down his throat. He just kept trying, harder and harder, until he finally found release. As he watched the dark brown sludge of chocolate and champagne spew from his mouth, he saw all the things he was trying to avoid, hurling down into the porcelain bowl; rolls of fat, love handles and double chins. It was like his imperfections were flushed away, along with the content of his stomach.

For a short while he felt redemption, like he'd been given absolution from his sin of gluttony and granted his skinny body back, like it had been irretrievably lost before, when he was counting calories.

But the joy was short-lived, like most joys are. When he was done purging and had flushed all his sins away, he sat on the floor, next to the toilet and felt broken.

This was not how sane, normal people acted, he knew that. But he also knew that he was too ambitious and too self-important to settle for the life of a normal person, so he was willing to put up with a little insanity, in order to be something more.

He knew there was something warped about his perception of himself, but he also knew he was closer to his ideal of beauty, than people with so called 'healthy' relations to their body and food. Usually, he found solace in the myths surrounding classical Hollywood actresses and royals like Joan Crawford or Empress Sisi of Austria, and the extremes they'd gone to for beauty's sake. Empress Sisi had had odd eating habits too, eating almost nothing but the occasional spoon of gravy, an egg or orange and who would wrap herself in raw veal to treat her skin.

Mishka felt better, thinking about the work, sacrifice and obsessiveness behind other people's beauty treatments.

It made him feel less alone, like he was supported by history. History taught him that no one became extraordinary, by conforming to the ordinary. He wanted beauty and beauty, everyone knows, is pain.

With that in mind, Mishka picked himself off the floor, dressed in an oversize linen shirt, with matching pants, some boating shoes and went for a run. Sweatshirts and running shoes weren't in Mishka's wardrobe, he never dressed for comfort or practicality, not even when exercising.

Today Mishka ran as fast as he could to ward off the fat cells he imagined forming on his underfed body. He was already sweating excessively, when he reached the gate of the graveyard, despite it being only about fifty meters from his apartment. According to a quick google search, he had to run for about two and half hours at a moderate pace, to burn off his surplus calorie intake. So, he set the alarm on his watch to go off in three hours and continued running.

Mishka always ran at the nearby graveyard, where he'd run in and out the different paths and lanes, rushing between headstones. The graveyard was usually empty, so he could run in peace, without being seen sweating. He also saw something poetic, in maintaining and training his body, among the decaying bodies underground. It made the whole exercise routine seem like a memento mori.

Now, when he was running, there was nothing else to occupy his mind, then Michael and the paranoia started all over again.

Why did Michael force himself on him, had he led him

on?

He had flirted with Michael and he had found Michael attractive.

Was it his own fault? Had he not made it clear enough, that Michael had gone too far?

He'd kept saying no, he'd even screamed and he'd tried pushing Michael away!

What more could he have done to prevent it?

And why had no one reacted?

Had the people in the bar known, that he was being... well, raped?

Was that what the bartender had meant when he'd asked if he'd enjoyed his evening?

Had the bartender been mocking him for letting himself get raped!

How awful people can be!

Historically, people were always behind terror and cruelty. People had been behind the holocaust, the Russian pogroms against the Jews and almost every other historic injustice had been thought up and executed by people.

People were the real problem here, it was bigger than Michael!

Mishka envied the dead for their peace and their security. The dead were beyond that sort of brutality. Their problems were all over, behind them. He was in the middle of his problems.

Mishka fastened his pace, until his sides hurt and he could barely breathe at all. He ran and forced himself on and on, until his alarm finally went off and his legs instantly gave out.

There he lay, gasping for air among the headstones, trying to make sense of his life and gain control of his experiences and his body.

From another perspective, Michael's actions were a compliment. The compliment being that Michael had wanted him too much, to accept a rejection. But, that explanation didn't feel quite right.

Mishka's body remembered how Michael had held it tight, immobilized it and forced it up against the wall. Once again, Mishka was stunned by the powerlessness he'd felt under Michael's muscles. The memory hurt, but it was like an epiphany to Mishka. All he'd been to Michael, was a release. That's why Michael had given him nothing in return, other than a flaccid and useless 'thank you'.

That was what desirability really was, that's what it truly means to be beautiful and desired, it reduces you to a thing, a thing other people judge to be useful in satisfying their wants and needs. Beauty isn't about how you look; it's about how you're viewed. Beauty really is in the eye of the beholder. In its most primary sense, beauty is not about aesthetics, it is sociology, founded in a social relation.

That's why he had a hard time gaining control over his narrative, because it wasn't up to him, it was up to his viewers and followers – his fellow man. The realization made him crave autonomy more than ever, he no longer wanted to be under someone's direct control again, like with Michael or with his patrons before that.

What he really needed was to take control over the situation and create some distance between him and his audience.

If he wanted to gain power, he had to be in tune with his audience. That's what he'd gotten wrong in his mishandling of the scandal. He'd continued, like he was still performing for a single patron at a time. But the scandal had brought him into the public eye, which meant he was facing a mass audience and he needed to play on the needs and desires of the masses. What he needed to do was find a demographic and adjust himself to their collective gaze. It was all just about marketing.

The scandal had given him notoriety and if he could resonate with a large demographic, then he might be able to generate revenue from them, somehow and money meant power.

Mishka fled from his current reality into fantasies for his future. It was an old and fundamental coping mechanism. Throughout his childhood, he'd escaped his bullying schoolmates and the un-understanding adults around him, by planning a bright and shimmering future, that resembled the glamorous lives of the characters in his beloved books and movies.

As he ran home, he envisioned a bejeweled and solitary future, where he could buy anything he wanted and could live for the pleasure of his own gaze. He could live in happy unison with his reflection, away from the grapy hands and violent thrusts of men like Michael. He could live for the pleasure of his own gaze.

Chapter 17

In the days following his rape, Mishka barricaded himself at home and retreated into himself, to analyze his past and plan for his future. He especially wanted to know, where he had gone wrong with Michael. It was easier, he thought, to find faults with himself and work on those, rather than work on bettering the wide, chaotic world. What other people did, was beyond his control, he could only control his own actions and be tactical, when dealing with the world.

The crucial thing was to identify the reason, why Michael had completely ignored him, when he'd said no?

No had been the first word, Mishka had learned to say, as a child. He'd learned it out of self-defense, because he wanted to be left alone, even then. Back then, people were either fussing over him or trying to hurt him. He remembered an older local boy, who had tried to strangle him to death, when he was about three. When the older boy had been caught and stopped by a neighbor, he had said he just wanted to see, what it would be like to strangle Mishka. Perhaps there was something in that, maybe he was just a person people wanted to hurt, out of simple curiosity? That was probably what explained all the hurt, that had been inflicted on Mishka. All those men had just wanted to see, what it was like and Mishka just happened to be an ideal victim. Maybe, that was the role he had played, when he'd enabled his patrons to play out their fantasies, he'd created himself as a victim and served himself up on a silver platter, with Michael, with Mr. P, with Phillip?

Mishka also wondered, who he would have become if his mother and his childhood had been like the other kids' in his hometown, normative, small and… beige. His adult life would certainly have become more normative, but also bland and tasteless. No, he preferred a childhood of coffee cakes, uncertainty and hard philosophical views. The truth was, that his mother had made him feel exceptional and superior, because he, unlike most people he'd met in his life, knew his view of the world was warped by his perspective of it and therefore, he took nothing to be objectively true. This uncertainty allowed him room to maneuver in his life, to change tone, appearance and tactics at the drop of a hat. Because his beliefs were never fixed, neither was his personality and it allowed him to take on new personas, when he thought it convenient.

He found hope in that. It meant he could always change and be something else.

To do something proactive, he prepared himself for his new directive; trying to form himself in the image of someone engaging to the general public, so he could spin his notoriety to his own gain.

Mishka researched his audience, scouring through all the stories about him in connection to the scandal. He paid special attention to the user engagement of his digital footprint, trying to figure out, what people wanted him to be. To gain more specific insights into his target demographic, he also went through his own social media accounts and analyzed the comments on all his posts.

Mishka found a big gap, in the engagements on his own posts, to the coverage of Mervin's scandal.

His own content had mainly attracted engagements from middleclass to wealthy men, between 30-80, who were either gay, bisexual, or bi-curious. There was also a secondary audience of straight, white girls, between 20-35 and a small group of outraged incels. Most comments were enthusiastically sleazy, with strange men directly outlining the sexual act they wanted to perform with or to him and why they wanted to do it. Other comments were from straight glamour-girls that were trying to brand themselves as supporters of the queer community. However, there was also some negative engagements in form of slut shaming, sexist comments blaming him for being 'obviously a fag' and a few comments questioning his styling choices.

The stories that the media had brought of him, in connection to Mervin's scandal, mainly had negative rhetoric, however the engagements on the stories were very divided. The commentators could be divided into two groups, consisting of the closed minds of the great unwashed masses of 'normals' and their open-minded counterparts of bohemian creatives. Both groups made comments, that centered on their own world view and were clearly made to support their own social identity. The 'normals' either pitied him or denounced him as 'disgusting'. Either way, they focused on his homosexuality, on the fact that he had been with a married man or the financial side of his relationship to Mervin or all three things. What annoyed him was that they didn't seem to get the subtleties and extravagance of his lifestyle. They simply saw him as a whore, no different from a street walker.

The other group, of open-minded bohemians, didn't seem to understand him any better. They painted a picture of him as a progressive sex worker, who was rebelling against society's condemnation of sex work.

No one mentioned his style, his attitude or his looks. He concluded that they all wanted him to be a trope and this he could work with.

He would take charge and paint a different picture, that could fascinate them and they could relish in condemning or celebrating. Like Andy Warhol, he would simply measure his press coverage in inches. It wouldn't matter if people liked him or not, it just mattered that they wanted to see more of him. After all, in the digital media age, all that mattered was that he would be able to get attention and be a polarizing figure, that could drive up user engagement.

So, he'd recreate himself in his own image, of an unapologetically gay, pretty boy for hire. He'd be a male femme fatale – a homme fatale – like a cross between Dorian Gray and Gilda.

As preparation he consumed every movie and book he had with a sexually depraved main character, studying their polarizing characteristics. He worked hard to adopt some of the characters' behavioral patterns, mannerisms, and rhetoric. He practiced his body movements, his facial expressions and his diction, until he simply became a new character.

To make the finishing touches, Mishka reorganized his closet. He curated his collection to fit his new public persona, that would dress exclusively in extravagant evening wear. It was important, that he looked queer, expensive, and somewhere between horny and oversexed. To this end, he also studied new makeup looks, as he tried to create a signature look of bed chamber eyes, tussled hair and big, expressive eyebrows.

When he felt he was ready for his first performance, he

made a call to Nickolaj, the guy from The Society Chronicler, he'd met at Balthazar, the evening of his rape. Mishka invited him over that evening to discuss his offer of doing a story on him and Nickolaj accepted.

Mishka was determined to set the right scene for Nickolaj and project the lifestyle he had before the scandal. Just like he'd done with his patrons, Mishka prepared the apartment to look like a den of gluttony, fornication and vanity.

Mishka wanted to sell Nickolaj the story of himself as the spendthrift and promiscuous young dandy, who lived on the expense of others. He was transforming himself and his home into a trope.

His heart was pounding and he had butterflies in his stomach, as he ran through his rooms, scattering empty champagne bottles, his most expensive clothes and accessories and the bags and boxes he'd received them in.

Everything depended on Nickolaj's impression of him tonight and it was through Nickolaj's eyes, Mishka tried to see himself and his apartment.

A half hour before Nickolaj's scheduled arrival, Mishka was set. He had curated a playlist of party music, which was playing on full blast. It caused his downstairs neighbor to bang against their joint floor/ceiling, but Mishka didn't care.

Dressed in a tight-fitted Tom Ford smoking jacket, with no shirt underneath, super skinny pleather pants and dress slippers, Mishka sat down at his dressing table to prime himself. He fixed his hair and put shine on his face and exposed chest, while he rehearsed poses and lines in the mirror, as he waited for Nickolaj. When he inspected his reflection, he was satisfied. The shine made him look like he was fresh from a sweaty round of fucking and his clothing made it look like he was on his way to a nightclub. It seemed perfect for the story he wanted to sell. Still, he was nervous, like when he lost his virginity to a horny old man and his money. Just like then, he didn't know what he was in for and it scared him.

He was startled and excited when he heard the buzz from the front door. Mishka buzzed Nickolaj in and did a final inspection of his reflection, as Nickolaj walked up.

Mishka stared into the eyes of his reflection and nodded. This was it. Everything was ready.

Mishka smiled nervously, as he greeted Nickolaj and escorted him into the living room, treating him to a scotch, like he was one of his patrons.

It all made an overwhelming impression on Nickolaj. The mess and shaggy décor, mixed with high end fashion labels and empty bottles from expensive wines, all of it drowning in the deafening volume of Mishka's pretentious music. This was a world apart from Nickolaj's and he had no idea, that a world like this actually existed. Of course, Nickolaj had both read and written about it, but he had dismissed both as exaggerated marketing ploys, but Mishka seemed different to him. To Nickolaj, Mishka seemed like a fictional character come to life.

Nickolaj was still turning his head, exploring the surroundings, when Mishka started in on him.

"I'll get straight to the point. I want you to help sell my story. I'll give as many details as you think necessary, names, positions, even taste descriptions of different board member's cum, but I want to be the headline, not just a side story," Mishka explained earnestly.

"Yeah, I don't think that's going to be a problem. Could

you turn the music down? It's really loud," Nickolaj said.

Mishka strutted slowly over to his speaker and turned the music off.

"You don't have to try so hard, you know! The business with Eugene Irvine is still in full swing and it'll continue until they find him. You could make good content. Show people where the money went," Nickolaj said calmly, as he examined Mishka and the clutter.

"Is that so," Mishka said, breaking into a smile. That was exactly the character he had been preparing himself to play. He had been right.

"You know, I have no idea how much he actually spent on me over the years," Mishka boasted.

Nickolaj turned to him and smiled.

"That's beautiful. You should say that in the article, just like that. It's the sort of thing that'll rile people up," Nickolaj laughed.

"Fine, should we do it now?" Mishka asked, while he opened his jacket, showing his naked torso and suggestively adjusting his pants.

Nathen furled his brows and chuckled in response, overwhelmed by Mishka's aggressive performance.

"I meant the article... mostly," Mishka said with a smile.

"The article, mostly. Okay. Yeah, let's do it," Nickolaj said and sat down in a chair, setting up a writing station at the coffee table, with a laptop, paper notes and his phone recording.

Over a couple of hours, Nickolaj questioned Mishka, about his relationship with Mervin and tap, tap, tapped the answers on his laptop. It annoyed Mishka, that Nickolaj never took his eyes off the laptop, that the work had more allure, than he did. It didn't occur to Mishka, that Nickolaj was actually there for his work, because Mishka's ego didn't allow for that. The more distant Nickolaj seemed, the more provocative Mishka answered his questions. But no matter how depraved or detailed Mishka's account was, Nickolaj still kept his eyes on his work. Occasionally Nickolaj reacted with a 'that's great' or an ambiguous 'hmmm', but through the whole séance, Nickolaj never once looked at Mishka or asked him anything that wasn't pertinent for the article.

When Nickolaj completely stopped asking questions and just typed on his laptop, Mishka felt sidelined by the article and by Mervin. The whole thing seemed to be focused on Nickolaj's scoop and Mervin's scandal, it still wasn't about him. He desperately felt the cold, of being just out of the limelight and he desperately wanted to be center stage.

"I actually sucked him off, while he sat in that chair. That was one of the last times we were together, before he left. He sat right there," Mishka noted casually and pointed to the chair Nickolaj was occupying.

Nickolaj looked suspiciously down on the chair and then on Mishka and Mishka couldn't help but laugh.

It egged him on, that he was finally the object of Nickolaj's gaze, so he walked slowly over to Nickolaj and sat down by Nickolaj's feet.

"And I was right here," Mishka whispered.

Nickolaj closed the laptop, so he could get a clear sightline of Mishka.

Mishka brushed Nickolaj's legs with his hands.

"What are you doing? I didn't come here for that, okay," Nickolaj said in an annoyed tone.

"This kind of is the story, isn't it. It's what I do. That's how I got everything in this apartment. It's why Mervin installed me in this apartment, in the first place," Mishka said calmly.

"Just stop for a moment," Nickolaj said and got up from his seat.

"You don't want me, do you? You just wanted the story?" Mishka sulked.

"Well, yeah. This isn't a date. It's work. I thought you knew that?" Nickolaj rationalized in his confusion.

"Well, this is my work. My work is to seduce and make men feel pleased, that's what I do." Mishka argued with pride, still sitting on his knees, in front of the empty chair, Nickolaj had fled from.

Nickolaj took a deep breath and it dawned on him, the life that Mishka had actually led and how different it had been from his own sense of normality. As he looked at Mishka again, he now saw a sad little boy, that had been pushed into the bed of countless old men and been told that he belonged there and how Mishka had believed it. So much of Nickolaj's work was reporting carefully calibrated gossip, manufactured by PR agents and celebrity managers. Nickolaj had forgotten the truth and trauma, that was behind 'a good story'.

"It doesn't have to be. You're a good story. I can get you a good deal for an exclusive on Eugene Irvine. That will set you up for a time, until you figure things out." Nickolaj comforted him.

"Thank you, that would be lovely," Mishka said placidly and got up off his knees.

Mishka lit a cigarette and sat down in the chair, Nickolaj had been sitting in. Staring at Nickolaj, he started to negotiate. "How much can you get me? For an exclusive?"

Nickolaj was surprised by the change of mood, but also

relieved, that he didn't have to be so obviously confronted with Mishka's pain.

"I don't know, a couple of thousands. It depends on what you give me." Nickolaj shrugged.

"No more? What would I have to do for something like 50,000 kroner?" Mishka raged.

"Dirt! And exclusive rights to your stories about Eugene Irvine. You specifically have to talk about the money he spent on you and everything you did for him in return. Also, I need permission for us to set the narrative and it will be harsh. You won't get a read-through before we spread the story and you won't be able to contest, how we represent you or what you've said," Nickolaj recited factually, waiting to see Mishka's reaction.

"Well, what do you want to know, that I haven't already shared? I've already told you, I'll share anything," Mishka said nonchalant.

"It has to be blacker and whiter. When you talk about Irvine, you make him sound like a generous benefactor, which is too much like the Eugene Irvine people knew before the scandal. When I say dirt, I mean I need details of him as an adulterer, a money fraud and closeted gay man. You need to give me a story, that people can be outraged about," Nickolaj lectured Mishka.

Mishka swallowed his scotch and started telling a new story of Mervin, one just as true as the one he told before, but unkind and without nuance.

Nickolaj got his computer and wrote eagerly, as Mishka recounted each single trinket Mervin had ever bought him, remembering the labels they were from, their retail price and the acts he'd performed to deserve them. Mishka explained his routine with Mervin, explicitly clarifying Mervin's sexual tastes and preferences. Even the nickname was revealed, as well as the booze Mishka would pour for Mervin on his visits. Mishka talked with fervor, as he thought about how his statements would make him look to the public. He shared any detail, he thought people wanted to hear and strained to be scandalous enough to catch their attention. This time, Nickolaj shifted his attention between his computer screen and Mishka, as Nickolaj would nod enthusiastically or whisper 'great' at each anecdote.

When Mishka could think of no more outrageous things to say and the room became quiet, Mishka remembered how kind Mervin had been to him.

Nickolaj was typing up the last part of Mishka's monologue, when Mishka unawares whispered: "I'm sorry he went away, we had a good thing going".

"What, you and Eugene Irvine? You're kidding me? You really wanted that to continue? Wouldn't you rather... well, anything else?" Nickolaj laughed.

Mishka shook his head. "He was nice to me and he really wanted me. We had a good relationship. It worked for us," Mishka explained calmly.

Nickolaj chuckled in disbelief. "Come on. I mean you no offence at all, but 'nice'? He was in his 70s and you're, what 20, 19? It's creepy, just admit it, it's creepy. He could be your grandfather. Of course, it didn't work for you. Of course, it didn't. He used you, he totally used you. It was abuse." Nickolaj argued fervently, shocked to see Mishka's disapproving face.

"You weren't there! What do you know what it was like? I liked him, he did a lot for me." Mishka sulked.

"Yeah, of course he did a lot for you, so he could have his way with you. He was a horny old man." Nickolaj said, looking confused at Mishka.

"What's with the middleclass morality? Don't be so uptight. Sexuality is a fluid thing and sex can actually just be for fun." Mishka deflected.

Nickolaj looked at him seriously. "Was it though, was it fun for you?"

"Yes, it was fun to be so wanted. I liked how much he liked me." Mishka said.

After a few minutes of silence, where Mishka's vanity filled the air, Nickolaj finally replied: "Yeah, I don't get that. But I guess it's part of what makes you a good story".

Mishka took it as a que. 'A good story', that's what he was now. It was eerie how much this interview resembled his relationship with his patrons. Nickolaj was just as commandeering as they had been and, in both cases, he was playing a part in their fantasy. It puzzled Mishka, why this was more respectable, than having sex. This felt like more of a sellout, than the sex had done. This was a new type of submission for him, but it seemed very similar to the submission his patrons had demanded from him. He wondered, why the world seems to differentiate so much between giving your body and giving your will. If you can sell one part of you, why not the other?

Mishka took a deep breath. "I can do that. I can be a good story." he said meekly.

"Great. Now, we need to schedule a photographer, to take some pictures of you and all the stuff Eugene Irvine bought you and maybe shoot a video." Nickolaj replied.

They made their plans, Nickolaj finished his questions, a few days later photos were taken and a video was shot and

Mishka was paid for his exclusive.

Mishka didn't hear anything from Nickolaj or the magazine, until they released the story online, with the video and the full interview in their printed magazine.

In both versions, Mishka was portrayed much as he'd hoped, like a male Anna Nichole Smith, with the spendthrift of Imelda Marcos. The features were full of pictures of Mervin's expensive gifts and the text detailed the transactional nature of Mishka's relationship with Mervin, alongside details of Mervin's sexual appetites. However, this still left Mishka with the label as Mervin's property and this disappointed him. He'd hoped the story would help him break out from Mervin's shadow. It was like Mervin was still fucking him, like he was trapped underneath Mervin's sweaty body and he had to steal breaths of air, as he waited for Mervin to finish with him.

It wasn't that Mishka regretted his sexual past or that he felt he'd done anything wrong in exposing and trashing Mervin. Mishka just felt overlooked, like he'd gone missing while in plain sight and he was tired of not being seen, despite his best efforts to gather people's attention.

The press he'd gotten from Mervin's scandal had highlighted a general problem for Mishka. He had not been aware of it before, but there was something wrong in his relation to the world around him. There was something passive and disconnected about his existence, but he couldn't quite put his fingers on it. People only saw, what they wanted to do to him or get from him.

As Mishka read Nickolaj's story, he felt like he was crawling the mind of one of his patrons. When he had been with his patrons, he had always had to guess their fantasies and what they wanted from him. With the interview, Nickolaj had told him upfront and now he could read the fantasy, through

Nickolaj's perspective. Mishka wondered if the feature portrayed him, like his patrons had actually seen him.

For several days after the release, Mishka read and reread the feature to his reflection, until he knew it by heart and could recite it on command. He roamed around his apartment, chanting Nickolaj's words and tried to epitomize them, as he groomed, dressed and styled himself.

He regarded the feature as an advertisement and desperately wanted to live up to what he was marketed to be.

The story got a lot of engagement on social media and just like Nickolaj said, it was spread out of people's outrage.

However, it was various things that caused outrage for different social groups. Their outrage seemed more like a performance, than actual displays of emotions or morals. Reading the user engagement on the story was like being in a hall of mirrors. He could see so many reflections of himself, it was completely disorienting. It was clear to see the users' social performance in their engagements. Some claimed to be outraged by Mervin's spending. Some by his relationship to Mervin, either because they were of the same gender or the age difference. For others, the outrage was caused by Mishka's lifestyle, looks and fashion sense. The cause for outrage didn't seem terribly important, just like it didn't seem to need much cause at all. People wanted to be outraged. Even people's outrage caused further contradictory outrage and it didn't take long, before the story of Mishka became a large political debate, on social media, about the justice system, sexual minorities and consumerism. People seemed to see all sorts of things in Mishka.

It dawned on Mishka, that he'd always been so focused on being desirable, that he hadn't taken into account, whether people wanted to feel desire or if they preferred to feel something else. Suddenly, the transaction of his previous relationship became clear to him. Nickolaj was wrong, when he saw Mervin as exploitive, because he had been exploitive himself. He had not only used his patrons for their money, he'd also used them as a mirror to reflect in, to see his own desirability. This explained a lot about the behavior of his patrons towards him and his own behavior towards them. All his relationships had been about objectification, were both parties objectified and used each other. None of his patrons had really seen him and he hadn't bothered to see them either.

Perhaps he was better suited to a relationship with a mass audience, where he wasn't confronted with the messiness of an actual individual?

He could give them what they wanted.

If they wanted to be outraged, he could easily be outrageous. It could empower them both. He would give them a cause for their outrage, so they could act out their social identities and they would give him their clicks and attention, which could make him feel like he mattered and gain him profits.

Now that he gave it some thought, most historical characters seemed to be outrageous. In fact, they had become historical because they were 'good stories' and that had given them some social capital, that bought them their place in history.

Maybe outrageousness is what it takes, to be noticed and be allowed to live by your own rules.

To be a good story, he needed to be outrageous, that's what he took away from this experience. He needed to be a subject to debate.

He would start by entering the dialogue, by answering people's comments to the story on the magazine's social media channels. It was hard at first, to just say something outrageous to people's comments and not consider their comments sincerely. He read people's comments as ques for what would cause further outrage and thought of his answers as entertainment for them. Once he got into it, he had fun turning people's words on them, poking fun at everything and taking nothing seriously.

In his eyes, he was arguing against a wall of absurd self-assuredness and the blind egotism of the average user. The point wasn't to convince anyone of anything, the point was to get people's attention and get them to care about him.

Days went by, as Mishka was mesmerized by his reflection in other people's comments and he just sat at his screens, antagonizing them for more views. He answered comments, shared people's reactions to the article and posted selfies and videos, where he addressed people's notions about him. It was clear to Mishka, that every single comment, was also a mirror for the one who wrote it. But as Mishka thought about it, he realized the same could be said of his patron's sexual fantasies and their general treatment of him. Their sexual fantasies and fetishes were always a mirror of their personal traits and social ambitions. Mishka was feeding people's desire for outrage and provoking them to either salute, laugh at him or denounce him.

In a matter of days, the story had been picked up by other news sources and the story took on a life of its own.

Suddenly the conversation became about him and not about Mervin or his scandal.

He was seen by the general public.

Chapter 18

Times had changed for Mishka and he was living in a new era, where he felt seen and recognized.

His image was almost unavoidable, both online and in print.

People came up to talk to him and take selfies with him, when he was out shopping, visiting a museum or walking in the botanical gardens. When he walked down the street people parted and made room for him. The press stopped him and took his picture and asked for quotes.

Wherever he went, there was someone to reflect in, someone who wanted to share their version of him and his image.

He had become a good story and people were engaging with him, both on- and offline.

As the obsession with him grew, even his home became a public place. People started taking pictures of him, through his windows, when he was walking around his apartment.

At first, he'd kept his curtains pulled, for privacy, but he soon grew tired of being alone in the dark. It made him miss the close nature of his patrons and he decided to recreate it with the public. He had started to value the attention and gaze of strangers, more than he valued his privacy or comfort. Because he wasn't comfortable with letting people see him out of character, he started living as if he was always being watched. Everything he did now, was on brand and camera ready, even when he was home alone.

To help himself stay in character, Mishka had covered his walls with mirrors, in every shape and size. They worked as a disciplinary tool. That way, he could always see himself from every angle, in every room of his apartment. It kept him on his toes and made him always perform for his reflection. As he moved around his rooms, he held his reflection in his gaze, constantly analyzing himself. Now, his stomach was always sucked in, every hair was always in place and he only moved in poses.

The mirrors scolded him, if he did anything that didn't look good, which forced him into a life of aesthetic habits. Mishka no longer wore things that weren't camera ready, he never slouched and he'd completely stopped eating.

He was on a strict liquid diet, so no one should be able to take a snapshot of him, with food in his mouth or stuffing his face.

To keep up the appearance of a shameless and spendthrift homme fatale, he always pretended to be drinking, even when he wasn't. He lived on water with olives, juices and cold coffee mixed with sugar and either heavy cream or raw egg whites, all of which he'd drink out of cocktail glasses.

All parts of his life, except his bathroom habits, was now a front stage performance. The only backstage he had, the only place he was ever alone now, was his bathroom since it didn't have a window.

However, there had been some overlap between his private person and him as content. His mother had called him.

The press hadn't gone over well with his parents. They were from another generation and of a class, that valued privacy and calm, above all else. For them, the greatest privilege was to live at peace, away from the world. That was their version of elitism, to be separated from the world and left to their own devices. So, his mother had been worried about her son and the family reputation, when Mishka had become a news story.

First, his mother had called several times, in distress, to comfort him, but found Mishka unmoved and unfeeling. His parents didn't understand, that Mishka wanted the attention, in fact preferred it to anything else. They didn't acknowledge his restless urgency and distaste for peace and quiet, which left room for all the thoughts, feelings and bad memories he tried to avoid.

After that, she called several times to try and understand his joy for his situation and his appreciation of his growing recognition. When they failed to reach commonality, she stopped calling altogether. It had pained and embarrassed her, that she couldn't understand him anymore, this creature she had created. To her, the fact that she couldn't understand was a horrible failure on her part, so she had stopped calling, so she could avoid failing. He was no longer her good little boy and he wasn't the man she had envisioned him to become. She had tried to create a perfect being, an uber-mensch, but had ended up with a shiny surface of a person, that filled itself up with everybody else's fallacies. Unlike Mishka's patrons, his mother noticed it, when he just repeated back her words and mirrored her and she hated the distance it created and the control it took from her.

The recent press and Mishka's encouragement of the press had created a chasm between him and his family, which they didn't have the emotional vocabulary to breach. Not because they didn't want to or because they didn't love each other enough, but because they simply belonged to different worlds and no longer spoke the same language. The chasm wasn't created out of Mishka's lifestyle, his sexuality or even his sexual promiscuity or prostitution, but because he no longer hid, what he was doing. It was Mishka's desire to be seen and it was his exhibitionism, that set him apart and isolated him from his family. They no longer had common means or common goals and so, they separated from each other, so they could each pursue their own ambitions.

All Mishka had now was his audience and his reflection, so he lived to please them both. His posing and pretending worked and made him a staple in the gossip columns and on social media. There always seemed to be a new detail to him, that people could read about and discuss on online forums.

His notoriety had been perceived by the PR-agents and firms, which got him on some exclusive invitation lists, with great party favors. While other people were socializing with friends, lovers and family, Mishka went out to events and tried to be a good story. Because he had no one else to see and thirsted for company to reflect himself in, Mishka accepted every single invitation he got. At every event, he tried to behave outrageously and scandalously, flirting shamelessly with everyone, drinking heavily and doing everything he could to draw attention to himself.

Whenever someone responded to his insincere flirtations, he let them do whatever they wanted to do to him and boasted about it afterwards.

All parts of Mishka's life were a pose and truth was no longer a concept he recognized. To Mishka, his reflection was his entire world, whether it was the reflection of his image in the mirror, the media or people.

With his patrons, Mishka had guessed what they wanted and done it. Now, Mishka guessed what people would want to see and share on social media and did that. It was amazing how fast it became habitual for him, to make a spectacle of himself and gather the crowd to revel at his every action.

Without the complexity of a real person, but with the one-sidedness of a pornographic image, Mishka's momentary notoriety snowballed into a sort of internet celebrity.

With his newfound celebrity came endorsements, sponsorships, the occasional modelling job and even new patrons. Unlike before, when he hid his lifestyle and his patrons hid him, it was all out in the open now. The new patrons seemed to delight in the attention they borrowed from him. For them, he was not just a thing of amusement, he was a tool to demonstrate their wealth and social position and strengthen their brand.

Everything Mishka did now, earned him money. The drinks that he drank, the selfies that he took, the comments he made, the places he visited, the men that he slept with, the clothes that he wore and the underwear he sullied and sold online.

He felt rich, although he didn't make much more, than those of his childhood friends, who had grown up into respectable middle-class jobs, working in management, advertising or consulting. But unlike them, he was alone and had all his money to himself, which gave him a nice spending budget. He even got an agent, an accountant and hired a cleaning woman, who came twice a week.

As the attention on him grew and he became overbooked and had fewer financial worries, he could devote all his attention to himself, his looks and ambitions.

Always, he wanted more. More clothes, more expensive things, a thinner body and a more youthful face. Over the years, as his finances became increasingly stable and comfortable, he became a megalomaniac, a perfect consumerist. He would go shopping at least two to three times a week, carefully collecting perfumes, beauty products, clothes, accessories and jewelry for his ever-growing collection of things. Adding to this, he constantly pressed his patrons for gifts, while his agent pressed everyone for more cash. In the end, his carefully curated collection became too big for his old apartment. With the approval of his accountant, he found a new, much bigger place, only to fill that up too.

His new home was an old, majestic apartment, built in the 1850s to house an upper middleclass family. Like many of those apartments, it was built like a labyrinth of connecting rooms.

The apartment included a dining room, two sitting rooms and a library, which were attached with large archways and French doors. There were also three bedrooms, a master bathroom, a guest bathroom and a kitchen and former maid's chamber, that were hidden away at the very end of a long, narrow corridor. The ceiling and walls all had white stucco and the floors were aged hardwood, set in decorative patterns.

Instead of housing a family, like it was built to do, it housed him and his things. The extra bedrooms were used as closets and the former maid's chamber was repurposed to a walk-in jewelry vault.

Mishka had all the rooms decorated with busy House of Hackney wallpaper, crystal chandeliers, heavy velvet curtains in every window and doorway and even heavier antique furniture. The whole thing looked like a caricature of a nineteenth century bordello and Mishka half expected to run into Toulouse-Lautrec, when he drifted around the apartment.

His new apartment was less of a home and more of an extension of his personal brand. It was a stage set and it had its intended effect on the people who saw it. Everyone who saw his new place, recognized him as something out of the ordinary, something exotic, that required special treatment.

In his new place, he settled into a new routine.

Each day he got up late, then spent around four hours in his bathroom, where he'd exercise, shower and minutely groom every single inch of himself. On a good day, when he was especially pleased with his looks, he'd rub up against his bathroom mirror and fuck his reflection, until he and his reflection came together. It was the only real sexual intercourse he had. When he was with his patrons, he usually didn't orgasm at all, it was impossible for him. Most of the patrons neither noticed nor cared, since they used and viewed him as a thing, not a real person.

In the late afternoon or early evening, he would finally emerge from his bathroom and parade around in his rooms, hoping a reporter would take shots of him through the window. Often, he'd pass the time by going shopping, get some sort of cosmetic treatment, visit the museums or just go strolling around the city parks. He always went somewhere he could either make himself look better or where he could be seen.

His evening was spent out at events or with his new patrons, where he'd promote himself, his various sponsors and beg for any scrap of attention he could get. Him and his patrons didn't really speak or connect at any human level, they just used each other as props in front of the camera. They gave each other press and furthered each other's branding strategy. When they had sex it was the same, it was a separate experience. Mishka would go numb and let them take possession of his body. The patrons would use him like a sex toy and masturbate in him, by either skull fucking him or penetrate him anally, as he lay flat on his stomach. Mishka no longer took joy in being had sexually, it didn't matter to him, when there wasn't any cameras around. He didn't want to be had, he wanted to be desired and the patrons he had now, didn't desire him, they just used him. Still, he enjoyed the money and gifts and still measured his worth, by how much he could get from his patrons. The only reason he continued having patrons was to boost his brand and measure his worth.

This was his life now and one day grew into another and so did the weeks and months, until there had gone a little more than a year.

At that point, his shopping had expanded his collection so it even filled his new place, which ironically meant, he couldn't afford to move to a bigger place. Out of need and greed, he organized and categorized his collection, until every room doubled as a treasure chamber. Shoes, perfume and accessories were stowed away between his beloved books in the library. Half the kitchen cabinets were filled with clothes and the other half with stemware and porcelain. He used his oven, freezer and refrigerator to store the jewelry, he couldn't fit into his walk-in vault. The sitting rooms were filled with standing trunks, holding his excess suits and in the dining room, every chair was covered in coats, jackets and fur pieces.

The sheer mass of his collection of luxury goods overwhelmed the senses and the expense of it was incomprehensible to most. The press loved to show pictures of his home and made features and interviews about the most trifling things, just so they could have more pictures of him together with his collection.

He discovered it had a special effect on patrons too. The minute they saw the opulence of his home, they became competitive and left bigger and bigger wards of cash by his bed. As a result, he always brought back his patrons to his place, to raise his worth and he always told them, who had left the biggest amount, so he could profit from their rivalry.

Even on social media, people took notice. His apartment was no longer just a backdrop for his selfies, it became a story of its own, but one which strengthened his image. It earned him a new, widespread reputation, as the new Marie Antoinette, which some people celebrated him for and others condemned him for, but all of them watched him and engaged with his content. As long as he got clicks, he felt invincible.

He had become a symbol of consumerism and the selfie generation. This brought even further attention from the press, that came and took more pictures, interviewed him about his lifestyle and spread the word of his decadence.

Mishka didn't just enjoy being watched and followed, it had become a premise of his existence. Everything he did, he did to be seen and to reflect himself in other people's gazes, comments and behaviors towards him. Other people's judgement of him, became his god. He worshipped every compliment and every critique.

While some thought of him as an influencer, it was in fact his audience that influenced and defined him. He was, whatever people wanted him to be, whether it was what they wished or feared he'd be.

As the world forgot his former connection to Eugene Irvine and Mishka became a name recognized on its own, he got back in touch with Jason, after they met by chance at the launch party of an artisanal gin.

Jason had been following Mishka in the media and even admitted to occasionally cyber stalking him. Mishka was touched that Jason still gave him attention and loved the way Jason looked at him. They set up a date for the following week, on a Tuesday, when Mishka had no event to go to.

They had agreed to meet at the National Gallery and Mishka had shown up uncharacteristically early.

As he stood between the large columns of the National Gallery's entry way, he felt anxious. It didn't feel like a meet up between two old friends or a rendezvous between two lovers, but like an exam. Mishka had chosen their meeting point, but he hadn't told Jason, that the National Gallery was one of his holy places. It felt right to Mishka, to meet Jason in a sacred place, since Jason was the only one left, that still saw humanity in him and not just the image of him. Everyone else had left him or he had pushed them away. As he waited, he got some performance anxiety, which was unusual for him at this point.

Perhaps he was anxious because he actually had to engage in a real conversation. He'd gotten rusty at making conversation, these days he only spoke in one-liners, the press could quote him for, otherwise he merely wrote paratexts for his social media posts, spoke at his followers in videos or barked orders at waiters.

His fear for an actual dialogue made him aware of how much of his personhood he'd weeded out, to make room for his image. It reminded him of Bette Davis' speech in 'All About Eve', when she talked about the things she'd given up for her career.

He pouted as a group of visitors sneaked a picture of him, as they walked past him into the museum. He didn't know why, but he had a gnawing feeling, that Jason was to be the judge, that would pass sentence on the validity of his new form of existence, whether he was a success in life or a failure. It was a lot of pressure, even if the pressure was strictly internalized. Personally, it made him proud, that he was able to turn off his humanity, he saw something godlike in it, but it also made him wonder, what he'd gotten in return.

Just as he was deep in thought he felt two hands clasp his shoulders, as Jason sneaked up behind him.

Mishka was shaking as he turned around.

"Oh, it's you," Mishka sang, over-pronouncing each letter, like he was trying to impress Professor Higgins and Colonel Pickering.

"Yeah, here I am. I'm glad you wanted to meet, but why here?" Jason asked, with happiness in his voice.

Mishka looked up at the building, like he was surprised himself and re-thinking his choice. "I just like it here," Mishka answered, deciding not to share the significance of the place, fearing Jason wouldn't understand it.

Jason nodded and smiled, like he understood anyway. "It suits you. I thought so as I walked up and saw you standing there, calmly between the columns, with your straightened back. You looked so proper... but I know better."

Mishka looked at Jason and smiled, as he wondered whether Jason was complementing or insulting him. Not able to reason it out, Mishka suggested they went in.

Jason walked a step behind Mishka, as Mishka showed him all his favorite paintings and shared gossip about the artists or the people portrayed in the pictures. Mishka ended the tour with the portrait of dowager queen Juliane Marie.

"This is my favorite. She founded the Royal Copenhagen porcelain factory in 1775 and still, she was very unpopular with the people and in court. But just look at her! She's so proper and elegant in her white silk, lace and all of her frills. Don't you just love her!" Mishka exclaimed, completely entranced by his associations with the portrait.

Jason just watched Mishka, as he talked. He loved Mishka's passion. "No, I don't love her. But I love how much you do," Jason explained in a calm, friendly tone, as he watched Mishka watch the portrait.

Mishka looked back at Jason. Jason's eyes felt like projector lights to him and he was warmed by Jason's interest in him.

"Do you remember when I told you I loved you and you laughed?" Jason asked.

Mishka started walking around the room, feeling uneasy. "Yes, of course. What about it?" Mishka said, facing away from Jason.

"Why didn't you take it seriously?" Jason had changed his tone, it was harder now, but still calm.

"You always told me in bed. It's hard to take a declaration of love seriously, when covered in various bodily fluids." Mishka deflected, but still meant every word.

"Why? Why shouldn't I tell you I love, after we've had sex? We were naked, lying close up against each other. Isn't that the perfect time to be honest, about how I feel about you?" Jason asked without plan or menace, but simply to discover Mishka's point of view.

"And the others? I know you always spent time with other boys too, you were never mine exclusively. Did you say the same thing to them?" Mishka said, turning around to see it land on Jason.

Jason just shook his head. "What does that matter? You weren't mine exclusively either. Besides, I'm not talking about everyone else, I'm talking about you and me. I told you I loved you, because I did, because it was how I felt, because it was true. It wasn't true about anyone else, so I didn't say it to anyone else. You were different, are different, than everyone else. You're special to me," Jason said almost robotically, like he was reciting his phone number. There was no passion, blame or feeling in his voice at all. He was simply relaying information. Mishka posed and stared at Jason, to give himself time to think things through. Jason's delivery made Mishka wonder, how Jason related to his own feelings. Not that he was questioning if Jason had feelings, but he didn't recognize how Jason processed feelings and put them into practice. It occurred to Mishka, perhaps he didn't recognize the mechanisms of Jason's feelings, because he himself worked so hard to separate feeling from action.

Mishka didn't know what to say, so he turned away from Jason and walked around the room, then stopped at the portrait of Juliane Marie and fled into it.

"Do you think she knew, that she'd be admired here some day? That over two hundred years later, we'd still be dining on her porcelain?" Mishka asked, staring at the painting.

"You always run away from me," Jason reproached him, continuing, "If things don't suit you, you just run away. It's hard to keep your interest. Whoever ends up with you, will have to work hard to keep you."

Mishka knew Jason meant it as a critique, but he couldn't help feeling flattered by the description.

"And you think this is a problem?" Mishka asked triumphantly.

"I hope it won't be, for you or me." Jason stated.

A thousand potential futures filled the room, as Jason and Mishka looked at each other, wondering what to do. Mishka was reminded of Sylvia Plath. He hated Sylvia Plath, but right now he understood what it was like to starve underneath a fig tree, because it was impossible to choose a fig to eat. Maybe that was his future? No, he had an agent to choose figs for him.

Mishka looked intently on Jason, wondering what he was feeling, if he still wanted him.

Jason broke into a smile. "You're so beautiful. My little monster. But, you're still too skinny, you really should eat something. Let's get out of here. I'll take you out and feed you," Jason winked.

Without waiting for an answer, Jason put his arm around Mishka's shoulder and led him out of the museum. On the way out, Mishka noticed a custodian, who intently followed them with his eyes.

Jason kept his arm around Mishka, leading him into a nearby bistro and Jason didn't let go of Mishka, until they sat down at a table. As usual, Jason took charge and ordered for the both of them, while Mishka scanned the room.

Every time someone in the restaurant touched their phone, Mishka was camera ready. A few people did sneak a few photos of him, which he had a good feeling about, but most were just checking their messages or Instagramming their food.

During the meal, Mishka drank every drop of wine he was served, but did his best to ignore the food. It was only at Jason's insistence that Mishka carefully took a few bites, tasting the things he really liked and leaving the rest. It was hard for him to eat, but he did it out of politeness. As he thoroughly chewed the few bites he cautiously put in his mouth, he was reminded of how hungry he always was. He could feel his bowels starting up again and his stomach was growling for more. His system was no longer used to solid foods and he started to feel sick. He tried to distract himself with smiling, nodding and posing in response to Jason's slightly monologist attempts at conversation.

Jason was distracted by the sexual suggestiveness of Mishka's eating poses and didn't see the pain Mishka was in. All Jason saw was a young boy, just troubled enough to be fascinating, a boy he desired and who he had sitting right across from him. To Jason, Mishka was a pretty face, with a limber body and a manner compliant enough to keep him satisfied. It was something he'd never found in anyone else and that was what made Jason love Mishka.

At the end of the meal, Mishka excused himself and calmly went to throw up in the bathroom. His system was rejecting the food and it pleased Mishka. Despite its insistent instinctual hunger, his body was still compliant enough to reject food on its own now. To Mishka it felt like his transformation was complete, that he'd shed his base humanity and had truly transformed into a spotless object of desire. On his way back to Jason's table, Mishka tested his hypothesis, by analyzing how many eyes fixated on him, as he got within their eyeshot. Yes, they all looked at him, he caught everyone's eye and their eyes followed him and wanted to see him.

It made him feel like he really was something and it made him smile, as he sat down, opposite Jason. It appealed to Jason, that other people wanted Mishka too and he enjoyed watching other people gawking at Mishka.

As they sat there at the table, bathed in the gaze of the other guests, Mishka took off his left shoes and let his foot travel up Jason's leg. Underneath the long tablecloth, Mishka massaged Jason cock with his foot. Jason welcomed it, as he liked sex in public places and Mishka just liked the attention and being made use of. But, when Jason accidentally let out a moan, a waiter resolutely brought them the check. This little passive aggressive insistence on the waiter's part, was enough to rush them out, without a word. Jason quickly paid and left a big tip, as an apology to the waiter.

But Jason was determined to see his pleasure to the end and shepherded Mishka out of the bistro and hurled him into the first cab he saw.

Mishka was confused by the commotion, as Jason frustratedly yelled: "The address, the address. Come on, quickly".

"What do you mean?" Mishka timidly asked, afraid of doing the wrong thing.

"Your address. Your new address! I don't know it. Give it to the driver," Jason said, frustrated that he wasn't orgasming now. He'd been close, when the waiter interrupted them. Now, Jason felt an unmitigated anger at anything that delayed his ejaculation, including Mishka's slowness.

"Oh," Mishka exclaimed and quickly gave his address to the driver.

As the car moved them towards Mishka's bed, Jason and the general mood calmed down, as Jason could see he'd have his pleasure soon.

"Why are we going to my apartment?" Mishka asked out of general curiosity and slight boredom.

"Uhm, we just can't go to my apartment right now." Jason dismissed him.

"Why not?" Mishka insisted.

"We just can't right now." Jason tried to brush him off.

"You've got someone living there, don't you? You installed one of your other boys with you," Mishka asked, intrigued with the sudden drama over an address.

"Come on, let's not," Jason said and kissed Mishka, to shut him up.

Mishka pushed him away. He wanted to know what was going on. It was important to him, that he should be the epicenter of Jason's sexual interests and romantic feelings. A live-in-boyfriend threatened his star status, so Mishka pressed on to measure his level of importance in Jason's life.

"That's it, isn't? You're living with someone?" Mishka sneered.

"Don't be like that, Mishka. We were having a good time," Jason pleaded.

Mishka shifted in his seat, trying to get as far away from Jason as he could in the backseat of a cab. He fled into himself and Jason felt the mood making him limp.

"He doesn't mean anything to me. I was going to break up with him, when we scheduled our date, but I wasn't sure you'd show up, so I put it off. I didn't want to give up my relationship, if you were going to stand me up," Jason explained calmly.

Mishka tried to go through Jason's reasoning. It flattered him, that Jason thought him so fickle and that he seemed so ready to dump his boyfriend, just for a date with him. Mishka felt empowered by it, that he held the future of Jason's relationship in his hands.

"But I did show up? So, are you going to dump him now?" Mishka dared Jason, to see how far Jason was willing to go for him.

"What? You think I'm lying, that I won't do it? I'll do it right now, see," Jason said, as he took out his phone and made a call.

To egg Jason on, Mishka moved closer to Jason and started stroking Jason's crotch, reawakening Jason's erection.

Jason was brutal on the phone, saying it was over and that he expected the guy, whose name was apparently Thomas, to move out by the next day, at noon. Mishka applauded himself, as he listened to Jason's ruthless breakup and heard the tears of the now ex-boyfriend. As the cab neared Mishka's apartment he stroked Jason's crotch faster, to motivate him to end the call, but he didn't. Jason kept talking, as he paid for the cab and followed Mishka into his apartment and then to his bedroom. The boyfriend was determined not to be an ex-boyfriend and kept questioning Jason, in a desperate attempt to find meaning and continuity in their relationship, that was ending so suddenly and without warning.

Feeling Jason's attentions shift from him to his ex-boyfriend, Mishka felt lonely and couldn't wait anymore. Without any preamble, Mishka unzipped Jason's pants and sucked his penis, while Jason continued to talk his way through his breakup with Thomas. Mishka was pleased as Jason's penis grew bigger and stiffer in his mouth and Jason got more and more distracted. He could feel Jason's interest going from his breakup and his boyfriend to him. As Jason neared climax, he forgot himself, moaned and dropped the phone as he came in Mishka mouth. Mishka simply continued sucking away, until Jason had emptied himself in his mouth three times.

Jason was his now, he'd won him from his boyfriend.

Chapter 19

Mishka and Jason had been dating for months now and Jason was practically living part time with Mishka, in Mishka's apartment.

They were officially in a relationship and it caused trouble, like changes usually does.

At first, they had been happy. Mishka found some calm and security in a constant companion and Jason even enjoyed Mishka's capriciousness and constant need for sexual confirmation, because it led to an endless string of orgasms for Jason. They found common ground, in their enthusiasm for Mishka's popularity and infamy. Their relationship gave Jason the power rush of a child, that is monopolizing the most popular ride on the playground. In response, Mishka felt flattered, understood and appreciated. Their commonality made Mishka confide in Jason and let Jason watch him, when he fucked his own reflection. Mishka's reflection became actualized in their relationship, as a third partner. They were effectively in a throuple – Mishka, Jason and Mishka's reflection. Over time their fantasies gave way to the cruel realities of a relationship. They began to fight, mostly over Mishka autonomy.

Jason had become envious, when Mishka was with someone else or even received attention from other people and he became obsessive, trying to keep Mishka at home, as much as he could. But, when they were alone together, Jason became bored of Mishka and irritated at Mishka's neurotic and self-destructive behavior. Mishka's exoticism and fascination had ended, when Jason came close enough to see the weak and insecure person underneath the well-constructed surface. Jason had discovered the bitterness, that every lovelorn person discovers, when they get together with the object of their sexual fantasies. When fantasy becomes reality, the fantasy dies.

The more Jason tempered his expectation, to better match reality, the more Mishka felt like he was failing to be beautiful enough, thin enough and agreeable enough. The more he felt he failed, the harder Mishka tried to fit the fantasy, by dieting, exercising, and grooming himself.

Mishka tried so hard to keep up with Jason's fantasy. When Jason wasn't at Mishka's apartment, Mishka just waited for him and prepared himself for him. Mishka no longer had a life away from Jason, he existed in a vacuum of Jason's gaze and at Jason's pleasure.

Mishka had started running twice a day and only ate, when Jason was there to see it. After each meal, he'd take ipecac syrup, the first chance he got. Mishka visited his beauty clinic several times a week, every time he felt, he'd let Jason down. Mishka would get his face peeled, micro-needled and tightened, just as his body was peeled, lasered and frozen. It didn't matter what the treatment was, Mishka took any treatment the clinic offered him, in the desperate hope of living up to an impossible fantasy. Jason had become the epicenter of Mishka's world and insecurities. Mishka lived and died by Jason's evaluation of him.

To deal with the pressure of Jason's fantasies, Mishka had also started drinking more and regularly took small doses of ketamine, not enough for him to hallucinate, but enough to calm him down.

The sex had changed too, it was no longer intimate. It had become completely one-sided and was no longer an activity they did together. Mishka was like an automat, that gave Jason his orgasms, like a vending machine dolls out snacks at request. Jason received his orgasms, careless and unengaged. He enjoyed his orgasms, but he had them needlessly, without having hungered for them.

To Mishka sex was just something he did, it was part of his role and he performed his sexual favors out of routine and unoriginality.

The relationship had completely soured for them both, but neither of them had the determination to quit each other. They just stood still, in a fog, refusing to take a step in any direction, because they couldn't see a clear path.

As Jason domesticized Mishka, it changed Mishka's narrative. Mishka was no longer seen at every event with an open bar and he no longer appeared with other famous or infamous personalities. Instead of a wild and glamourous life of sexual escapades, Mishka's social media accounts started to feature pictures and selfies of quiet nights in, drink recipes and beauty tutorials. The change of lifestyle and the clear fading of Mishka's forced joire de vivre lost him followers, on all his accounts. Suddenly, endorsement deals were offered less frequently and paid less. As much as it bothered Mishka, he didn't see the need to do anything about it. He didn't have the confidence to deal with it, because he was too hurt from Jason's declining interest in him.

It wasn't until his followers on Instagram dropped below a million, that he felt a call to action and insisted on meeting his agent. She would have to handle it.

Mishka's agent was a cynical and commanding woman, with a very wispy, Scandinavian look. While her personality clashed with her looks, her name somehow seemed appropriate for both; Ingeborg Lundqvist. A former model, Ingeborg detested being objectified or handled in any way and had become an agent out of the same perverse compulsion, that causes abused children to become abusers themselves. It was this perversion, that made her get along with Mishka. She wanted to be the one to handle things and Mishka wanted to be handled.

To prepare himself for Ingeborg's judgement, Mishka put on his armor of designer labels, jewelry and perfume. He spent hours meticulously choosing his outfit and doing his makeup, nervously sipping martinis as he worked on himself.

Mishka stomped groggily into Ingeborg's office, dressed in black tweed, gold, diamonds and pearls.

"What's this about?" Ingeborg barked, before Mishka had time to greet her. Ingeborg was one of those efficient types, that hates small talk and never participates in meetings, unless they serve a specific point.

"I want to know, what to do. I'm losing my relevance," Mishka said, like a child admitting to accidentally kicking a ball through a window.

"You need to re-establish your brand. That will require sacrifice on your part, okay!" Ingeborg sighed.

Mishka nodded in response, while he looked at his shoes.

Ingeborg looked up at him, annoyed, and sneered: "You know what the best deal I've gotten for you in the last four months is? Hm? It's an offer of 2000 kroner for a sponsored video, about bamboo tube socks. That's what you're worth now, 2000 kroner. People are going off you, Mishka."

Mishka let the verbal bitch-slap land without protest. He knew he deserved it. It had been months, since he'd answered any invitation or went out, where he could be seen.

His agent saw the unspoken criticism land and gestured for him to sit down.

"You need to act now, if you don't want to lose them! Dump the boyfriend!" she ordered with the superiority of a school head master.

Mishka was hesitant to give a response and instead just stared at her coolly. It didn't feel final enough for him. He needed a better sense of direction, if he was going to get out of the fog of his relationship with Jason.

Ingeborg closed her eyes and sighed exasperated. "You've changed your lifestyle and it's not tracking. You're a lifestyle influencer, Mishka and you became one, by appearing in sex scandals. A relationship, it's too normal... And boring. People don't want you to be normal. They don't want you to be spending your Fridays on the couch with your boyfriend, watching some crappy Netflix true crime story or listening to some dumb podcast, about a serial killer. No, no. They want to see pictures of you, caught sucking the cock of a married politician or doing coke at the counter of a Chanel boutique?" she proclaimed adamantly.

Mishka looked defiantly at her and asked, "What should I do?"

Ingeborg took no notice of Mishka's stare, she kept her eyes peeled on her computer screen.

"Something shocking, that's worth gossiping about," Ingeborg proclaimed, as she tapped on her keyboard.

Mishka unsuccessfully tried to seize her gaze and asked

the question, he always asked himself, before he did anything: "What's in it for me?"

"More views, more clicks, more attention and more money," Ingeborg stated.

They both knew, that Mishka was going to do what she asked. He always did what she said and they both prospered by it. He did things and she got her percentage. They both worshiped money, because they thought money could remake them. She measured her independence and power in money. Mishka used money to measure his worth. It was a commonality they both recognized, but never spoke of.

This was all it took for Mishka to dump Jason. Ingeborg had shoved him out of the fogginess of his 'real relationship' and pushed him back under the blinding stage lights.

On his way home, Mishka called a locksmith to change the lock of his apartment.

Conveniently, Jason was at work, so the locksmith could change the locks in peace. In the meantime, Mishka blocked Jason's phone number and blocked Jason on all his social media accounts, then he gathered all Jason's things and had them messengered to Jason's address, together with a note, that simply said: "Sorry, I'm done."

As soon as the locks were changed, he went out to celebrate and to revitalize his career. It was in the afternoon and all the fashionable bars were closed, so he did a tour of hotel bars, where he was determined to be promiscuous.

Because it was the afternoon on a weekday, there were only few people at the bars and they were all guests of the hotel. At each place Mishka strutted in, trying too hard to look promiscuous and conspicuous, as he ordered a glass of champagne and flirted overtly with every man in his vicinity, including the waitstaff.

Mishka's determination and desperation attracted the men, who couldn't cope with the murkiness of a genuine personality. He was approached by men, who enjoyed thinking of and treating their sexual partners like objects.

In a matter of seven hours, Mishka visited five hotels, where he performed as a sexual object to a string of men. He was fucked by a bartender in a storage space, got picked up for a threesome, by a couple of gay tourists, visited the hotel rooms of two different visiting business men and he gave a hand job to some random guy in a public bathroom. After that, the nightlife started to open up and with traces of cum on his clothes, face and in his hair, Mishka went out to paparazzi-ridden, fashionable night clubs and partied on. Goading every reporter he met, Mishka did and said everything he could think of to appear scandalous and sexually explicit. Mishka loudly and casually offered sexual favors to men, did drugs openly and named everyone he could remember having an affair with – all in front of the paparazzi. He even went so far, as to suck off one of the photographers in the alley, while the photographer filmed it.

As the clubs shut down, Mishka went to harder and harder places and when they closed down at dawn, he went to a gay cruising park, where he ended up in a labyrinth of hands, tongues, mouths and anus', belonging to himself and four other men. The group mingled with each other, stroked, sucked, rimmed and fucked randomly, as opportune body parts encountered each other.

Mishka didn't come home until the early morning, only to find Jason asleep outside his apartment door. He tried unlocking the door, without waking Jason, but he was too loud in his drunkenness.

Jason opened his eyes and looked up at Mishka, anxiously trying to open the door.

"Is the lock broken? I couldn't get in, either," Jason asked half asleep. Laughing and yawning at the same time, Jason said, "You know, I thought you did something. That you just changed the locks and shut me out."

Mishka was looking for the right words to say, but he was drunk, high and tired and his thoughts were slow and unsteady.

As Jason woke up, he noticed how Mishka looked and he smelled the stench of sweat and sex, wafting off Mishka.

"The note," Jason said with furrowed brows. "So, this is how it is, you're just done?"

"I'uhm. Afraid so. It just didn't work for me," Mishka said haughtily and as he heard his own words, he realized how true they were. He did need things, people and relationships to work *for* him, to promote him.

Jason got up from the floor, so he could meet Mishka's gaze. With an angry expression, Jason examined Mishka, looking for a way to crack through Mishka's thick facade. Mishka felt it and felt violated by Jason's attempt to see what was deep inside him. It made Mishka feel like he was losing control and it also made him worry about his true worth.

After a few moments, Jason nodded to himself.

"Well, I guess I always knew you'd move on. Whenever I didn't look directly at you, you were always getting away from me. You have to be watched, Mishka… and minded. A single moment of boredom and you're gone. You always use freedom to escape," Jason said calmly and walked out.

Mishka stood for a moment to process Jason's evaluation of him. Was it good or bad?

He liked the idea of being high maintenance and elusive, but he feared it also boxed him in, limited him. It was like the ending of "Breakfast at Tiffany's", when Paul Varjak tells Holly Golightly she's in a cage of her own making. Mishka feared that Jason was his Paul Varjak and he should run after him, like Holly had run after Paul, but he just stood there and listened to Jason's steps, as he left the building.

He took a deep breath, shook off Holly Golightly and went into his apartment. Once inside, Mishka posed up against the closed front door and did a story for his Instagram only fans account, where he showed off the cum stains and tried to count, how many men he'd been with and encouraged his followers to guess who they might be. He posted the video, cleaned himself off and went to bed, feeling used and hopeful for the future.

He only got a few hours' sleep, before he awoke to the annoyingly persistent sound of his telephone. The apartment was flooded with light, he'd forgotten to close the curtains, when he went to bed. His head screamed in pain, his body throbbed from being over-used and a stream of dried blood ran from his nose to his pillow.

He slowly reached for the insistent telephone, swiped to answer it and held it up to his ear.

Someone was screaming at him, he didn't know who it was, but they were going on and on about something.

As he somewhat regained consciousness and the world crept in on him, he recognized the authoritative screams of his agent Ingeborg.

"Ingeborg, it's you!" Mishka shrieked in surprise. "So, how did I do last night. Am I relevant again?" He asked in a hoarse and tired tone, as he slowly sat up in his bed.

Ingeborg sighed aggressively, annoyed that Mishka was just now joining the conversation, when she was half-way through it. She hated wasting time and repeating herself, because it made her feel out of control. "Ogrh! You did okay. Lots of mentions of you online media and it's gaining some traction on SoME. Hopefully we can build on that, if you don't fuck it up."

"So, I did good," Mishka asked, sounding like a toddler seeking approval from a beloved nanny or a favorite teacher.

"Mmm, it's more on brand, but let's see how the sex tape plays out," Ingeborg answered coldly.

Mishka could hear she was tapping on her keyboard and messing with some papers. She wasn't fully invested, not impressed, even after all he'd done. He'd have to try harder, he thought, as he tried to get up. It hurt, as he stretched out his worn body and he couldn't concentrate on Ingeborg's stream of words.

Ingeborg sensed his distraction.

"Mishka!" she yelled through the phone. "You're showing a double chin in some of these photos. Especially in the sex tape, it's a bad angle, you look like a pyramid. Remember your posture and lose some weight, okay. No one wants to see a fatty's sex tape." Then she hung up forcefully.

Mishka was relieved. He'd gotten directions and he felt Ingeborg saw him, like he saw himself; as a thing, a tool, a body to be manipulated to reach certain goals and gain certain advantages.

He moaned as he staggered to his bedroom door, listened for the maid, but there was no sound of her. Concluding he was alone, he threw on a black, red and gold kimono, grabbed his phone and made his way to the kitchen.

As he put on the kettle for his habitual morning pot of French press coffee, he checked his phone.

He'd gotten a lot of new followers and a ton of likes and comments on Instagram.

Then he saw all the Google Alerts for his name.

The photographer, he'd given a blow job, had released a pixilated video of it. Between that, the other things he did in front the paparazzi and the story he'd posted this morning, Mishka was once again noteworthy and a small part of the news cycle.

Throughout the day, the stories of Mishka's scandalous behavior spread from media source to media source, each sensationalizing his actions, by outlining everything he did and speculating about his motivations and mental state.

Social media users spread the story in awe or horror. Some users proclaimed their regret, that they didn't get a piece of him, others shared him as a symbol of sex positivism, while a lot used his actions to share hate speech about sexual minorities, to flag him, as a threat to family values or simply to call him disgusting.

Mishka was pleased, with good and bad mentions alike. He was talked about again, the subject of clickbait articles and social media debates. It made him feel special, like a modern noblemen, a thought that was reinforced by the knowledge, that he was starting his morning routine, while 'normal' people were nearing the end of their work day.

He prepared his morning tray, with a pot of French press coffee, a bread plate filled with health supplements, beauty supplements and sedatives, a glass of water and a glass of juice. To celebrate his re-found notoriety and his break away from Jason, he spiked his juice with champagne and took his tray into the living room. While he enjoyed his breakfast, he took a closer look at his digital representations.

His evening of flaunted debauchery had launched a myriad of stories, which had spread wide. Mishka's ego and self-assurance grew parallel to the story, with each new mention of his depravity. He felt like he was part of the world again and it made him make more of an effort.

Mishka started to put his heart and soul into his routine, instead of during it mechanically. On his daily run, he ran faster and longer, than usual. There was even a happy spring in his step. Once again, he was exercising for a point, not in a desperate attempt to be a little more pleasing to Jason, but to please the gaze of a vast mass of men.

It was even a breeze to stay away from food, he didn't even mull over, whether to eat or not. Once again, starving himself came naturally.

Now, when people noticed him again, things seemed worth doing. He felt the pressure of other people's expectations and he wanted to be perfect for them, to recreate himself in line with their fantasies.

Throughout the day, he analyzed his past and strategized his future.

Jason had taught him the folly of seeking the love of another person. One person could never give him the amount of attention he needed. Besides, being in a real relationship was way too close, for Mishka to cast his spell. He'd learned that intimacy wasn't free, it could only exist at the cost of mysticism and unequivocal adoration. To be intimate, meant losing the distance that made him appear to be magical, beautiful, and otherworldly and he'd never give that up again. He started to think of himself as a piece of art, that only made sense, only became clear and beautiful, when admired from a certain distance. Up close, he was a mess of paint clots and splats. Distance was necessary. To come close to him, meant to love him less. True, unmuddied love only existed, when it was unrequited and remote.

When he woke the next morning, hungry, sore and lean, his agent had already lined up a string of promotions, endorsements, collabs and collected several offers for odd jobs for him.

Over the following months, Ingeborg egged on Mishka's careless scandalousness and turned it into money, lots of money. It was a very lucrative time for Mishka and his agent, which was largely due to Mishka's blind obedience to Ingeborg's every command. If she told him to lose weight, he did. Ingeborg controlled him completely and molded him into whatever could get her a big commission. Mishka threw himself into his work, body, scheme and heart.

The only competition his agent had, for absolute power over Mishka, was with Mishka's patrons.

Mishka had become less selective with his choice of patrons, in fact he didn't select or choose them at all. He was afraid to turn anyone down, who'd pay for him, in fear they'd go off him. They had all become the same to him, Mishka no longer saw the individual patrons, anyone who'd pay for his company became his patron. Mishka had started to view people as segments of a demographic. Everything was business to him and he viewed people through the lenses of a business manager and a marketing agent.

His way with patrons was different too, in fact he no longer had a way with patrons, they were in control of him. When Mishka heard a demand for something, he mechanically delivered it.

Mishka seemingly had no will of his own, anymore.

For his agent he was a soldier, who blindly commanded orders.

For his patrons he was a doll, that put up no resistance. They talked to him, petted him and emptied themselves inside him, while Mishka remained completely passive.

For his followers and the media he was entertaining content, they could easily attach their opinions too.

Mishka had dreamed of fame and financial comfort, but had no idea what to do with it, when it arrived. He was terrified of losing his position, his newfound wealth and his social relevance. He never did anything, he wasn't explicitly asked to do. At events, he behaved as scandalously as Ingeborg had told him to and said the things, Ingeborg had told him to say. Having sex with his patrons, he moved like they told him to, touched and licked what they told him to and moaned in the way they told him to.

A change had occurred during his time with Jason, though it was imperceptible to Mishka, it was clear to everyone else. Mishka had transformed himself, from a courtesan to a vending machine of human interaction and of course he was used for sex and entertainment. That's all privileged people want, sex and entertainment.

The cause of the change was partly due to his long standing fear of failure, but also an increased fear for intimacy.

Mishka's newfound opaqueness empowered him and strengthened his career as an influencer and spokesperson. He'd learned that he had to be apart from everyone else, to stand out. It was necessary to keep a line between him and his audience, so they could love him. That's why performers were on a stage, to set themselves apart. So, he cut ties with the general populous, isolated himself and built himself a stage to perform on.

Mishka became obsessed with keeping the public at bay. While his agent was busy minding his career and taking in capital, Mishka used the money to build borders between him and the rest of society.

He hired a bodyguard, to keep people at arm's length in public.

He bought a house, that was situated close to the sea, in an isolated part of northern Zeeland and had renovated it and equipped it with every security measure he could buy.

He now had a home, where he could be truly alone and where the press couldn't peak in.

All the windows had mirror foil, there were security cameras all around the grounds, a massive gate and fence around the property, locks, and silent alarms, loud alarms, light sensors and all the things, that were necessary for a modern fortress.

In his new, large house he felt safe. He decorated it differently, than his other apartments. The place was large enough to house his enormous collection of things and so, they were all neatly organized and stored in closets, drawers and cabinets. His other places had all been overstuffed, messy and cramped spaces, where everything was out in the open. In his new place, everything was carefully arranged and all his things were hidden away. His new home was dominated by order and open surfaces. It was a place he would not invite the public in. Even the maids were surveyed by his bodyguard, to ensure they didn't go snooping or take any pictures, they might share on social media or with the press.

The only people he trusted now, was his bodyguard and his agent. Neither of them let him down.

The bodyguard kept an impenetrable border, between Mishka and the rest of the world. His agent kept making bigger and bigger deals, making Mishka increasingly rich.

Mishka finally had the capital to live the lifestyle he'd always dreamt of, but he no longer had the nerve or the will to do it.

Most of his free time was spent in his home, his fortress, drinking alone with his reflection. It was social media, that kept him in touch with his audience, posting selfie after selfie, endorsing products and spreading his image, as much as he could. His followers' reactions were his only look into society and a world outside of himself.

With Jason out of the way, his reflection was once again his main companion, as well as his obsession. Each night, Mishka would dress up for his reflection, dance with it, drink with it and make love to it, while the bodyguard stood outside his bedroom, protecting them.

Mishka shifted between worrying about what his bodyguard might hear through his bedroom door and relishing the thought of the bodyguard listening in.

For years he found all the comfort, love and nourishment he needed in his reflection. It was a perfect relationship of mutual love and respect. He and his reflection loved each other, lusted for each other and eventually became monogamous lovers. They worshiped each other and together, they spent hours and hours each day worshiping each other and maintaining Mishka's beauty.

As the years went on, their relationship soured, little by little.

His reflections started scolding him, as Mishka discovered spots and creases on his hands. Despite all the creams, all the exercise, all the sacrifice and all the procedures – Mishka was starting to age and his reflection was bearing witness to it. Mishka's reflection had turned on him, instead of celebrating his beauty, it started to portray his sins, like Dorian Gray's portrait.

As small laugh lines started forming around Mishka's eyes, he and his reflection fell out of love and started hating each other.

Mishka found it harder and harder to look at himself. Something had to be done, sanctions had to be made and security covers had to be applied. He had all the mirrors in the house covered with black chiffon and dimmed all the lights. Whenever he was with someone, even the maids, he covered his eyes with sunglasses and wore gloves.

Mishka's tastes and styling became increasingly expensive and he covered himself in designer labels and high-end jewelry to compensate for his body's betrayal. He still posted selfies, but was very careful to manipulate his image with filters and retouches, to maintain the illusion of an ageless face.

To everyone else, Mishka was still nineteen years old, even though he was actually ten years older. There was a growing divide between Mishka's self-perception and the way others perceived him. Compliments started to have a new meaning to Mishka. Previously compliments had flattered him and he'd used it as research into other people's perception of beauty and done his best to live up to it. To inhabit what they wanted to see in him. Now, he took compliments as veiled threats, because he could no longer recognize himself in them and no longer had the confidence to hope he'd ever live up to it. He felt the aging process taking hold, and just like an expected income stream, Mishka used it in advance. Mishka felt and started to act middle aged, as he anticipated the loss of his youth, beauty and sexual appeal. This was everything he'd based his existence, social identity and social media branding on and now it was disappearing – his one USP. Stubborn and spoiled as he was, he refused to accept a world or an existence outside of his wishes. He expected the world and his physique to change and fit into his wishes and wants, like it had done throughout most of his life, but now he was beginning to sense his own powerlessness. But, this was all happening inside of Mishka, outside of him the world idolized him.

As his success grew, so did the gap between him and the surrounding world.

The more compliments he got, the more frustrated he became, which in turn made him feel mad. Madness is to some extent a disagreement of realities and his reality didn't match the way others still perceived him. He became mad at himself and the flatterers, as he desperately tried and failed to reconcile with his own gaze. While he had started to hate his reflection, he still respected it, as the most credible source on his looks.

The gap between his own knowledge of his decay and other people's positive view of him, made Mishka depressed.

It started slowly, at first he just felt so tired and he stayed in bed longer and longer. Much to his agent's frustration and anger, it took bigger and bigger deals to motivate Mishka to do any work.

His social and emotional detachment attracted people and enabled his success, materializing in bigger deals and projects, which bored Mishka and caused him to retract further into himself.

Mishka was spoiled and like all spoiled people, he unconsciously sought his own destruction and kept testing the limits of his seemingly limitless terrain.

Without any real push back and without a fight worth fighting, Mishka became so tired of everything, that he decided to retire and retreat from the ugly and boring world.

He'd noticed, the more unhappy he was, the more pleased the world seemed to be with him. It seemed, to be successful and pleasing, you had to be miserable. That was the secret, to endure misery to gain the world. Life wasn't contra mundi, but miseri mundi.

After he'd talked it over with his accountant and the accountant had made the necessary changes to his finances and investments, Mishka was officially retiring.

Chapter 20

For his great escape into retirement, Mishka both endured and basked in the twilight of his fame, by selling exclusive interviews, about his upcoming retirement, his affair with Mervin or other aspects of his life. It was like he was making the rounds at a private party, saying goodbye.

Once everything was arranged and dealt with and his retirement actually started in effect, he was quickly hit by his own pointlessness.

He'd spent most of his life mentally preparing to become this persona of Mishka Balzac, he'd been busy performing in the role and gathering the funds to acquire his independence. Now, that he was entirely independent, he could no longer remember, what he wanted to use his independence for.

Raised as a member of the middleclass bourgeoisie, Mishka wasn't really fit to lead a life of leisure. With his maids, his bodyguard, an investment adviser and his accountant doing all the necessary things to keep up his lifestyle, Mishka didn't know what to do. Without patrons to please, he didn't really see the point of himself. With no purpose, Mishka crept about the house like a ghost, trying to find something to do.

His unsettlement seethed throughout the house. It scared the maids and made them overly cautious in their work. In order to distract themselves, the maids kept the house spotless and in strict order, working harder, than they'd done anywhere else.

The bodyguard, a man of few words and sentiments, felt uneasy too. He couldn't quite put his finger on it, but he felt haunted by an unspecified and relentless sense of danger, which made him paranoid.

Even the delivery guys felt something weird, when they came by with groceries or the spoils of Mishka's online shopping.

No one spoke of it, but everyone felt that Mishka was causing some sort of sinister imbalance. Nobody dared even hint at it, because they simply couldn't put their feelings into words or even specify what caused their feelings, but it was there, whatever it was.

Mishka was completely unaware of the effect he had on the staff; he was too occupied by himself.

Most of his attentions was on his looks. Even though he never left his house, he did a lot about his appearance. He was always impeccably dressed, always styled with fingerless gloves from Karl Lagerfeld and dark designer sunglasses, to hide his aging eyes and hands. Every day, Mishka would put on some sort of suit or Chanel-looking tweed outfit, which he wore throughout the day, until it was time to change to evening wear. Every day at five p.m. sharp, he would be ready for a predinner cocktail, he'd consume in his library, dressed in an extravagant interpretation of a tuxedo.

In his boredom, Mishka had learned punctuality. His routine had evolved into obsessiveness. Any deviation from his schedule, caused him anxiety. His anxiety had fixed itself on the possible loss of his social position, his wealth and the public's interest. All alone, he struggled not to lose face. He constantly felt like he was in danger of some sort of attack or invasion, but he didn't know what the danger was or where it was coming from. To stay guarded he kept up his formal ways and tried to hold on to everything he could, while he waited impatiently for someone to come and save him.

To hold on to his figure, he had once again stopped eating solid foods. He now sustained himself on a strict liquid diet, consisting mainly of alcohol. He'd start with his morning coffee, then be served endless trays of tea and coffee, throughout the day, switch to cocktails at five p.m., before dining on soup and wine, ending the evening in a parade of after dinner cocktails and cigarettes.

Despite not caring what the staff thought of him, Mishka instinctually hid his day-drinking, sneaking whiskey into his morning coffee or just drinking it straight out of a coffee cup.

It was part of his middle-class morality, which forbade him to drink openly before five p.m., which caused him to hide his growing consumption of alcohol. He didn't do it out of consideration, embarrassment or even to save face for the staff. It simply didn't occur to Mishka, that he could drink openly, before five p.m.

It was strange, but the clocks kept sounding louder and louder to Mishka and it started to bother him. When the house clocks started to become too apparent to Mishka, he'd fill the house with music, startling the staff with the sudden tones of Stravinsky or Nina Simone, played at maximum volume.

When Mishka had retired, he'd thought of his reputation and of people's view of him, he hadn't thought of his wellbeing or made plans for what he should fill his time with. As a result, Mishka lived entirely in the past, obsessing, analyzing and creating new narratives for everything that had ever happened to him. He was organizing his memories and processing his experiences. It was hard for him to find any real meaning in his life, he only found purposes and functions he'd filled in the past.

He'd become desperately lonely, but he didn't know how to reach out to people, how to meet someone new or to relate to someone, outside the guidelines of his former relationships of patron and sugar baby.

Mishka had never bothered to learn how to be a friend, a boyfriend or a family member. He'd never felt or seen the need for it. But now, in his loneliness, he felt the price he'd paid for his life. He was like an abused dog that desperately needed care, but didn't trust anyone enough not to bite them, who came near him, fearing what people would do to him. Not knowing what to do about it, he did nothing. Never going out and only seeing people who worked for him or serviced him in some way, Mishka lost his social graces – he lost his tact and so, danced alone to his own beat.

Secretively, he longed for company and fans to perform for, like he'd performed for his patrons, but he was too afraid of his reputation to seek people out. He couldn't understand why no one seemed to see the slow disappearance of his looks. People still saw and treated him as the beautiful nineteen-year-old boy he'd been, they didn't seem to see the nearly thirty-year-old pompous skeleton he'd become.

He wanted to be remembered as he'd been: young, beautiful and shameless, a flapper of the twenty-first century. If the cost was isolation, he was willing to pay it and so, he kept his distance from the world.

It was only the dead, who stayed as they were, he'd become aware of that. How lucky they'd been, the beauties who'd died young. Mishka became so envious of the dead.

Often, he'd be lost in thought of their luck, James Dean, Marilyn Monroe and others like them, who'd died young and lived on frozen in time. Sometimes he'd wake up from these thoughts to see nervous maids standing before him, asking him something trivial.

The deeper he went into his retirement, the more he drank.

Instead of looking at his emotions and weaknesses and work through them, he drank increasingly more, so he could be beyond caring. In his drunkenness he became mean, transferring his misery and failures to his domestic help, constantly thinking up punishments for his maids and the delivery people. It was always childish things, like hiding an expensive piece of jewelry and accusing the maids of stealing it, pressuring them to name one of the others as the thief. When the jewelry was later found, he'd apologize for his 'honest mistake' and give them some sort of gift in reimbursement. Once he cut himself with a knife in front of a delivery man and then accused the delivery man of attacking him, pressuring the delivery service to fire them or he'd sue the company and press charges against the delivery man.

He'd hide around to see the chaos and pain he caused and secretly giggled at it, like a mischievous child. Afterwards he'd lie to himself and his victims, until everyone involved was convinced it was clumsy accidents or they'd actually done, what Mishka had accused them of. No one had the malignant mind to recognize the creative psychological sadism in Mishka. They didn't want to see Mishka for what he was, they'd rather accept the responsibility and believe themselves to be guilty of crimes they hadn't committed, than accept the evil in Mishka.

In his boredom and misplacement, Mishka turned his

recluse sanctuary into a madhouse of passive aggressive horrors, that destroyed the common sense of reality of everyone who entered it.

Nothing was perceived like it was.

Mishka kept his looks to a strange degree, like a wax figure. Instead of wrinkling and fattening, he thinned, elongated and whitened. Yes, he looked as ageless as humanly possible, but he didn't see it himself.

Every day, he thought he saw his reflection age horribly. He imagined himself getting fat, bald and wrinkled. As a result, he kept starving, kept exercising and got more and more injections, treatments and surgery.

He ended up looking timeless. His delusions were so exceptionally strong, that they spread to all his staff and they became an echo chamber, that simply repeated his delusions back to him, confirming his madness as reality.

Chapter 21

Mishka was nearing yet another birthday, in just a few days' time. Preparing for the day, Mishka had tried on all his clothes and picked two favorite outfits, he'd wear on the day – a daytime outfit and an evening outfit. He'd gone to the tailor to get them taken in, to fit tight over his exposed bones.

Over the years, Mishka had gotten thinner and thinner and often had to have his clothes taken in, to fit properly. Rarely, did clothes fit him straight off the rack.

As Mishka posed in front of the mirrors and flirted with his reflections, a bit drunk from his morning green tea and gin, the tailor disrupted his interaction with himself.

"Excuse me, sir," the tailor politely tried to penetrate Mishka's self-absorption.

The interruption was unusual and out of routine, so Mishka simply ignored it. Mishka had gone to the same tailor for years, an empathetic and intuitive man, he had quickly figured out Mishka's style and usually did his work, with very few instructions or questions.

"Umhmm." The tailor loudly cleared his throat and repeated himself. "Excuse me, sir."

"Mmm," Mishka hummed and tilted his head slightly indicating he was listening, even though he never broke eye contact with his reflection.

"I'm afraid we can't take it in any further. Not again. We've already altered it twice and taken it in, as much as we could. There's barely room for the pockets as it is and the shoulders would only look odd, if we take it in at the arms or sides again," the tailor meekly said, fearing Mishka's reaction. The tailor knew, that vain people could be dangerous, when their image was scratched, however slightly.

Mishka's face dropped, as he stared at his reflection, inspecting the body, that was constantly betraying him. It was strange, Mishka couldn't help but feel betrayed by his body, whether it gained weight, stayed at its weight or looked different when it lost weight. Mishka felt like he was worth more, was more desirable if he took up less space, so weight loss kept being important to him, no matter how much his ribs stood out from his body. But, Mishka didn't like it, when his weight loss caused changes. Having to change his plan for his birthday outfit was small, he knew that, but as the plan disintegrated by the tailor's logic reasoning, it felt like his whole future disappeared and he was floating in midair, not knowing if he was falling or flying.

Mishka gained control of his face and looked like a carefree boy again.

"Well, isn't that something. I guess, we'll have to think up a whole new outfit. Two new outfits, to show me off. It's for my birthday, what can you do?" Mishka chirped in an eerily cheery tone.

The tailor was relieved and fell back to his routine, showing different samples of fabric, designs and decorations to Mishka.

For a daytime outfit, Mishka ordered a three-piece, slim fit, grey suit and a cream colored silk shirt, which he planned to wear with a grey and silver leopard bowtie he already had at home.

For the evening, he chose a classic smoking, which he would have sewn up in black silk and the jacket would be embroidered all over with faceted black jets pearls of various size, small white fresh water pearls and silver thread. He also ordered a new black chiffon shirt, with a matching oversize butterfly to go with the smoking.

As Mishka was measured and had sample sizes fitted to him, he stared himself down and imagined himself in the clothes he'd ordered. Shopping was the only thing that gave him optimism. When he ordered lavish and glamorous clothes, he could fetichize himself and think of himself as well-kept and good-looking. It also reminded him of his affluency, that he had become the rich man, that he had previously wanted to marry for money.

Despite his usual reproaches to himself, his shopping reminded him, that he was enough on his own.

On this occasion, the things were also to soften the blow of his upcoming birthday. A way to flaunt and cherish his looks while he still had them. He felt like he was holding on to his appearance with his fingernails, like it was being yanked away from him, by some unseen, malevolent demon.

Everything was so still and stable in the tailor's old fashioned store front. It made him remember how things used to be, back when a standard size could still fit him tightly. The quietness and slowness of the tailors was in stark contrast to the noise and fast-paced fashion boutiques he had used to frequent. The loud noise of the other customers, who would ask for a selfie with him, the on-brand music pumping in the background, the slithering and insistent service of the pretentious sales clerks and the occasional press, following him from store to store.

Now, his life was calm and quiet. The noise had stopped. The only noise was the tailor's sporadic queries about the fit and Mishka's robotic denials and reassurances, which Mishka always made with the same passive and flavorless smile his mother had taught him. It was a smile designed to reveal nothing, a polite piece of armor against society.

The lack of conversation made Mishka feel embarrassed. It was so strange for him to have an actual conversation. Mostly, Mishka was alone. The few social events he went to, to remind people he was still alive, were more about being seen and photographed, then actually engaging with each other socially. His staff was satisfied with orders or to be left to their own devices, scared of what Mishka might say or do to them. His social media followers were satisfied with pictures, videos and paratexts. It hadn't dawned on Mishka until now, that his self-isolation was costing him something. He felt embarrassed again. Embarrassed by his lack of social contact, his loss of social skills. He'd set himself apart and made others see him like something special and now he was so separate from the world, he'd settled into his own special way of being.

When the tailor had finished measuring Mishka and noting necessary changes to the standard sample size, Mishka paid, arranged times for fittings and went out into the street.

There was no press, who'd gathered outside, no one had done some digging or followed him here. He was alone.

Missing his former busy life, Mishka put on his sunglasses and took a few selfies, to bask in his own attention and hopefully that of his followers. People walked around him in a circle, like he was doing a piece of performance art and in a way he was. Out of the corner of his eyes, he saw a few people recognizing him, pointing and taking pictures of him, as he finally took a selfie worthy of posting.

It was small, but it was good to be noticed and it resonated with Mishka. Over the following days, Mishka went through his regular routine with more vigor and joy, than usual. He had an afterglow of someone who'd been wanted and loved, that's what he'd gotten from being the object of a few people's gaze, outside the storefront of his tailor.

Desperate to recreate the feeling, Mishka had been posting even more selfies, than usual. He'd take picture after picture, as he tried to pick out outfits, every morning, when he'd choose his outfit for the day and every evening, when he changed for dinner. Throughout the days, he'd post selfies, documenting his strict routine of leisure.

His followers saw Mishka's odd and leisurely life, of ceremonies meals, he didn't eat, to walks and runs around his estate and festive, solitary evenings. From the outside perspective of his followers, Mishka's life looked like a nonstop, one-person party, which they could only immerse themselves in through the frame of Mishka's posts.

Mishka closely followed the likes, comments and shares. Counting each engagement and measuring its qualitative value, so he could figure out his own worth and track his social decline.

It gave him the confidence to admit, that he might have made a mistake retiring and he was brewing up an idea for a comeback, but it wasn't ready yet. In the meantime, he prepared for his upcoming birthday. He'd invited no guests and was not expecting visitors, but he planned an elaborate event. He scoured the internet for brand name champagne from the year of his birth and bought up case after case. He'd ordered a birthday cake, that looked like a wedding cake for

Marie Antoinette, along with gold macaroons from La Glace. Most of his evenings were spent listening to and preselecting music, that he would listen to on his birthday.

Mishka didn't know why, but he felt a need to celebrate his life on this particular birthday and he felt he needed to do it alone.

As he prepared for the birthday, he went through his memories, sorting his life, like it was a messy storage space.

It gave him insight into himself and gave him a glimpse of who he really was.

His entire life had been a fight for more. Being a gay, effeminate, bourgeois white man put him in the intersection between privilege and minority. He'd known enough privilege to have acquired a taste for it and enough violent opposition to his sexuality and his femininity to know, that privilege and equality was not in his direct reach.

So, he'd taken a non-direct, passive aggressive approach to life. In his experience, most of the people who objected the strongest to his sexuality and femininity, also had a perverse need to possess it and often had some sort of sexual desire for it.

He'd worked hard to fit into other people's images of perfection, because he'd so often been told by society that he was wrong. As a 'fuck you' to society, he'd used his sexuality and his femininity to fuck his way to a position of power, weaponizing the parts of his identity, society had tried to erase. He'd sought and won affordances, where society had tried to restrain him.

He'd lived his life in spite.

Every day, several times a day, he'd been informed that he shouldn't exist, that he was wrong and often, that he should seize to exist.

As a child it had been a piece of information given to him from his schoolmates, at times their parents, even parents of his friends and also from strangers yelling from their cars.

As a teenager and as an adult, he'd been told by people at bars, friends of friends, even by boyfriends and patrons, social media trolls, random passersby on the street and from strangers yelling from cars. Always strangers yelling from cars.

He'd been continuously told off, because he wasn't attracted to women and didn't seem masculine enough for patriarchal society, because he liked glitter and because of a thousand other little things, he wasn't meant to like or do or be.

But, he continued to like glitter in spite. He'd lived in spite of the fact, that many people actively wanted him dead or just preferred he didn't exist. Every day he had decided that everyone else was wrong and he had a right to be who he was, despite what anyone said.

He'd continued to live and had lived in the shadow of the continued threats to his life and to his autonomy. He'd been able to do this, because of his spitefulness and because he'd hid, in the desire of acceptable men, men who were more masculine than him, men who passed.

Spite had been a fixed condition of his life. Spite had been a thick wall between Mishka and the rest of the world. As a result, he'd existed in a vacuum, in a continuous fight for his own existence. Not a direct, bare knuckle fight, but through a series of tactical maneuvers.

Yes, he'd lived a life, an interesting life.

It gave him the idea to write his memoir. After all, that's

what fascinating people did in their otium and he had indeed lived a fascinating life. The book could give him a chance to sample a comeback and if it didn't amount to that, well, then it would be a nice way to retire for good.

He worked and worked on an outline for his book and even finished a few sample chapters, to show the tone of the book. Like Mishka, the book was confused, pretentiously existential and way too choreographed to be real. But Mishka didn't see any of that and naively sent it to his old agent.

His followers' interest in his posts filled him with a false sense of confidence, that made him believe his book was brilliant. He couldn't wait for the book to be realized and he wrote every day, as he waited for his agent to get back to him.

But, to his great surprise, his agent did not hurry to answer his call, like she had done when he was in demand. Mishka was sensitive to snubbing and feared it meant a loss of influence and relevance. However, Mishka wasn't the type to accept defeat, so he continued to call her and continued to find her unavailable, again and again. He took his insecurities out on his agent's assistant, passive-aggressively harassing her, hoping it would make his agent finally call him back. In the meantime, package after package arrived at the house, in preparation for Mishka's birthday party. But one day it happened, his agent did call him back. It was the day before Mishka's birthday. Mishka had had his final fitting at the tailors and had just gotten home, with his two new outfits in hand, when his agent called and asked for him. A maid, who always screened Mishka's calls, handed Mishka the phone and whispered the word 'agent'.

As Mishka lifted the phone to his ear, he could hear his agent taking a deep breath and exhaling wearily. It wasn't good news and Mishka had a strong impulse to throw the phone across the room, but gathered himself and went through the scene, like a good boy.

"Hello, darling. I'm so sorry for haranguing your assistant, such a sweet girl, but I've been so very anxious to hear from you, darling. How is it? Interesting, right. It has potential?" Mishka rambled, desperately trying to lead his agent, even though he knew she wasn't the type to rear off script, no matter how hard anyone tried to lead her astray.

"I'm afraid it's not really the time for this sort of thing," she said patiently and insistently.

Mishka didn't answer, he didn't want to make it any easier for her to turn him down.

When Mishka remained silent, she continued.

"The timing is off. No one really reads memoirs anymore. Maybe if it was a sort of scandal story, a tell-all, but everything you'd done has already been broadcast everywhere, we made sure of that. Besides, you've been away. You retired," she stated firmly.

Mishka nodded, feeling ready to kill someone. "I think people are still interested. They still engage with my posts. People care…"

"Just enjoy what you have." She cut him off.

Mishka got angry, practically yelling into the phone "People care! They…"

"Sure, they do. Anyway, I have to go. So great to hear from you," she said and hung up.

Holding the phone, struggling to find a comeback, Mishka noticed the maid was still standing beside him, holding out her hand for the phone, eyes full of sympathy.

Mishka dropped the phone to the floor and sneered,

"Don't you have another mess to clean up," and hurried up to his bedroom, with the outfits for his birthday tomorrow.

Slamming the door and acclimating to being alone, Mishka led his guard down, placed the garment bags gently on his bed and took out a bottle of whiskey he'd hidden under his bed and poured himself a glass, which he swallowed instantly. Refilling his glass, Mishka drank a second glass and then poured a third. He felt calmer now, not that the whiskey helped, but it was something to do, something that was simultaneously self-indulgent and self-destructive.

Calmer, he put on some music, found a hidden stash of Sobranie cocktail cigarettes and placed himself by the window. Smoking a whole rainbow of cigarettes, puffing the smoke out of the open window and sipping his whiskey, he immersed himself in the loud tones of 'Don't rain on my parade', which pushed its way through the speakers. He had no nearby neighbors, but still, he thought the music was loud enough to bother the faraway ones. He wanted to be a little difficult now. The upbeat and happy music was a pleasing contrast to his state of mind. Sometimes it's nice to be contradicted, he thought.

His agent had not so subtly told him of his obsolescence and irrelevance and he believed her, the way most people instantly accept bad news as true, without evidence or argument.

Even though he accepted her premise, he still didn't understand how or why he'd been forgotten so fast, after everything he'd done *for* people and *to* himself. All the work he'd poured into his looks, his style and his promiscuity. He'd gone hungry, he'd exercised till he vomited from exhaustion, he'd spent so much of his patron's money on his wardrobe and dermatology and he'd let them fuck him till he was raw and bloody. All of this, only to be forgotten as soon as he left their line of sight. He hated them, people, for forgetting him. He hadn't minded being treated like a thing, but he objected to being treated like nothing, to not be thought of or considered at all.

The cigarette burned his finger and he dropped it, down his suit. He'd smoked it to the filter, without realizing. He licked the small burn mark and took off his clothes.

As he undressed, he caught sight of himself in the vanity mirror.

Fuck it, he thought. His social identity had gone up in flames, but his self-concept was still very much alive and frankly, all he had in his current position of social irrelevance.

He turned off the music and finished undressing, slowly and deliberately. Taking his time, he went over every inch of his reflection, as he slowly exposed himself to his mirror.

With small and gentle steps, he walked over to his vanity mirror and kissed his reflection, with a sloppy and wet kiss. He just kept kissing his reflection more and more, while his kisses became wetter and more ravenous.

Shutting out all other thoughts than of himself, he lost himself to his reflection and gave in to self-love, pressing himself up against the mirror, until his cock stiffened. Lubricating his cock with his spit, he made his body glide up against his reflection, making the hard surface of the mirror feel softer and more agreeable. It was like the mirror disappeared and he melted together with his image.

As he gave himself up to his reflection, he lost all sense of a world outside of himself and his own enjoyment of his reflection. He fucked his reflection, hungry for his own approval. Fucking until he grew limp, without reaching the point of joy he was thrusting for.

Tired, he stepped down and looked at the smudged mirror and disorderly table. All his little beauty helpers were spread across the table, like the little jars and bottles had been dancing, until they'd collapsed randomly about the table top.

Mishka carefully cleaned off the mirror and put all the bottles and jars back in their place, until he'd recreated order and the vanity looked like itself again.

Looking in the clean mirror, he saw dried streams running down the eyes of his reflection. He'd apparently cried at some point. Oddly, he hadn't noticed he'd been crying and had no memory of it.

He took a deep breath to regain a sense of calm. Everything felt out of place, even though his things were once again arranged neatly.

Remembering 'The Bell Jar', he took a long hot shower, to set himself right. The hot water loosened his weak and overstrained muscles and cleared his mind.

The book had been a stray thought and he'd started writing it on an impulse. How had it become so important to him all of the sudden? Why did it seem so paramount, that he should get it published?

Why wasn't he satisfied without it, why did he need a book deal? He had enough money, a good investment adviser, a great house and a wardrobe that almost rivaled Imelda Marcos'.

Why was this such a defeat? Why was his life not enough for him?

Then he remembered what his mother had philosophized to him: that he'd never be happy, because to be happy meant being satisfied with the status quo and he was never satisfied with anything, he always wanted something more.

It was true, she'd spotted the truth of him.

He felt sorry for his mother. She had tried so hard, every millisecond of his upbringing, to create the perfect man, by always trying to make the best of things, by being as honest as she could be and by stitching together all the different pieces, that fit into her fragmented idea of perfection. However, she also tried to warn him, not to expect too much, not to think the world was perfect or ready to receive him. Only fools think the world is fair, she used to say.

His father had merely tried to get him out of the way, by shouting, shaming, ignoring or slapping him. The sentence that would always remind of his father was: "Sch, what will the neighbors think?"

Remembering the terrible hold those words had in his childhood, he rolled his eyes and groaned, much like his mother had done, each time his father had said it. Sentiments like that, was what tied him to middle class morality, which he'd never quite been able to clean off, no matter how much whiskey, cum or money he used.

Mishka got out of the shower and put on a kimono. He was thirsty, even more than usual.

Opening the bedroom door, he listened for the staff, not sure if the coast was clear. He stood and listened a while and decided, they must have gone home. Tiptoeing his way to the kitchen, he noticed how far the preparation for his birthday had gone. There were deliveries all over the place, the wine fridge was stocked full of the champagne he'd ordered, the gold macaroons were already placed on porcelain trays and the birthday cake had arrived as well. Mishka was a bit blown away with the grandeur of it all. All of this for a birthday, he intended to celebrate alone, all for one person – just for him.

He was amused by his own silliness and self-indulgence. He really was too much, just too damn much – like Joan Crawford. It made him realize the extent of his ego and vanity.

In the end, he was the only one left, who could love him. Mishka picked out his favorite champagne glass, opened one of the bottles meant for the morning and took it with him upstairs.

Behind his closed bedroom door, he put on some Rosemary Clooney and played it loudly. Getting giddy from the champagne, he went to his closet and inspected its grand contents. Giving in to impulse, he started trying on all his clothes, rating the individual pieces and judging his styling skills. Item by item, Mishka emptied his closets, as he tried on suits, shirts, t-shirts, trousers, shorts, shoes, furs and jewelry. As soon as he was satisfied with a look, he'd toast himself, post a selfie to show off the outfit, tagging the brands, then undressed and threw the items about the room. His once organized bedroom quickly started to resemble a disorganized warehouse sale, with countless items lying everywhere.

Mishka kept going, ferociously, with the upbeat music playing loudly in the background, until his closet was empty. Not knowing what to do now, he stood naked, in the middle of the mess he'd made and drank continuously, losing all sense of time.

He was startled when the antique clock, his great, great grandfather had made, struck midnight. It was odd, he thought, that he heard the clock. It was placed in a hallway quite a distance from his bedroom. Then he noticed how quiet everything was and he heard the unfamiliar absence of music.

The playlist had stopped, run out of songs to play.

Midnight! It was his birthday now. He was officially older. Although it only mattered to him since he always lied about his age to other people. If something was accepted as true by enough people, it became the truth – a social truth, Mishka mused. He knew truth to be inherently political, so in a democratic society truth was merely a matter of numbers. He raised his glass to toast himself, but found it empty, so was the bottle.

It felt like a cruel injustice and to rectify it he went down to the kitchen and opened another bottle. Taking a stroll throughout his house, he inspected it and for the first time, he saw it for the opulent symbol it was.

His house was more like a temple, than a home. It was an extravagant place of worship of his own brand and beauty, built on the generosity of his true-believing benefactors. It occurred to him, that he'd never really appreciated it, never really lived in his house, but merely situated himself in it, like he was an icon. Out of curiosity, he walked around the house and tried all the seating, smelled every bouquet and studied every trinket. For the first time, he tried living in his house, rather than just performing in it. As he returned to the kitchen, he even sampled the macaroons and ate a big chunk of his birthday cake.

Emptying the bottle, he opened another and went back to his bedroom and dressed for his birthday.

He put on the smoking, he'd ordered from the tailor, with the chiffon shirt and bow, which he paired with a twenties' style Tiffany's pearl necklace, a white gold diamond collier and lots and lots of cocktail rings, which he scavenged for, among the mess he'd made earlier.

As he looked in the mirror, he became sad. There was something anti-climatic about everything.

As he sat there in front of his vanity mirror, a glass of champagne firm in hand, he suddenly understood that he'd never be happy, that nothing would ever be enough for him. He'd never be good enough for his own gaze. There would always be something more to strive for, to have and to be. He'd never be lazy or careless enough to be happy.

His mother really had been right about him.

As soon as Mishka reached a goal or a new level, he instantly found it dissatisfying and tried to move on to the next. He no longer knew what that meant and it saddened him, because he no longer had anything to strive for, no more to be. His time was over.

He was too thin to fit standardized clothing, he had financial security and an abundance of things and he'd never ever be younger than he was now.

He wanted to fight it, to change, but how exactly do you challenge your own nature to a fight? To fight against your own nature is a slow, continuous battle, where one kills oneself bit by bit. Mishka was not one for slow, prolonged processes, he needed things to be demonstrative, dramatic and to yield instant results. So, he did a demonstrative and dramatic gesture, to prove to himself, he wouldn't stand for his unhappy nature and he called his mother, the informant of his unhappiness.

As the phone rang, he contemplated why his mother's statements bothered him so much, why he still cared. What really bothered Mishka was, that his mother really saw him, that he couldn't hide or pretend with her. She had created him and she saw him, even the parts of him that hadn't turned out the way she intended them too, when she stitched them together.

"Hi, darling. What a lovely surprise!" his mother chirped at the other end of the phone, interrupting Mishka's trail of thought.

As he heard her voice, Mishka froze and became uncertain.

"Darling, are you there?" his mother inquired, alarmed by the silence.

"Hi." he answered timidly.

"Happy birthday my sweet boy. Are you celebrating, having a party?"

"No, I'm just, just thinking. Trying to get my life in order." Mishka said, as he looked around at the mess he'd made of his bedroom.

"Well, birthdays have that effect, don't they." His mother instinctively de-dramatized.

Mishka took a big gulp straight from the champagne bottle, to regain his nerve.

"I don't like it." he spat out to his mother.

A few moments passed in silence, before Mishka continued.

"My life, I don't like it and I don't like me much either, the me you created." he said groggily.

His mother realized that he was drunk and wanted to calm him down, to prevent a scene.

"Oh, darling. You're such good company, always so agreeable. You always seek the middle, to fit in. That's not something to sneeze at. Not everyone can do that. It's a gift, your gift." she said in a soothing, pedagogical tone.

Her lack of understanding felt like a rejection.

Unknowingly and most unwillingly his mother was tossing him aside.

It had always been a problem for him, with everyone.

His inability to connect.

He always lived detached and it was the detachment that hurt, when he talked to his mother. He didn't want to be separate, but he simply couldn't breach the space between him and other people. There was a moat around him and he had no idea who built it or how to lower the drawbridge.

Mishka knew she meant well, but he needed more from her. He knew she didn't withhold anything, that she wasn't denying him. What he needed from her, just wasn't in her nature to give, just as it wasn't in his nature to ask for it directly.

With nothing polite to say, Mishka simply said, "Thank you, Mother." And hung up the phone.

He was disappointed and he wondered why he had thought the conversation would have gone any differently than it had.

He'd never been good at confronting people or standing up for himself.

He wasn't that explicit.

Weighing his mother's words, he decided she was right, as she most often was. He often was agreeable. Even now, his grand gesture of opposition was to avoid more confrontation, by hanging up the phone.

A deep feeling of regret flushed his entire inner universe and he desperately wished that things had been different.

All he wanted was to be beautiful, to be worth something.

Suddenly the paradox of his life dawned on him. As suffocating as he found other people's company, he needed people for their gaze and admiration.

He needed others, because it was impossible for him to realize his aesthetic ambitions on his own.

He remembered his earlier realization, that it was impossible for him to be beautiful alone.

Beauty seemed to be a social construct.

If beauty is in the eye of the beholder, then surely beauty is a social relation, based on objectification.

Almost Lacanian in nature, he reasoned to himself.

To be beautiful, he required someone to gaze upon him and find him beautiful. He needed to be an object of their gaze, an image for them to admire, as a visual projection of their desires.

To be beautiful, therefore, requires submission and he had made a career out of being submissive and letting himself be objectified.

That was what his patrons had paid him for, for him to set aside any human complexity or will and instead be a passive tool for them to use, as they wished.

In his adaptation to the fantasies of his patrons, his followers and to anyone else who could make him feel worth something, he had slowly killed off his own identity. It was only natural that he was so disgruntled in his isolation. On his own, he wasn't happy, because he wasn't anyone anymore.

He had reduced himself to an image, instead of growing into a real human being.

His grooming routine, exercise, styling, shopping, the constant inspection of himself in the mirror, all the selfies and all the ways he had prostituted himself to his patrons and to the press, it had all just been ways for him to utilize himself and to recreate himself as a beautiful image. Without noticing, he had been dying for a long time. He'd been killing himself for years, reducing his humanity to a one-sided image of beauty.

The truth was, that he didn't exist at all anymore, he was a fantasy and fantasies aren't real.

Alone he was nothing. By cutting himself off from society he had effectually killed off his own sense of self. Alone he was not beautiful, he didn't exist at all.

He saw no other options left to him, no other men to submit to, to tempt or to please, other than the god he had stopped believing in so long ago.

He gave the room a glance and reviewed all the luxuries he had collected. This was what his life had resulted in, a pile of expensive consumer goods that he had cared for more, than any person in his life. The luxuries he had amassed, made by people kept in slave-like conditions to produce his clothes and accessories and to mine out the precious stones and metals of his extensive jewelry collection. He felt neither shame, regret or pleasure, it was simply fact.

He scoffed, as he saw his treasures. Even his goals had been a form of submission. He was a consumerist, that wanted all the things the media told him to want. All his references and aesthetics were simply collaged out of media content, from fashion magazines, classic literature and classic movies.

Mishka went back to his vanity mirror and stared into his reflection. He felt betrayed.

All his achievements had been born out of cowardice. He'd been too afraid to be someone and had fled into the comfort and nonchalance of being an object. He'd let everyone patronize him and use him. What had he gotten in return? Nothing but trinkets, alcoholism and loneliness. He was like a

Hollywood starlet, who'd lost their momentum, like Joan Crawford out of the spotlight.

He suddenly remembered that night Mervin had made a drunken visit to his apartment and looked him so persistently in the eyes. At the time, it had felt uncomfortable and like an intrusion. Now Mishka knew why. The intense and prolonged eye contact had confronted him with his own lack of humanity. Mervin had tried desperately to connect and Mishka hadn't been able to do it.

Mishka looked at his reflection and all he saw was a façade. His eyes were empty and emotionless, with their large, dilated pupils.

Mishka put on his makeup one last time. When he was satisfied with his face, he took a selfie and posted it with the tag: "This is it".

Afterwards, he took out a new bottle of scotch, hidden in the drawer and placed it on the makeup table, along with his whole collection of pills, which he organized neatly on the table top.

He took a pill from a random bottle and began to pray. At the end of the prayer, he placed the pill carefully on his tongue and washed it down with a sip of scotch. It felt good to pray, to submit himself once again to a man of higher standing, so he continued praying, over and over again.

With each prayer, he took another pill and downed it with another sip of scotch, growing groggier each time.

He continued praying, drinking and popping pills, working through nausea and fighting not to fall asleep too soon, until finally, the world started to disintegrate and disappear.

Catching a last look of himself in the mirror, he saw his

frail, well dressed body and his bony bejeweled hand clutching the scotch bottle, as his eyes got droopy and eventually closed. Still, his mind raced. He wondered which selfie he'd posted tonight, would get the most likes, which look people would respond to. He hoped someone was masturbating to one of his selfies right now. As his grasp of reality lapsed, his thoughts went back to his old apartment and he could almost hear the footsteps of a patron in the old hallway and the sound of keys rattling in the door and he instantly felt his penis harden, before his mind slipped from him.

It was early morning now and everything was busy downstairs.

The maids were rushing in the kitchen, to arrange everything as Mishka liked it. The bodyguard had been sent to town, to deal with the baker and get a new cake, to replace the one Mishka had eaten during the night. The doorbell kept ringing, as flowers and gifts were delivered and filled the ground floor. As Mishka was draped across his makeup table, dying from neglect, his maids were struggling to find the space for all the birthday presents and flowers people had sent Mishka, to celebrate him.

When everything was ready for Mishka's exacting standards, they waited for Mishka to show himself downstairs at the usual time. As the hours went on, they became nervous at the unprecedented disturbance to the usual routine.

When the bodyguard finally came to check on Mishka, it was too late and Mishka was dead.

The bodyguard looked around at all the things scattered around the room, all Mishka's things, the empty champagne bottles and Mishka, lying over the makeup table of his vanity mirror. It seemed almost supernatural to the bodyguard, like some sinister, mythological creature was at play.

He had never understood his employer but had always been intrigued by Mishka and his opaqueness.

Unlike Mishka himself, the bodyguard saw a young, beautiful, and irresistible boy, in Mishka. He decided to kiss Mishka, out of respect. But, as soon as his lips touched Mishka, he couldn't help letting his hand explore Mishka's cold, unresponsive body. It pleased him to finally have Mishka's body to himself, without having to worry about what Mishka would have thought of him. He put his hand down his pants and noiselessly pleasured himself, as he filled his gaze with Mishka's inanimate body.